Los Angeles, late Septemb
are blowing, covering the c
the Mojave and Sonoran d
That night, there are three

The official view is that they are all unrelated. The deceaseds had no connection, and all died in different parts of the city.

However, Police Detective Sam Leroy has other ideas, and begins to widen the investigation.

But he meets resistance from the most unexpected quarter, and when his life and that of his loved ones are threatened, he faces a choice: back off, or do what he knows he must do…

Philip Cox is married with two children and lives near London. A former Bank Manager, he pursued a career in banking and financial services until 2009, when he took a break to become a stay-at-home father. In between numerous school runs, Philip wrote *After the Rain*, which appeared in 2011. *Dark Eyes of London* and *She's Not Coming Home* followed in 2012. *Something to Die For*, which introduced the maverick LAPD detective Sam Leroy, was published in 2013. *Don't Go Out in the Dark* was published in 2014, and *Wrong Time to Die*, the second Sam Leroy story, was published in 2015. *Should Have Looked Away* followed in 2016. *The Angel* is the second story featuring reporter Jack Richardson, whom we first met in *Don't Go Out in the Dark.*

Also by Philip Cox

After the Rain
Dark Eyes of London
She's Not Coming Home
Don't Go Out in the Dark
Wrong Time to Die
Should Have Looked Away
No Place to Die
The Angel

SOMETHING TO DIE FOR

PHILIP COX

For Alison
And for Ella and Iona

ACKNOWLEDGEMENTS

All I did was write the book! Other people helped in the process. I want to thank Kelly Burney and Martin Romero of the Los Angeles Police Department, Michaela Wood of the California Hospital Medical Center, the managements of the Ronald Reagan Medical Center and Los Angeles County Hospital and Emilio Grube of Grand Central Market. Also thanks to Anne Poole for her help with the text, and Ron Reiring (main picture) and Jason Ralston (insert) for the cover images.

Finally, not forgetting the REAL Sam Leroy...

The author is British, but the story takes place in the United States, and most of the characters are American. So: British English or American English? The narrative is in British English, and the dialogue is mostly American English. So US readers please note that some words may be spelt differently, such as tyres for tires, centre for center.

CHAPTER ONE

THE SANTA ANA winds are dry and warm - sometimes hot – winds that affect coastal Southern California and northern Baja California from September to March. In fact, they range from hot to cold, depending on the temperatures in the region of origin, namely the Great Basin, which stretches from the Sierra Nevada range in the west to the Wasatch Range in Utah, and Northern Mexico up to Oregon, and the upper Mojave Desert.

The air from the Mojave Desert is relatively dense owing to its coolness and aridity, and tends to channel down the valleys and canyons in gusts which can attain hurricane force at times. As the air descends, it not only becomes drier, but warmer. The southern California coastal region gets some of its hottest weather of the year when the Santa Anas are blowing. At these times it is more often than not hotter along the coast than in the deserts.

Tonight was no exception. A warm and dry blast of air blew down the mountain passes. Warm and dry, and easily exceeding 40 mph, they brought with them a thin layer of reddish dust. They were hot too: the Santa Monica weather station's instruments were recording 98 degrees.

The man staggered along the empty road. Dressed only in torn white shorts, he weaved back and forth across the yellow centre line. He could make out some kind of reflection on the wet road below. He felt down and rubbed his leg. There were scratch marks down to his ankle from the tumble he had taken down the hillside from above. He stopped and looked round, disorientated, blinking.

Where was he?

Somewhere high up, he was sure; he could hear, or thought he could hear, the muffled rumbling of traffic below.

But where exactly?

And how did he get here?

He stopped and looked around. He could make out lights above and below, but the road he was on was devoid of any buildings. It was only the light from the moon which gave him any form of illumination.

There was mist around: as the road disappeared round a bend ahead, and behind as it receded into the dark.

He felt cold, even though the strong winds blowing down the hillside were hot. He wiped the dust from his eyes and continued along the road.

He needed to find shelter, some help.

After a few more yards' shuffling, he stopped again. A dog was barking. He looked around, trying to figure out where the sound was coming from. A dog would mean someone's house.

The barking seemed to be coming from below. Maybe the lights below were from a house. That meant a phone.

A phone. He could remember using a cell phone earlier that evening. Could remember putting the phone back onto the belt clip he used. Involuntarily, he felt down to his waist. All he could feel was the elastic of his torn, dirty shorts.

Where were his clothes? How did he end up here?

He started to walk again, this time towards where he thought the barking, which had now stopped, came from. He rubbed the side of his leg and looked at his hand. Blood. Then looked at his leg. The scratches were bleeding more; not profusely, but they would need attention.

He veered over to the right hand side of the road, so now he was walking partly on the road, partly on the bumpy verge.

He paused as he could make out a new source of light. They got closer. Two small separate lights, slightly diffused in the mist. Then the sound of a car engine.

By now he could make out the vehicle as it came round the bend. It was not coming at him very fast, no doubt because of the mist, which seemed to thicken as the road went downhill. He staggered over to the centre of the road as the car came round the bend. Feebly, he waved his arms in the air. The driver braked, and the car skidded slightly as it came to a halt around ten feet past the man. He ran up to the driver's door. A grey haired man was driving, with a woman of similar age sitting in front with him. The driver wound down his window.

'What in hell's going on?' the driver asked. 'I could have...' He stopped as he noticed the figure was wearing only shorts. 'Jesus H!' he exclaimed.

'Please, I need help...' The man rested his hand on the car roof and leaned over.

'Look, I'm sorry, I....'

'Can I borrow your cell phone? I need to make a call.'

The woman leaned forward and saw him. 'Tell him to go away, Gus.'

Gus looked over at her and back at the man. 'I – I, er…'

'Please, mister. Go away. You're scaring us,' the woman said.

'I just need a cell phone for a minute…'

'Sorry, pal,' said Gus as he wound up the window. 'We don't want any trouble.'

'But I just…'

Gus wound up the window and the car sped away into the darkness and into the mist.

He watched as the red tail lights faded away into the mist. After a few moments' pause, he continued to shuffle on. He cried out as he stepped on something sharp. He lifted up his leg and pulled out a sharp stone which had gotten embedded in the sole of his bare foot. Then moved on again.

Looking down, he could make out some lights. Maybe that was where the barking was coming from. This was the direction from which he could still hear the rumble of traffic.

He slowly stepped off the road and began to climb down the slope. It was steep in places but he was able to grab onto some bushes for support. As he climbed further down, the undergrowth became thicker. He tried to make out what the vegetation was. The smell seemed familiar: maybe buckbush. As he got further down, he realised he had lost sight of the lights. He panicked slightly as he lost his bearings. Looked around again. No sign of any lights now, but the ambient sound of the traffic below was still there.

He moved on again.

After twenty yards or so, the traffic noise was getting louder. Perhaps he should head for there; on a busy road he would stand a better chance of flagging someone down.

Then he missed his footing. Tried to grab a bush for support, but missed. Landing on his back, he slid down the slope. He cried out as his back was lacerated by the shrubs and rocks as he skimmed over them. He hit an obstruction, a tree stump maybe; rather than stopping his descent, it served to knock him sideways so now he was rolling down. He tried to put his hands in front of him to protect his face, but his momentum was too great. As he rolled down, one side of his head hit some hard ground. Just then, his fall stopped.

He lay there, dazed. He thought he had reached the end of the drop as he was now lying on level ground. He felt up to his temple: it was wet and sticky. His vision was blurred. He stood up and moved on. Suddenly under his feet he could feel not ground and brush, but a smooth surface. Not unlike the road above. Still disorientated he staggered forward.

His last sensations were a blinding white light, a loud, deep blare. Then, a microsecond of intense pain as something weighing 35000 lbs slammed into him.

Then nothing.

CHAPTER TWO

SO FAR, JAY Wang was not having a good day. At least it was just after seven, so it would not be long until the next, and hopefully better, day.

Ironically, this was a day he had been looking forward to for many weeks. It was his girlfriend, Kiera Alvarado's twenty-third birthday. He had splashed out $111 for two terrace seats for a Norah Jones concert at the Hollywood Bowl: not his first choice for an evening's entertainment, but she was quite insistent. Then there was the meal: somewhere nice, somewhere stylish, but not too fancy, either before or after the show.

It was looking as if it would be after the show: after getting off work early, rushing home for a quick shower and change of clothes, and then making the five mile journey down to Kiera's place in ten minutes, they had experienced nothing but gridlock since they joined the Hollywood Freeway. Now they were headed west on Santa Monica

Boulevard, where the traffic was still slow, but less so than on the freeway.

'We're not gonna make it in time,' Jay muttered, impatiently tapping his fingers on the steering wheel.

'I told you we shouldn't have used the freeway,' Kiera retorted. 'Not at this time of day.'

'We'd get held up at this time of day whichever route we took.'

'Not if we'd used Wilshire and Highland.'

'Bullshit. Freeway, residential: it's all jammed up. Friday rush hour, remember.'

Kiera snorted and looked out of the window. She swore under her breath as a green light turned amber, then red, before they could get past.

'And what about eating?' she asked. 'I can't wait till after the show. If we ever get there.'

'Jesus, I thought we were going to eat afterwards.'

'Are you serious? It'll be eleven before we get out.'

'Where do you want to go then?' Jay snapped back.

She squinted as she peered ahead, then pointed. About a hundred yards in front of them, across the street, was a large illuminated Denny's sign.

'Go in there,' she said.

'Denny's? We don't have long, remember?'

'I don't care. I just need something quick. I've not eaten since midday.'

Once they reached the parking lot entrance, Jay paused for a break in eastbound traffic and pulled in.

'Busy here tonight,' Jay said as he drove around looking for a space.

'I don't believe this,' Kiera moaned as it was quite clear the lot was full.

'What do you want me to do?'

'It's no use driving around the lot. Let's go.'

'Okay.' Jay eased the Chevy out of the parking lot. The lights at the intersection with Van Ness turned red, so he was able to cross the eastbound lane easily and get back into westbound traffic.

'We're going to be even later now,' Kiera grumbled, checking her watch.

Jay accelerated slightly as the signals they passed changed to red. 'Not necessarily. We're at Gower already.'

'And?' she asked. 'The show starts in an hour; we have to get all the way to Highland, *then* find somewhere to park. Plus get something to eat first.'

Jay looked at his watch, then at the LED clock on the dashboard, as if it was going to tell him an earlier time.

'Tell you what,' Kiera said. 'Just get me a burger and fries. Just something quick.'

'Burger and fries? But it's your birthday – don't you want something special…?'

'That would have been nice, but I'd rather get to the concert in time.'

She looked over at Jay and saw the disappointed look on his face. She reached over and held his arm.

'I know you wanted to make tonight special, baby,' she said softly, 'but it will be. As long as we get there in time. Think about it. There was no way we were going to get home from work, change, get out here, eat, and get to the Bowl by eight thirty. Not on a weekday.'

Jay nodded. 'Okay, baby. If you say so.'

Both remained silent for the next couple of blocks, then Jay said, 'There's a McDonalds on Hollywood, just before Highland.'

Kiera laughed. 'Looks like we might have to. You can pull up outside and run in for something.'

'McDonalds,' Jay scoffed. 'Okay, if that's all right with you. Sorry. I'll make it up to you another time.'

She put her hand on the top of his leg and moved it up to his thigh. 'Oh, I know you will.'

Jay laughed and indicated right, then, turned onto Vine Street. Just past Selma, the traffic ground to a halt again.

Jay swore and put on the brake.

'I knew we should have used the Red Line,' Kiera said, sitting up in her seat so she could see any cause for the delay. There was a row of red tail and brake lights right up to the intersection with Hollywood Boulevard, and the traffic there seemed to be at a standstill.

'It's gridlock everywhere,' she wailed. 'Jay, you need to do something.'

'Do what?' he asked. Do what exactly?'

'I don't know,' she replied, settling back down in her seat. She rested her elbow on the door and her head in her hand.

'Jesus Christ,' Jay muttered, looking around at the traffic. Then he noticed something. He indicated left and turned into the oncoming traffic.

Kiera sat bolt upright in her seat. 'What the fuck are you...'

'Just relax. Trust me.'

Some of the traffic coming down Vine Street blew their horns, but Jay was eventually able to get to a ninety degree angle and make it across the two opposite lanes. Gripping onto her seat handle, Kiera could see he was headed for an alleyway alongside the Stars on Vine restaurant.

'Where does this lead us?' she asked.

'No idea,' said Jay as he drove along the darkened alleyway. 'But I'm guessing it'll take us away from this traffic. We're running parallel with Hollywood Boulevard now.'

Jay switched to high beams as the alleyway got darker. Rather than leading directly to the next cross street as he had hoped, the alley turned right at a ninety degree angle.

'I don't like this, Jay,' said Kiera. 'Where are we going?'

'Relax; it has to come out somewhere. And we're going in the right direction.'

'Right direction for where?'

'For Highland Avenue. It's over in that direction.'

Jay continued slowly along the alley. Over the tops of the buildings he could see the glow from the streetlamps on Hollywood Boulevard and could make out the sound of traffic and horns.

The alley led them to a small open space. About fifty feet square, it seemed to be a small parking lot belonging to some of the buildings surrounding them. One car was parked up against a wall. Two dumpsters were alongside another wall.

'Great,' said Kiera. 'A dead end.'

'Shit,' muttered Jay. 'I'm going to have to turn round.'

'There's no way we're going to make it now,' said Kiera, sitting back and folding her arms in protest.

Jay ignored her and turned the car as far as he could to the left, engaged reverse, and fed the steering wheel the other way. He reversed twenty feet or so into a recessed area between two buildings. Just as he did so, the rear of the car bumped up and down, causing Jay and Kiera to bounce in their seats.

'Jesus, what was that?' Kiera called out.

'Probably some garbage,' Jay said. 'There are dumpsters everywhere.'

He put the Chevy into Drive and moved forward slowly. The bump again.

'Jay, you need to check what it was,' said Kiera nervously.

Jay put on the brake and released his seat belt. 'What are you expecting: a body?' he snapped as he got out of the car.

Kiera sat back in her seat and began playing with her phone. She sat up with a start when she heard Jay crying out.

'Oh my God, Oh, Jesus. Oh Jesus.'

Kiera released her own belt and got out. Jay was standing at the back of the car, holding his head in his hands, wailing and looking down at the ground. She looked down too and put her hand to her mouth when she saw what Jay was looking at.

Lying partly underneath the Chevy, naked except for a torn pair of black briefs, and dark tread marks on the skin where the tyres had run over it, was a man's body.

CHAPTER THREE

'GO ON, GABBY; have another.'

Gabriella Rider recoiled slightly as a slightly inebriated Lance Smart loomed over her, with an opened bottle of California Chardonnay wavering above her glass.

She looked up, gave him a smile, and held the palm of her hand over her glass. 'I'm okay right now.'

Lance Smart shuffled his feet around to steady himself. He was not going to give up that easily.

'Go on Gabby. Just a drop more.' He leaned over further, grasping the bottle in his right hand and holding his left arm out to balance. Gabrielle was beginning to be concerned he might collapse on top of her.

Eventually she took her hand off the glass.

'All right,' she said. 'Just a drop.' She held the glass out.

'Just a drop,' he repeated, slurring. He leaned further over and deliberately poured more wine into her glass. Not just a drop as Gabrielle had asked, but refilled the glass.

'No, that's en -' Too late.

Lance Smart gave her a drunken smile, turned, and staggered off.

Gabrielle shook her head and took a sip. She checked her watch: it was just after nine. Biting her lip, she began to figure out at what time she could leave. She didn't want to be the first to go; however the sooner she could get away the better. This was as boring as hell, and Lance Smart had had too much to drink. As usual. If he was anybody other than a senior partner in the firm… It wasn't that he ever said or did anything inappropriate: he was just a pain in the ass when he had more than two glasses.

She looked around at some of her colleagues, willing one of them to finish their drink and go.

'Not eating anything, Gabrielle?'

She looked up and saw Cecil Reed, the CEO, standing over her. He had a drink in one hand and a plate of canapés in the other.

She looked up at him and smiled. 'Not that hungry, Mr Reed.'

'Nonsense. You must eat something. You must be hungry. Otherwise you'll be merry after one of those.' He indicated down to her now full glass of Chardonnay. 'And not fit for work tomorrow.'

He was right. Gabriella was getting hungry. She just felt that if she started eating here, that would mean getting to leave later. She stood up.

'That's the spirit,' Reed said, holding both wine and plate in one hand and guiding her over to the buffet table with the other. 'Why not try something? The Dim Sing are delicious.'

'Dim Sing?' she asked, as they walked over.

'Yes, those little dumpling things. Chinese, I believe.'

'Oh, you mean Dim Sum,' she laughed.

'See, I told you you were hungry.' He led her to the buffet.

Gabrielle looked around at the food laid out on the white linen tablecloth. There was a printed label by each dish, presumably so those who were not versed in Chinese knew what they were eating. Har gow shrimp dumplings, chicken and vegetable congee, steamed dumplings, rice noodle rolls, sweet and sour pork, and Cha siu bao, a bun filled with barbecued pork. She studied each food for a moment, then picked up a paper plate from a small pile at the end of the table and helped herself to some shrimp dumplings and noodle rolls. As she turned to return to her seat she found herself staring into Cecil Reed's eyes.

'That all you're having, my dear?' he asked, looking down at her half empty plate in disbelief.

She nodded. 'Not much of an appetite tonight, I'm afraid.'

Reed shook his head. 'You young ladies,' he muttered. 'Always worrying about your figures.'

Gabrielle smiled again and returned to her seat. As she walked away, she could still hear Reed mumbling something about size zeroes.

As she sat down, out of the corner of her eye she could see Lance Smart still staggering around topping up people's glasses. He saw her and turned in her direction.

'Oh shit,' Gabrielle muttered under her breath.

As he came over, she caught the attention of two women colleagues who were chatting three seats down. She moved her seat and joined them.

Gabrielle had only been working as an admin assistant at LaVerne & Marshall, a medium sized attorney firm based in offices in Century City, two weeks, and so had not had much of a chance to get to know her co-workers that well. Quiet and introverted, she had kept herself to herself, and had stayed off everybody's radar.

Except that of Lance Smart, whose radar had picked her up at work, and certainly had here. If she was hoping that by joining the other two women, she had escaped his attentions, she was mistaken. He kept coming.

'More wine, ladies?' He stopped around three feet from there they had congregated and stood swaying, with a bottle in each hand.

Gabrielle's colleagues both said no, and turned away from him. She followed suit.

'Are you sure? We have gallons in the cellar.'

The older of the two, who Gabrielle was aware was called Monica, looked up at him.

'Piss off, Lance. Go get some black coffee.'

He froze, with a hurt look on his face, then not saying another word, turned and shambled away.

'Well done, you,' said Stella, Monica's colleague. They both laughed, Gabrielle joining in.

For the next half an hour, the three of them chatted. Chatted and laughed about the firm, about their jobs, their families, until Gabrielle noticed a few people the other side of the room preparing to leave.

'I think it's my turn to say goodbye,' she said, standing up. 'Sorry.'

'Don't apologise, honey,' said Monica. 'I'm leaving soon. I've always hated these office receptions.'

'Me too,' added Stella. 'If the big boys want to celebrate closing a big contract, why don't they go celebrate? No need to keep us here longer than we need to be. See you in the morning, Gabrielle.'

Gabrielle said her goodbyes, visited the restroom, and then picked up her coat and bag. Much to her dismay, as she made her way to the door, she was caught by Lance Smart again.

'Why are you leaving so soon?' he asked, leaning against the door frame.

'I'm tired, and need to go home,' she said walking off

to the elevator. He stood up and followed her.

'But the night's so young,' he smirked as she punched the elevator call button. 'I was hoping we could have another drink here, then head back to my penthouse for a nightcap.'

'Er – I don't think so, Lance.'

To her relief, the elevator doors opened. She quickly stepped in and hit the P2 button, praying that he would not follow her.

'Well, that's your loss,' he said, chasing the remaining gap in the doors as they slid shut.

'I'll try to get by,' she called out as the doors closed and the elevator took her from her office on the 15th floor to the second basement level parking garage.

There were no stops on the journey past sixteen floors and after a minute the doors slid open. Gabrielle stepped out.

The garage was around a quarter full, the remaining cars presumably belonging to the people still at the LaVerne & Marshall reception. Gabrielle felt a little uneasy: the place felt deserted, creepy. Her vehicle was parked at the far end, three spaces away from one of the whitewashed wall. She started to walk over, a little faster than usual.

As she approached a concrete column, she thought she could hear voices from around the column. Speaking quietly. She stopped walking. The voices stopped. Nervously, she fumbled in her bag and got out her keys. Held the key out and pressed the unlock button. There was a click from the end of that row of cars and the lights on her Mini Hardtop flashed as the doors unlocked. Relieved, she broke into a run.

'Good night, Gabrielle,' a woman's voice called out. Gabrielle skidded to a halt and turned round. The voice came from the other side of the column. She breathed a sigh of relief as she saw, sitting on the hood of the black sedan, her skirt hitched up to her waist, Melody from Accounts.

Standing facing her was a young guy who Gabrielle thought worked as an assistant to one of the partners. She laughed, partly out of relief, and partly as now she knew why they wanted to leave the party early.

'Night,' she smiled, and turned to walk to her car. Melody and the guy remained frozen: obviously they were going to let Gabrielle drive away before they continued.

Gabrielle had only taken two steps when she heard a cry – a man's cry – and a dull thumping noise. It was coming over from the other side of the place.

'What the hell -?' Melody's partner muttered. He stepped back and pulled up his pants. Melody adjusted her clothing and got off the sedan.

'Is anybody there?' Melody cried out, as she, the guy and Gabrielle slowly and cautiously stepped over to where they thought the sound had come from.

'You there,' the guy called out. 'You some kind of freaking perv-'

He was stopped mid-sentence as Melody screamed. Gabrielle gasped and put her hand over her mouth.

In the corner of the garage, a metallic blue Dodge Dart had been reversed into the space. There was a man next to the car. He was lying face down, at a ninety-degree angle, as if he was just about to open the door before he fell. The right arm was stretched out, as if reaching for the door. Except for a pair of red shorts, this man was naked. There were vicious looking scratch marks across his back.

Melody screamed again, her scream echoing around the whitewashed walls of the garage.

CHAPTER FOUR

IT WAS A Saturday night. The same as any other Saturday night. As any other Saturday night at the Marriott Hotel, Downtown Los Angeles. Guests moved around the lobby, making their way to or from one of the bars, or the restaurant. Some were sitting on one of the many armchairs, chatting over coffee or a drink, reading a newspaper, or just waiting.

There were three lines waiting at reception, each with two guests behind the person checking in. Once check-in had been completed, a bell hop appeared, to escort the guest and his bags to one of the bedrooms in the twenty-one storey hotel.

This night was slightly different, however, in that a raucous noise was emanating from one of the three function rooms. From outside, you could hear a man's voice, and laughter.

The man concerned was Henry Meriwether II, owner of a leather goods manufacturing firm, and father of the bride.

The bride, his only daughter, Holly, was the subject of his speech. A speech filled with tales of Holly when she was growing up, of his admiration for her new husband, Police Detective Ray Quinn, who was sitting laughing, and clutching his new wife's hand. The speech was also peppered with numerous jokes, ranging from harmless G-rated to deep blue. He seemed to have no concern that a large number of children were at the wedding. Maybe he figured the bluer jokes would go over the heads of the minors.

Then it was time for the groom to give his speech. Quinn stood up, coughed, pulled a folded sheet of paper from his pocket, and nervously opened it. Took a gulp of water, a deep breath, and began his speech.

Quinn's speech had no jokes. He thanked all those who had attended the ceremony, his in-laws, and his new bride, 'for having the *cojones* to put up with me'.

The speech over, he leaned down, and gave his wife a long, loving kiss. The guests cheered and clapped as he sat back down again. As he sat back down, he looked over to the guests, at one guest in particular.

At the far end of one of the tables, Police Detective Sam Leroy laughed and applauded as Quinn sat down. As Quinn looked over, Leroy returned his grin. Raised his glass to him.

Leroy and Quinn were colleagues working on the Homicide Desk of the West Los Angeles Area of the LAPD. More than colleagues: they had been partnering each other for two years now; Leroy was the senior partner, and had become a mentor to Quinn. And a good friend. So it was only natural that he would be here at Quinn's wedding.

After the speeches, the music began. The first dance was

of course for the bride and groom. Leroy remained at the end of his table, turning his chair around to face the dance floor.

'Your turn next, Sam,' Holly called out as they glided past his chair.

Leroy raised his glass to them. 'For what?' he replied. 'A dance or a wedding?'

Holly shrugged. 'Whatever,' she laughed as they glided away.

Leroy finished his drink, stood up and ambled over to the bar. There were already three other guests there, including Preston Patterson, a fifty-something career cop, known throughout the department as 'PP', and Leroy's captain.

Patterson stepped over next to Leroy. 'Put it on my tab,' he instructed the bartender.

Leroy took the drink and raised the glass to Patterson. 'Thanks.'

'No problem.' Patterson moved closer to Leroy. 'Look – I'm glad I caught you.'

'Oh yes?' Leroy replied, slowly and suspiciously.

'Yeah. Saves having to wait till Monday.'

'Go on.'

'The Lieutenant post.'

Patterson paused.

Leroy looked into his drink and said nothing.

Patterson continued, 'We've decided to give it to Perez.'

Leroy swirled his drink. 'Ah. Perez.'

'It's nothing personal, you understand…'

Leroy said nothing.

'It's just that you can be a bit…' Patterson tried to find the right word.

Leroy said nothing.

Patterson looked around, as if the right word was on the dance floor.

'A bit...?' asked Leroy.

'Goddam it Sam, you know what I mean. You can be a bit unorthodox, a bit...'

'I get results though, don't I?'

'Yes you do. And there's never been any criticism of your style. It's just that you don't always say the right things. Do you get me?'

Leroy said nothing.

'What I'm saying is,' continued Patterson, 'is that you piss people off sometimes. People whose opinions count.'

'Like the Chief?'

'Like the Chief, yeah. And others.'

Leroy said nothing.

'Maybe you're too direct where you should be tactful. *I've* no problem with you – I like that in a fellow officer. But...'

Leroy said nothing.

Patterson continued, 'But Perez on the other hand – he...'

'Is a good ass kisser?'

'I wouldn't put it quite that way.'

'But...?'

'Okay, Perez is a good ass kisser. But the higher you go up the food chain, the more important that gets.'

Leroy nodded. Said nothing.

Patterson straightened up in his seat and finished his drink. Looked over at Leroy. 'You didn't want it anyway, did you?'

Leroy shook his head, still staring into his drink. 'No.'

Patterson stood up, clearly relieved that the conversation was over. 'Well, have a good evening. I guess I'll see you Monday. I'm assuming you're not back till Monday?' He nodded his head down at Leroy's drink.

'Monday.'

Patterson nodded and returned to two women further down the bar. One of them Leroy recognised as Patterson's wife; the other seemed too old to be a daughter…

Leroy shrugged, finished his drink, and turned round. Quinn and Holly were coming towards him.

'She wants the next dance with you,' Quinn said.

'Oh, it's okay. I don't really….'

'No excuses,' laughed Holly as she took him by the arm and led him to the dance floor. Quinn went to the bar.'

'You like to get your own way,' Leroy said as they began a slow dance. 'I hope Ray knows what he's getting into.'

Holly looked up at him and smiled. 'Oh, don't worry. He does. And what about you, Sam?'

He looked down at her, frowning. 'What about me?'

'When are you going to be getting into something again?'

'Excuse me?'

'You know what I'm talking about. It's been well over a year since -'

'Fifteen months to be precise.'

'Well, surely it's time for you to get out there again.'

'I will when I'm ready.'

'I never met her, but Ray told me about her. I'm sure she would want you to.'

'The trouble with you married guys,' Leroy said, 'is that you can't bear to see other people on their own. We might prefer it.'

'How so?' asked Holly.

'What's best: to be in a relationship you don't want, or where you're not happy; or not to be in one?'

Holly thought for a moment, then nodded. 'Okay. Sorry. But don't leave it too long. It's such a waste.'

'In any case,' he went on, 'you're spoken for. So what hope have I?'

'I'll tell my husband you said that,' Holly laughed.

'I'll tell him myself. Excuse me…' Leroy said as he felt his cell phone vibrate in his pocket. Holly let him go, and

Leroy took the call.

Quinn remained at the bar while Holly and Leroy were dancing. He noticed Leroy excuse himself when he answered his phone and walk away from the floor as he took the call. Holly wandered over to a couple of girlfriends. Quinn slowly put his drink down and walked over to Leroy. As Quinn approached, Leroy ended the call and put the phone away.

'What's up, Sam?' Quinn asked.

'What's up? You just got married. That's what's up.' Leroy looked around. 'Look, Ray. I'm sorry, but I need to go.'

'Shit, Sam. Why? What's happened?'

Leroy looked around again. 'A body's been found. In a back street in Hollywood.'

'Well, that's a newsflash. What does that have to do with us?'

'Nothing to do with *us*. *You* just got married.'

'Okay – what does that have to do with you?'

'They want me to go over and take a look at the crime scene. You never know – I might be back later.'

'How many have you had, though?'

'A couple. I told them I can't drive, so they're sending a black and white over to pick me up. Asked me to take a look.'

'I still don't get what this has to do with you.'

'You know Bill Farmer over in Hollywood Division?'

'A little. Why?'

'He's asked me to go over. Says he would value my opinion.'

'Okay. Well, you'd better get off then.'

Leroy turned and faced Quinn. 'You know that John Doe we had the other day? The one in the parking lot? Just wearing a pair of briefs?'

'Over at Century City?'

'That's the one. That's why Farmer asked for me. They

just found his brother.'

CHAPTER FIVE

IT WAS NOT long before Leroy arrived at the crime scene. After his conversation with Quinn, he made his way to the front of the hotel. A taxi was pulling up, and disgorged a party of four, complete with suitcases. He stood to one side while the bell-hop met them, and wheeled their bags inside to reception. One of the party, a grey-haired man, paid the driver, and the cab sped off.

A few minutes later, a black and white pulled into the hotel grounds. Briefly acknowledging the two uniformed officers in the front, Leroy climbed in back, and the car sped off.

As they drove up the ramp to the Hollywood Freeway, they could see the traffic was moving slowly, maybe about thirty. The officer driving leaned over to the dashboard, and pressed a switch. Immediately Leroy could hear the siren wailing and could see the passing bushes illuminated by the red and blue lights.

'Hey guys,' he said as they joined the freeway and moved into the number four lane, 'there's no need for the siren, is there?'

The second officer turned round slightly. 'Sorry, sir, but Detective Farmer insisted. He wants you at the scene like yesterday.'

'Okay.' Leroy shrugged and sat back in his seat.

Twenty minutes later, they were travelling south down Vine Street. Just after the intersection with Hollywood Boulevard, they made a right to go down an alleyway. The entrance to the alley itself was cordoned off; the black and white slowed down as it approached the cordon, until a young female officer raised the barrier to allow them access. The driver switched off the lights and siren as they made their way along the alley. Round a couple of turns the road opened out. Leroy peered out of the window. Two cruisers were parked at one end of the opening, the red and blue lights on one still flashing. An SUV was standing adjacent to the opposite wall, next to a portable arc light, which was illuminating the scene.

The cruiser pulled up and Leroy climbed out. The officer driving wound down his window and said, 'We'll be parked over there when you're done, Detective. Take you back to your wedding when you've finished here.'

'All right, guy. Thanks.' Leroy patted the car roof and turned to face the crime scene. He noticed the cruiser back away as he walked up to the group of around half a dozen men milling around. One of them, a stocky, balding guy in his late forties, noticed him approach.

'Hey Sam, thanks for coming,' said Bill Farmer. 'Sorry to drag you away from the party.'

'No sweat. So what exactly do you need me for, anyway?'

'Come and look at this.' Farmer led Leroy through the small crowd. When the group parted, Leroy could see a car – he could recognise it as a Chevrolet, but couldn't make out the model – parked at a forty-five degree angle to the wall. A foot behind the rear nearside wing was a body. A man's body, face down, except for a pair of black underpants.

'Take a look,' said Farmer.

Leroy glanced over at him and knelt down next to the body. Under the lights from the arc lamp, he could make out a few facts. The guy appeared Caucasian, and must have been around five feet six tall, around a hundred and sixty pounds. The dark hair, which showed a few wisps of grey behind the ears, was cut short, no more than an inch. The back, which was smooth, except for a few dark hairs at the foot of the spine, appeared unblemished, although there were a couple of dirty marks, which seemed like oil stains.

Just below the underpants, at the top of both legs, were dark marks matching the tread of car tyres. It looked as if a vehicle had gone over the legs twice, as there were two tread marks, one being not quite superimposed on the other. Leroy looked over at the Chevy. The tyre treads matched. The lower legs were untouched also, but there were scratches on both feet, and it looked as if the soles of both feet had been bleeding.

Leroy looked up at Farmer. 'This the car that…?'

Farmer nodded. 'Drove over the legs, then back again.'

Leroy stood up. Stretched a little. 'Who called this in?' he asked. 'Who was driving this?'

'The two over there,' replied Farmer, indicating to a couple standing next to a pair of uniformed officers in a doorway. Leroy looked over.

They both seemed twenty-somethings. The guy was quite short – five feet, Leroy guessed – and looked Asian. The girl, same height but with a lighter frame, looked Hispanic. Both were smartly dressed: he wore a dress shirt, top three buttons open; she was wearing a short dark dress.

Leroy turned to Farmer. 'What's their story? Hooker and john?'

Farmer shook his head. 'No, no. Nothing like that. Guy out with his girlfriend. It's her birthday, apparently. He was taking her to a concert up at the Bowl.'

Leroy snorted. 'One present she wasn't expecting.'

'Yeah. Not even gift wrapped.'

'What were they doing back here, anyway? If they were going to the Bowl, I mean.'

'They said the traffic was all snarled up, and they were afraid they'd be late,' said Farmer. 'It was the guy driving, and he thought he'd take a shortcut.'

'Through here?'

'Says he was sure he could make it through to Highland this way. Said they arrived around here, realised they had taken the wrong turn. He tried to make a three point turn around here, and felt the axle go over something.'

Leroy nodded. 'Then moved the car again to get clear. Hence the two tread marks.'

'That's it,' Farmer said, then paused a moment. 'Anything you want to ask them?'

Leroy shrugged. 'Your investigation, Bill. In any case, I've been drinking, remember?'

Farmer nodded and Leroy knelt down again. Looked over the body.

'Cause of death?' he asked.

'Take a guess,' said Farmer.

Leroy stood up. Scratched his chin and looked down at the body.

'Don't tell me,' he said to Farmer. 'No obvious COD here, but tomorrow the ME will declare it was cardiac arrest.'

CHAPTER SIX

IT WAS JUST past midnight when Leroy eventually made it home. After looking over Bill Farmer's crime scene, and discussing with Farmer how similar this scene was to the one he had been to the previous day, there was nothing else he was able to do there.

'Appreciate you coming, Sam,' Farmer said, resting his hand on Leroy's shoulders.

'No problem, Bill. I owe you one anyway.'

Farmer laughed. 'Probably. Anyhow, I'll get that black and white to take you back to your guy's wedding.'

Leroy looked at his watch. 'Nah. Not worth it. They've probably left for their honeymoon now. I guess I'll just go home.'

'Whatever. They'll take you home. You still in

Venice?'

'Yeah, but don't worry; I'll take a cab.'

'Like hell you will. They were going to take you back Downtown, weren't they? What's a few more miles?'

'If you say so, Bill. It's just-'

'If it eases your conscience, don't put in for overtime for tonight, okay? I guess that kind of evens out the cost.'

Leroy shrugged and laughed. Farmer waved over to the black and white which was still parked fifty or so yards away. The headlights came on, and the car eased over. Leroy got in the back again and gave the officers his address.

'No sirens please this time, guys,' he said as he settled down in the seat.

They made their way onto the main streets and eventually headed west along Santa Monica Boulevard. Leroy felt a little disappointed about having to leave his partner's wedding early, but was sure he understood. He took out his phone and sent Quinn a text: *Sorry had to leave. On way home now as late. Have good honeymoon.*

After he had sent the message he said to the officers in front, 'Appreciate you taking me back, guys. I could've taken a cab.'

'Not to worry, sir,' the passenger replied. 'I know Detective Farmer was keen to get your opinion.'

'Let's just hope we don't get a call,' added the driver. 'Otherwise you'll have to get that cab. Or come with us.'

Leroy's phone bleeped: a text messaged was coming through. He checked the screen. It was Quinn.

No problem. Left ourselves. At our own hotel now.

Leroy nodded. Just as he put the phone back into his pocket, it bleeped again. Quinn again.

Btw what was at the scene?

Typical, thought Leroy, and replied, *Tell you when you back at work. Enjoy your honeymoon detective.*

Lmao came the reply.

Leroy frowned. *Lmao?*

Quinn replied, *Laugh my ass off.*

Leroy shook his head and put the phone away. Only Quinn would be asking about somebody else's crime scene on his wedding night. He reflected that if he was in a hotel room with Holly Quinn, a John Doe in a Hollywood back street would be the last thing on his mind.

Suddenly the car radio crackled and burst into life. 'Any unit, a 211 just occurred at West Pico Street at Sepulveda. Suspect was a male black, six-foot, approximately 180 pounds; shaved head, goatee, white t-shirt, dark baggy pants. Weapon used was a revolver. Code 3. Incident number 555 in RD 193.'

'That's the gas station,' the officer driving said. 'You coming with us, Detective?'

'No. Just drop me off here, will you?'

'Sure thing.'

The cruiser pulled up and Leroy got out. He had barely closed the door when the red and blue roof lights began flashing, the siren started, and the car made a U-turn in the middle of the traffic and headed back east.

Leroy watched as the red and blue lights disappeared into the distance, and the wail of the siren merged into the ambient sounds of the Saturday night traffic. He looked around to get his bearings: he was outside a music store on Santa Monica and 19th.

'Shit,' he said aloud. Nineteen blocks to the ocean. Then it was another three and a half miles to get home. He looked around again to see if he could see a cab. None. He squinted as he peered into the distance east. He thought he could make out a bus in the distance. He thought he could make out a bus stop on the corner of the next block, so sprinted down to 18th street. Sure enough, a bus arrived within seconds.

'Fantastic,' he said aloud, as he saw it was a Big Blue Bus, route 1, which would take him into Santa Monica, then it would turn left along Venice Main Street. He got on, paid his fare, and settled down in a seat halfway down the bus.

He alighted twenty-five minutes later at Windward Circle, Venice, and made the seven short blocks' walk home in fifteen.

Home was a second floor apartment in a small three storey building on 23rd Avenue, between Pacific Avenue and Speedway, a short walk from the ocean. The streets were deserted as Leroy made his way to his building and up the stairs to his floor. He let himself in, and flopped onto the couch. Checked his phone: at least no more messages from Quinn.

He sat up and leaned forward, rubbing his face with the palms of his hands. Now, the evening had not quite panned out as he had planned. He was kind of looking forward to his partner's wedding, but with the normal uncertainties he guessed most unattached people feel at events like this. Although he was happy for Quinn, he felt a tang of envy. If things had been different...

He sat back and thought about Bill Farmer's crime scene. Not his ideal Saturday night, but he was glad Farmer had called him over. The two cases must be connected; the similarities could never be coincidence. The day before - or rather now, two days before – he had been called to an office parking lot in Century City. Three people heading home after a party had discovered a dead male, wearing only underpants, lying by a car. As with Farmer's body, there were no signs of trauma. It was only at the preliminary autopsy – preliminary as it was late Friday night when the body was examined – that the cause of death was stated as cardiac arrest. There was going to be a full autopsy Monday morning.

He rested the back of his head on the couch and closed his eyes. After some very long shifts, he was exhausted. Sunday was to catch up on about three months' sleep deprivation. Monday morning, he will be talking to the ME about his and Farmers' John Does.

Within seconds, Sam Leroy was in a deep sleep.

CHAPTER SEVEN

REGULAR AS CLOCKWORK, Captain Preston Patterson
arrived at work at eight in the morning. Never, ever late;
never early either.

Except today.

Patterson made a $200 cash withdrawal at the ATM in
the red entrance lobby of the LAPD building on Butler and
Iowa and briskly walked in. The large analogue wall clock
showed the time as just after seven fifteen. The young
officer sitting at the reception desk and her two colleagues
milling around the lobby acknowledged Patterson's
greeting, then gave each other a look of surprise at his early
arrival.

Patterson made his way down the corridor of the single
floor building, feeling rather pleased with himself that he

was arriving at work so early. He was in early as he had a mountain of paperwork to finish, and would rather work early than late. And there was the weekly conference call with the other captains and the Chief of Police, where they would spend an hour and a half discussing each Division's crime statistics and clear up rates.

And today he had another call to make.

Despite his early start being of necessity than choice, he still could not help puffing his chest out slightly as he strode past the still empty desks to his own glassed-in office. He knew some of the lower ranks made a joke of his regular as clockwork arrival time, *so they'll be laughing on the other side of their faces when they arrive and see me at my desk.*

Patterson was just about to stride the last few yards to his office when he stopped dead in his tracks. Sitting at a desk, feverishly studying some paperwork and a PC screen, was Detective Sam Leroy. Leroy looked up at Patterson.

'Morning, sir,' Leroy said.

Patterson was temporarily taken aback.

'Morning, Sam. You're in early.'

'I could say the same, sir,' grinned Leroy.

'Yes, well; very funny. I have a mountain of paperwork to do. Plus a dozen or so calls.'

Leroy sat back and took a sip from a paper cup. 'Right.'

'So why the early start for you?' asked Patterson, resting his attaché case on an adjacent desk.

'It's this John Doe we had in Century City on Friday. Just trying to get to grips with it.'

Patterson frowned as he tried to recollect the case.

'Ah, yes. The guy in the parking lot. Just heart failure, as I recall.'

'So the preliminary examination said. The full autopsy is this morning. I'm planning on catching up with the ME later.'

'Seemed open and shut to me.'

'Captain, he was in a parking lot just dressed in his

shorts.'

'There was an office party upstairs, wasn't there? He probably picked up a workmate, they went to one of their cars for some action, and it was too much for him. How much alcohol in his system?'

Leroy shook his head. 'The prelim said there was a little; one unit maybe.'

'Like I said, seems open and shut. I wouldn't spend too much time on this one, Sam. How many unsolved homicides on our books?'

Leroy nodded and sipped more coffee. 'A dozen or so. I know. That's why I came in early.'

'Very commendable. Any case, Sam, Perez takes up his post later in the week. Should take the pressure off you.'

'I know, but Quinn's on honeymoon till the 26th.'

'All the more reason not to waste time on unnecessary cases,' said Patterson as he picked up his case and turned to leave.

Leroy scratched his chin and returned to his paperwork.

'By the way,' asked Patterson, turning round, 'you left early on Saturday?'

'Yeah,' Leroy relied, sitting back again. 'I had a call from Bill Farmer.'

'Hollywood Division, yes? What could he say to call you away from your partner's wedding?'

'He had his own John Doe that night. Back of Hollywood Boulevard.'

'Not unusual surely? A body in Hollywood on a Saturday night.'

'That was my reaction when he called and asked me to take a look.'

'And?'

'You want to know something, Captain? His John Doe was exactly the same as mine. Lying on the deck in his underpants, no obvious signs of death. Another heart failure, I guess. Another open and shut case.'

Patterson stared at Leroy a moment, then said, 'Well, I'll let you get on, then. You're obviously very busy. But don't forget those other cases, will you?'

'Of course not, Captain.'

Leroy leaned forward and resumed leafing through the paperwork on his desk. Patterson said nothing more, and walked to his own office. Went in and closed the door.

As he heard the door close, Leroy sat up. Something was different. He frowned as he tried to figure out what.

That was it. Patterson was one of those senior officers who normally left their office door open.

CHAPTER EIGHT

ONE OF THE dozen unsolved homicides was that of a homeless guy, found over a week earlier. Early one Sunday morning two joggers were running across Clover Park, a small city park, roughly one half block by three, used by local families for baseball, football, soccer and most other sports.

As the two tracksuited men passed a small brick building in the centre of the park, one of them began running on the spot.

'Can you hold on, Tyler?' he asked the other, who was also by now jogging on the spot. 'I need to take a piss.'

'Sure, go on, Will,' Tyler replied. He was now working out in the middle of the path.

The building comprised two small bathrooms, men's

and women's. To get access to the men's room Will had to walk - or rather jog – round a small partition and through a doorway with a pictogram of a man beside it. There were two urinals and two stall doors. Will opened the right-hand side door.

Outside, Tyler heard Will call out for him. He stopped working out and ran into the bathroom. Resting one hand on the wooden doorframe, he saw Will standing by one of the stall doors. The door was open, and sitting on the pedestal, slumped up in one corner was a man. He was wearing a dirty checked shirt and grubby dark coloured combat pants. Short, curly grey hair, goatee beard to match. He was staring, mouth and eyes wide open, up at the ceiling. There was a large black hole either side of his head, and a thick, black trace, now dried, running down his temple. The whole bathroom smelt bad.

'Fuck me,' said Tyler.

In terms of priority, the murder of a homeless person has very little priority in Homicide Division. In ninety-nine cases out of a hundred, the killer will never be found, and the Department does not have the resources to work such cases. So they stay on the books as an unsolved case, unless someone confesses later.

In most homicides, unless there is a reliable witness who is prepared to testify, one of the first areas the investigators look at is motive. Robbery was clearly discounted: he had no ID on him, and only a folded $5 bill in a back pocket. Leroy and Quinn canvassed the people using the park, and those living in a two block radius, but without success. The body was found early on a Sunday morning: the place would have been in use all day Saturday, so it must have occurred sometime Saturday night. The medical examiner confirmed this. But there was still the mystery of how this street person came to be there.

One theory that Leroy and Quinn had was that he originated from Santa Monica and had migrated eastwards. The night in question was unseasonably chilly - around 37 degrees – and he had sought shelter in the building. In any case, Clover Park is quite open, and he would have been hard pressed to find natural shelter for the night. He was sitting in a stall, but fully dressed, so was not using the toilet. Quinn suggested he might have been witness to some kind of encounter, maybe two gay men, and shot by one of them. Leroy felt the idea was not without merit, but he felt it unlikely he would be killed just because he saw two guys humping. In any case, whether it was that, or something like a drug transaction, even if he did report it, who would believe the word of a homeless old guy?

It was all academic, however; after two days, Leroy and Quinn were ordered by Patterson to leave the case as pending, and move on to the next case, where there was a better chance of finding the culprit.

'Street guy shot in the middle of a park middle of the night,' he had said. 'Chances of finding who did it – zero. Unless someone calls in and makes a confession, you're wasting the department's time and resources.'

So the Clover Park murder remained unsolved, and untouched.

Until this morning.

Leroy thought he would take the Captain at his word and focus on his twelve unsolveds. Clover Park began with a C, and was on the top of his list. He had decided he would spend one day on the case, to see if he could dig up anything more. Fresh pair of eyes syndrome. In any case, he was still uneasy about the guy being shot almost execution style just for witnessing something going on in a bathroom. Unless the killer did it because he felt like it.

Leroy parked on 25th, and wandered through the park, over to the bathrooms. He wandered around the buildings, then walked around the partition. The women's bathroom was to the left; the men's to the right. First of all he stepped over to the women's door, took out his badge, and then knocked on the wooden doorway.

'Hello? Anyone in there? Police,' he called out. There was no answer. He stepped in, and just as he got over the threshold, he heard a flush. He stepped back outside and momentarily a plump middle-aged woman stepped out. She stopped dead in her tracks when she saw Leroy, but relaxed when she noticed the badge he was holding out.

'Police. Sorry. Didn't mean to alarm you,' he said.

She muttered something, went over to the washbasin, washed and dried her hands and bustled past him. Once she had gone, Leroy looked around inside, pushed open the three stall doors with his foot. Looked around each stall. There was nothing of any interest here.

Then he went into the men's room. It was exactly as he had remembered it from before. A touch shabby, but generally clean, although with a slight odour of urine. Again, he pushed open the doors to the two stalls and looked around. Looking around the right-hand stall, he remembered the day when the body was found. He recalled that the bullet passed right through the victim's head. He had been shot at almost point-blank range, and the bullet also passed through the wooden stall wall to become embedded in the concrete wall some twenty feet away. It was a .38, he recalled. The hole in the wooden wall was still there; walking over to the far wall, he could still make out the spot from where it had been recovered.

He wandered around the bathroom, taking in the two stalls, the two urinals, the small hand basin under a mirror, which was surprisingly clean. The interior walls were still the same dark green he recalled from his first visit, slightly shabbier. He looked around, as if seeking inspiration.

He got none.

Normally, a homicide scene would have CSIs around it like fleas on a dog until they found something: this being a street person, he had doubts as to whether this scene received the same attention as the next unsolved on his list: a stabbing on a Blue Line tram on its way to Long Beach.

He wandered outside and looked around. This being a Monday morning, the park was fairly quiet. Weekends it would be filled with families, with kids playing ball games. Today, he could see two women pushing strollers, a man walking his dog along the park perimeter by 25th Street; another man the other side of the park, walking back to the parking lot. He heard an engine noise and looked up: he could just make out a single engine aircraft coming in to land at the municipal airport half a mile away.

He thought about the enquiries he and Quinn originally made: he himself knocked on the doors of three of the streets west of the park with a photograph of the dead man, but they all drew a blank. They made similar enquiries in Santa Monica itself, showing his image to the other street people congregating around Ocean Front Walk. But still the guy was a mystery. Then it all came down to resources: the likelihood of identification and conviction was so low, the case was left. An old story: not the first time that had happened, and Leroy was sure it would not be the last.

'Looks like you're going to stay unsolved, my friend,' he said quietly, looking back at the men's room. He turned and headed back to his car.

As he reached the edge of the grass and stepped onto the 25th Street sidewalk, his cell phone rang. Still walking down 25th to where he had parked his car, he answered. It was Russell Hobson, from the Medical Examiner's office.

As well as being colleagues, Leroy and Hobson were friends, and had been so for many years. By coincidence, they grew up in the same neighbourhood in Queens, New York City. They were born the same year, Hobson two months later than Leroy, and attended the same school. After they graduated from High School, their paths drifted: Hobson began medical training and Leroy joined the

NYPD. Then, eighteen months ago, to the surprise of them both, they met up again. Hobson, who had been working for the Chicago ME, applied for and got a position in LA; Leroy had transferred to the LAPD some years ago.

Leroy had been expecting this call. 'Talk to me Russ.'

'Sam, you need to get your ass down here right away.'

'Why? What's up?'

'That John Doe you brought in Friday. The one in Century City.'

'I know the one. Cardiac arrest, is it?'

'Well, yes and no.'

Leroy climbed into his black Ford Taurus. 'What do you mean, yes and no?'

'It's quite complicated. That's why I need you to come in. Can you do that?'

'Sure I can. Give me thirty minutes,' Leroy replied, starting the engine.

'Okay. See you soon, buddy.'

With that, Hobson hung up.

Letting out a deep breath, Leroy swung the car round and up to Ocean Park Boulevard. Although Hobson always did have a sense of drama, even they were kids together, there was something different in his voice today.

As he drove back to Police HQ, Leroy wondered what could be so urgent and dramatic about a cardiac arrest case.

CHAPTER NINE

THE AVERAGE ANNUAL rainfall for Southern California is twelve inches. As the silver Lotus made its way south-west along Mulholland Drive, it seemed to the driver that it was all falling that night. Just drizzle as he left the freeway; now it was raining hard. He had the wipers on full, but even then visibility was poor. The number of sharp turns on this stretch of road made it difficult to get above thirty-five in good driving conditions; now he could only manage ten miles per hour slower. He cursed frequently as vehicles approached from the other direction, headlights on full, dazzling him.

He checked the time. Almost nine o'clock. There was no way now he was going to get there on time. He cursed himself for not leaving home earlier, but it was becoming more and more difficult to get out, more difficult to find an excuse that sounded reasonable.

He considered taking a detour along Woodrow Wilson or one of the other side roads to make the journey shorter to cut out the bends, but tonight, in the dark and the rain, he was afraid he might miss the turning and a more minor road could be more treacherous in these conditions.

The traffic slowed almost to a stop at one really sharp bend, almost a one-eighty. He hoped that there had not been an accident; not from any concern about anyone involved, but that would delay him even more. So much so, that he would run out of time; that it would not be worth the remainder of the journey. He was expected home between eleven and eleven-thirty, and tonight time was not on his side.

The line of vehicles moved slowly up to and around the bend; as he turned the one-eighty, he could see a car had broken down, and traffic passing had to brake and wait for passing vehicles before they could overtake. After ten minutes he was able to pass the breakdown himself. Glancing out of the side window as he passed he could see a figure in a yellow hooded raincoat standing by the side of the car.

Once he passed the breakdown, he was able to pick up some speed, but still the rain and the twisting nature of the road made it impossible to get above twenty-five. As he carried on further, he wished he had had GPS fitted in the car. After all, he knew the ZIP code of where he was going. It was one of those things he hadn't gotten round to doing. He knew he was headed for the 8400 block, then next left. His stare went from the road ahead to the side of the road and back again, looking for his turning.

'Shit!' he yelled as he saw Edwin Way flash past. He knew his turning was just before Edwin. There was no way he could perform a U turn on this road: he slowed down to about fifteen and looked for a side road, either this side or the other.

Through the rain streamed windshield he made out a turning on his left. He slowed some more to let two vehicles pass, then carefully made a left. The street he turned into was unlit, and there were high bushes either side. He drove slowly forward, looking for a place to turn. After fifty yards or so, he could make out this was a dead end, but the road opened up at the spot where the driveways for two gated residences met.

He made a nine point turn in the tiny space, being careful not to damage his paintwork on the stone columns each side of the gateways. Then back down to Mulholland, waited for a passing car, and turning right.

A hundred yards later, he caught sight of his intended turn off. Another pause for passing traffic, another left turn, another darkened street. However, further up, he could make out lights from a building. As he got closer he could see that it was a large house, lights blazing from all its windows, and from a wide open front door. He breathed a sigh of relief. This must be his destination.

He took the car through an opened gate and as he got closer to the house he realised there was a figure standing outside the house, in the open doorway. As he parked the car, the figure walked out towards him. It was a man, clean shaven, tall and around 175 pounds. He was wearing an open necked shirt, and a pair of shorts. He leaned over to address the driver.

'I wondered if you had a problem finding the house,' he called out.

'You could say that.'

'Especially on a night like this. Not easy to find at the best of times. Come with me. You're getting wet.'

The man with the umbrella leading, they both walked into the house. Once inside, they went into what seemed to be a sitting room, but one from a different age. With the exception of a large flat screen television in one corner, the room was decorated and furnished as if it was the 1930s.

'Take a seat.' He shook the umbrella, folded it, and placed it in a rack. 'Would you like a drink?'

'Er – just water, please.'

'Nothing stronger?'

'Driving. And bad night out.'

'Of course. Still or sparkling?'

'Still, please.'

The host left the room and momentarily brought in a glass of water. Handed it over, and sat down on a couch opposite the man. He looked at his watch. 'I understand why you were late,' he said, 'but it does mean we don't have as much time. You don't anyway.'

'No problem. I understand.'

The host looked around. 'You could save time by seeing her in here. Rather than in one of the bedrooms. If that's okay with you.'

'That's okay by me.'

'Would you like her blonde, or brunette?'

'Er – blonde I think.'

'Black or red?'

'Excuse me?'

'Wearing black or red?'

'Black.'

The host stood up. 'Can I ask you to wait in the other room through there?' He indicated to a door. 'She will call you when she is ready for you.'

'Okay.' The other man got off the couch and went into the other room, closing the door behind him. This room was sparsely furnished, although in contemporary style. He sat on a black leather desk chair. Checked his watch: it was almost ten.

He must have been waiting five minutes when there was a faint knock on the door.

'Are you ready?' said a quiet voice. The door was opened slightly.

He slowly stepped back into the sitting room. The main light had been switched off; now the only illumination was from a small desk lamp. He closed the door behind him and looked over at the woman.

In the low light he could make out she was blonde, or at least not brunette. Her hair was shoulder length. She was wearing a shiny black dress, low cut and finishing just below her crotch, black lacy stockings. She was standing with one arm on her hip, the other on one of the couches.

'He told you we don't have much time, didn't he?' she asked, in a low, whispery voice.

'Er – yes. He did.'

'Better get started then. Come over here.' Running an index finger over the top of the couch, she took two steps round and sat down. She looked up at him and indicated for him to join her, but as he was about to sit down, she stopped him so he was now standing in front of her.

She took a deep sigh and reached over to him. He was already aroused and she began to massage the bump in his pants.

'We do have *some* time,' she laughed softly.

She massaged him some more, then unzipped his pants. He let out a cry, and put both hands on her shoulders for support. He closed his eyes tightly, enjoying the feeling. Opened them and looked down at her, working on him.

Then his eyes opened wide.

'No,' he panted. 'No way.'

CHAPTER TEN

IT TOOK LEROY twenty minutes to make the nineteen miles from Clover Park to meet up with Russell Hobson.

The medical examiner was based in one of the criminal laboratories in the Hertzberg-Davis Forensic Science Center on Paseo Rancho Castilla, just west of Monterey Park, and adjacent to California State University. Since 2007, and after two years' construction and costing slightly over $80 million, the imposing concrete and red brick building had been the home to the Los Angeles Crime Laboratories.

Leroy headed off the freeway and shortly pulled up at the barrier. Showed his identification to the guard who raised the barrier, and directed him over to a space. He walked quickly up the concrete steps to the main entrance.

A uniformed officer was exiting the building and nodded to Leroy as they passed. Leroy returned the nod: the officer's face seemed familiar, but he was unable to put a name to it. Their paths had obviously crossed in the past.

Once inside, he strode over to the four elevators: the doors for two of them were already opened. He stepped inside and jabbed at the 5 button. With a faint ping, the doors slid shut. He was momentarily on the fifth floor and walked down a corridor until he came to a white door with a plaque stating:

Laboratory 2

Dr Russell Hobson ME

Medical Examiner

Leroy pushed open the door and walked in. He had visited this laboratory many times before, and each time was taken back by the contrast between here and his own workplace. His offices were untidy, with desks and chairs everywhere, paperwork and box files piled on top of filing cabinets, notice boards covered with sheets of paper of varying sizes and colours. Here everything seemed so sterile - which is how it should be, he always reflected – and calm: no frantic hustle and bustle, no phones ringing constantly.

The laboratory was decorated in white, and the tables, cabinets and cupboards were all a shiny stainless steel. On one side of the laboratory were two tables, each covered by a green rubber sheet. Leroy could tell that each of the two sheets was covering a body.

Over on the far side of the laboratory, taking up the whole length of the wall, were three wide windows, providing, as he knew from experience, a vista of the San Bernadino Freeway. By one of the windows, at a sink busy washing his hands, was a figure in a white lab coat. The noise of the door closing caused him to turn round. He grinned as he saw Leroy.

'Well, you took your time,' he laughed, drying his hands.

'Very funny. There are such things as speed limits, you know,' Leroy retorted as they shook hands.

'Unlike you to observe them. How are you, Sam?' Hobson asked. 'How are you this fine Monday morning? Good weekend?'

'Nothing out of the ordinary.'

'Didn't your partner – Quinn…?'

'Ray Quinn, that's right.'

'Wasn't he getting married or something?'

'Or something?' Leroy laughed.

'You know what I mean. Wasn't he?'

'Yes, he was. Yes, he did, I should say. That's why I'm here on my own. He's off on honeymoon. I was at his wedding as it happened when I got a call about these.' He indicated over to the two tables. 'You did call about these, didn't you?'

'These? Only one of them is yours, buddy.'

'Don't tell me. The other belongs to Bill Farmer over in Hollywood Division.'

'How'd you know that?'

'That's why I had to leave the wedding early Saturday. Bill Farmer asked me to go over and look at the scene. Mine was the night before.'

Hobson nodded.

'Well, that would make sense,' he said as he took off his glasses and rubbed the bridge of his nose. 'Were the crime scenes similar?'

Leroy rubbed the back of his neck. 'Too similar to be coincidental. Two guys early middle age found dressed only in shorts – what do you think? Anyway, the preliminary examinations said they died of cardiac arrest, so at this stage we don't even know if it *was* a crime scene.'

'Oh, it was,' said Hobson as he pulled back both sheets. 'It *was* a crime scene.'

CHAPTER ELEVEN

LEROY LOOKED DOWN at the faces of the two dead men below. Both were white, early thirties. He recognised both faces, one from the Century City parking lot, the other from the Hollywood back street.

'The prelim exam said cardiac arrest. No suspicious circumstances, we guessed. After the first, that is.'

'And after Farmer showed you this one?'

'Thought it one hell of a coincidence to be sure, but that's why I was waiting on you. Is Bill Farmer coming over, by the way?'

'I called him after I had hung up on you. He's tied up in court this morning, hoped to make it over later.'

'Okay. So – are you telling me they didn't die of natural causes, then? How come the prelim said cardiac arrest?'

Hobson took off his glasses, put them in his lab coat pocket, then perched himself on a stool.

'Sam,' he said, 'cardiac arrest, heart failure: these occur every time someone dies. On death the heart stops. A prelim exam will only give you part of the picture; we have far more resources here than the guys on the ground. And if it hadn't been a weekend, we could have gotten all the facts sooner. Maybe.'

Leroy leaned on a wall and folded his arms. 'So what are you saying, Russ? It wasn't natural causes?'

Hobson sat forward, rubbing his hands up and down his legs. 'This is the – the sequence of events, as it were. They both died because their hearts failed. Right?'

Leroy nodded. 'Go on.'

'The next stage is to find out what caused the hearts to stop.'

'With you so far.'

'Sam, have you ever heard the expression *serotonin syndrome*?'

Leroy thought a moment. 'At the back of my mind, yes, but…'

'Well,' Hobson continued, 'serotonin syndrome is a drug reaction, potentially life-threatening, that can occur following therapeutic drug use, overdose of particular drugs, or the recreational use of some kinds of drugs. It's not hit or miss: it's predictable, and it's the result of excess serotonergic energy at the central nervous system and peripheral serotonin receptors. Some in the profession prefer to call it serotonin toxidrome as it's really a form of poisoning.'

'I see. I think. So basically, it's when someone has taken two different drugs at the same time, and they react.'

'More or less, yes.'

'So if someone had this – this syndrome: would they exhibit any symptoms?'

'For sure, yes. And quickly. Very shortly after

ingesting the second drug. And there are a lot of symptoms: sweating, shivering, shaking, twitching. And that's just a mild case. More seriously, we're talking about high blood pressure, hyperthermia, hypervigilance, diarrhoea, nausea. And the body temperature generally rises to over 106.'

'Jesus.'

'Quite.'

'So what sort of drugs could cause this state?'

'The list is endless, Sam. It could be a massive amount of one drug, or a combination.'

'Like what? Give me an example.'

'Antidepressants, painkillers, stimulants, recreational drugs. Certain herbs, such as nutmeg.'

'Shit. So what exactly is this – sero…?'

'Serotonin. It's a neurotransmitter, which means it's an endogenous chemical that transmit signals from a neuron to a target cell across a synapse.'

'Ah. Thought so,' Leroy lied.

'Basically, Sam, it's a chemical the body produces at certain times to produce a certain reaction, such as sleep, pain, appetite, depression.'

'O-kay. I think I'm getting it.'

'Good. Now, there's no actual laboratory test for serotonin syndrome.'

'Then how do you know…?'

'Hear me out. There's no specific test, and so we look at a diagnosis of the symptoms and the person's medical history.'

'Not much use with a dead John Doe.'

'Quite. But Toxicology were able to carry out screening tests on the blood and urine.'

'And?'

'In both cases, there were traces of drugs in both the blood and the urine. Of both guys, though more in – your guy.' Hobson rested the palm of one hand on the Century City corpse.

'Right. Now we're getting somewhere. What drugs were used, and how much?'

'Well, as you might know, narcotics tests take the form of colour tests and crystal tests. These are really screening tests, then we carry out a GC-MS...'

'Gas chromatograph-mass spectrometer...? Leroy said slowly.

'Good boy. So you do listen. Yes, you're right: we carry out a GC-MS and another similar test and we are able to identify the narcotics in his body.'

'Go on.'

Hobson picked up a printed report. Put his glasses back on.

'First off: alcohol. Zero in both cases.'

Leroy said, 'Go on.'

'They found - in both bodies, although as I say slightly more in your guy's – cocaine freebase, flunitrazepam, and lysegic acid diethylamide.'

Leroy whistled. 'That's one cocktail. Cocaine, rohypnol, and LSD. Am I right?'

'Correct.'

'So how much did they take? And isn't one person's tolerance different from another? These guys look quite fit, young, strong.'

Hobson referred to the printout again. 'Sam, don't forget that it's the reaction of the chemicals which causes seratonin syndrome.'

'Yes, but surely they snorted more than a row.'

'As far as the LSD is concerned: as you know, if you or I took say ten thousand micrograms, we'd go to the moon and back and be fine the next day. Kind of. We traced over a hundredth of a gram inside them.'

Leroy looked back at the bodies. 'Christ. That would cost a fortune.'

'I wouldn't know, but I would guess you have a point. Same with the rohypnol and the LSD.'

Leroy said nothing.

'One other thing,' continued Hobson. 'We also carried out trace evidence tests.'

'Not many personal effects.'

'No, there weren't. We just tested their shorts and the bodies themselves.'

'Powder on the nostrils, that type of thing?'

'That's one thing we looked for, yes, but that came up negative. The shorts on one of them - Bill Farmer's, I think – were soiled, but that's a common symptom of seratonin syndrome.'

'What did you find then?'

'Both bodies were clean; well, for our purposes. Except in both cases, we found trace on their penises.'

'Cocaine?'

'No. It was basically female DNA.'

'So they got laid before death.'

'Correct.'

'Any idea how long before they died?'

'DNA degrades quicker when wet. The fluid dried on them quite fast, so it's preserved very well. All I can say it, it's unlikely either of them took a shower between sex and death.'

'Can't you tell by checking the testicles?'

'The level in both sets was low. But as a test, it's not particularly conclusive, as different people refill at different rates. And the fact that we found a woman's DNA there suggests to me they had oral sex, otherwise they would have used a condom.

Leroy nodded thoughtfully. 'I understand. But why did you say it had to be a crime scene. Couldn't these two just have been to a party - albeit without alcohol – got stoned, very stoned, got laid, and suffered the cardiac arrest due to the drugs? Accidental death, though we can get the supplier.'

'On the face of it, that seems possible. But at the end of

the day, that's your job isn't it?'

Leroy nodded. 'Yeah. My job. I think missing persons is the best first port of call. See if we can ID any of these guys. Then maybe get their whereabouts.'

'You going to liaise with Farmer?' Hobson asked.

'Guess so. He's coming over later, you say?'

'U-huh. When he's done in court.'

'Okay. I'll give him a call in any case.'

'Right.'

Leroy touched Hobson's arm. 'Thanks for that, Russ. Be in touch.'

'It's nearly lunchtime. You…?'

'Some other time, buddy. Best get on with this.'

'Surely. Take care now.'

'See you.'

Leroy left the laboratory and made for the elevators. Back in the car, he turned on the engine. Looked through the windshield at the sun, high in the sky. So bright he had to squint. Took out his phone and called Bill Farmer. The phone went directly to voicemail; presumably Farmer was still in court.

Leroy pulled out of the space and, deep in thought, headed slowly for the main road.

CHAPTER TWELVE

AS LEROY TURNED off Butler Avenue at the entry to the parking lot behind Police Headquarters, he recognized the vehicle leaving. 'Oh shit,' he muttered as Captain Patterson stopped his car and wound down his window. He did the same.

'How are the enquiries going?' Patterson asked. Leroy knew perfectly well the enquiries he was referring to but pretended not to.

'Which enquiries, sir?'

'You were taking another look at some of the unsolveds still on your books,' Patterson replied. It always amused Leroy how if a case was successfully solved it was always on *our* books, and if it all went tits up or was unsolved, it was always on *your* books.

'I've made a start on the first. Street person found dead in the restroom in Clover Park. Been over the scene -'

'Street person? You sure you have your priorities right, Sam? I'm sure some of the other cases are more pressing.'

'I agree it's pretty low down the food chain, sir. Two priority points out of ten, I guess. Nevertheless, it is worth looking at again, even if only for a day or so. If you recall, we only spent a two days making enquiries. If the vic had been say a WASP, then -'

Patterson cut in with, 'Yes, well; don't wa- spend too much time on it.'

'As it turns out, sir, I got called away from the park. Hobson over at the crime lab wanted to see me about the John Doe we had in Century City Friday night.'

'The guy in the parking lot?'

'That's the one. And the one Bill Farmer had in Hollywood the next day.'

Patterson frowned. 'What does Farmer's case have to do with it?'

'They're virtually identical. Two men more or less the same age found dead and almost naked. Both had had sex recently and both were filled with a cocktail of drugs.'

'Drugs?'

'Yeah. Coke, rohypnol and LSD.'

'Hmm. Any sign of third party involvement?'

'Well, apart from the sex and whoever gave or sold them the drugs, no. Not as yet.'

'Hmm,' Patterson repeated.

'And it was a woman,' Leroy added.

'A woman?'

'Yes. It was a woman they had both had sex with. Unprotected, obviously.'

'Yes, of course. Otherwise, we'd never know. Same woman?'

'Not established yet, sir.'

'I see.' Patterson looked round and saw another car

behind him also waiting to exit the lot. 'Well, keep me up to date, won't you? Actually Perez - Lieutenant Perez – is back tomorrow, so once you've appraised him of things, he will keep me up to date.'

With that, Patterson wound the window up and drove off.

'Asshole,' Leroy muttered and moved the Taurus to his space. Once inside, he made his way to his desk, slumped into the chair and switched on his computer.

'Hey there, Sam,' said a voice behind him. Leroy swivelled round and saw Detective Eliza Domingo sitting at a desk in the corner.

'Hey,' replied Leroy. 'Didn't see you there.'

'Sorry to hear about…you know.'

'About what?'

Domingo shuffled in her chair. 'About you not getting the Lieutenant post.'

'Oh, everybody's heard then. I didn't think anyone even knew I'd put in for it.'

'Come on, Sam. You know what it's like here.'

'Sure. Anyway, Perez'll do a good job.'

'Yeah. Right.' Dead-pan, Domingo returned her gaze to her monitor screen, then glanced at Leroy and smirked.

Leroy grinned back at her and turned back to his screen. He keyed in his personnel number and password. At once a pop up appeared reminding him that he had to change his password in three days.

'Jesus,' he whispered, clicking on the *OK* button. The LAPD database opened. First, Leroy went to the reports of his and Farmer's bodies. He reread the preliminary examination reports, then notices that Hobson had already updated the system with his full report.

'You're on the ball, Russ,' he said out loud. He clicked on the folder for Hobson's report on the Century City victim, and read the report. Then did the same for the second case. In both cases, there was very little to add to what

Hobson had told him verbally earlier in the day.

'Going to get a coffee, Sam,' said Domingo who was now standing in front of his desk. 'Want one?'

He looked up. 'Yeah, thanks. Cream and sugar.'

'Coming up.' She wandered out of the office.

'Liza?' he called out. 'Just realised I haven't eaten today. Could you bring me back a sandwich?'

'Sure. What do you want?'

'Oh, anything. Cheese, bacon..?'

'Really. Anything.' Leroy turned back to his screen and read Hobson's reports again. When Domingo returned, he was searching the database for missing person reports.

'Thanks,' he said. 'How much do I owe you?'

'Forget it.' She rested her hand on his shoulder and went back to her desk. Leroy frowned. There was nothing on the two reports about either of the victim's wearing a wedding band. Not that the absence meant anything striking. Not every married man wore one, and a man living with a partner would be missed. And it was possible that they might have removed a wedding band before going to a sex and drugs party; in that case there would probably be a white ridge on the finger. Leroy's problem would be if the guy was single, living alone. It could be days before anyone reported him missing.

Leroy clicked on the folder icon and the missing persons database opened. He tabbed down the *Date Reported* column until he reached the date for the previous Monday. Then he slowly moved the cursor down over the entries, searching for matches.

'I wonder.' He clicked on the fifth entry down. It was for a man from Culver City, born thirty years ago. Leroy tabbed down to a photograph. 'Damn,' he muttered. The photographs were no match. The same again for the next entry. And the next. And the next.

Domingo called out, 'What are you looking for, Sam? Anything I can help with?'

69

He swung round again. 'No, I'm okay, thanks. Just searching the MPU database to see if I can come up with names for the John Doe I got last Friday. And Bill Farmer's up in Hollywood.'

'You had a John Doe on Friday?' Domingo asked.

'Yeah. And the next night, Bill Farmer up in Hollywood Division caught one in a back alley. Asked me to take a look at it on account of the circumstances being so similar to mine. Had to miss half of Quinn's wedding to get up there.'

'Both men?' she asked.

'Yeah, both men,' he replied as he swung back to his desk. 'Mid thirties.'

'Only wearing shorts, cause of death as yet not ascertained?'

Leroy pushed back against the desk, moving his chair back three feet as it swung back round to face Domingo.

Domingo looked up from her screen.

'We had one last night.'

CHAPTER THIRTEEN

'YOU HAD WHAT?' Leroy said. 'You had one of your own? Why didn't you tell me?'

Domingo cocked her head to one side. 'Sam,' she said, 'you only just told me yourself. I thought ours was a one-off.'

'Yeah – where's…what's your partner's name?'

'Connor. Judd Connor. Only been here three weeks. We were both up till one on this case. Told him to take today off. He has a family after all.'

'Don't tell Quinn that. The number of times we've been working till one *and* been in at eight the next morning.'

'Quinn?' she asked, looking into space in mock contemplation. 'Isn't he the guy you let off for ten days on account of his getting married?'

'Yeah yeah yeah. What was I supposed to do? In any case, forget about Quinn. Tell me about your body.'

She raised her eyebrows.

'You know what I mean,' Leroy grinned.

She picked up her paper cup and drained it. Leaned back in her chair.

'Black male, aged thirty to thirty-five, wearing only underpants, found by the side of the I-5 at Griffith Park last night.'

'Black, you say?'

'U-huh. Why? Is that important?'

Leroy shrugged. 'Probably not. The other two were white. Sorry. Carry on.'

'We figured he'd fallen or rolled down the hillside from Crystal Springs Drive. Or Griffith Park Drive. Both highways run about a hundred feet above.'

'Sure. I know where you mean.'

Domingo continued, 'We cordoned off the site last night and went back this morning once it got light. Found where he fell: scraps of material from his shorts snagged on a couple of branches and some blood traces.'

'Sounds reasonable. Did you establish cause of death?'

'That might take a while.'

'On our two it seemed at first that they died of natural causes. Cardiac arrest. But I saw the ME this morning and he tells me both their bodies were full of a drug cocktail. Roofies, LSD and coke. Massive doses.'

'Jesus,' said Domingo. 'ODs?'

'Clearly. But I can get my head round one person taking a massive OD, but *two*? Bit of a coincidence, don't you think?'

'Hmm. Maybe they were at the same party. Same age range. Maybe they were drunk.'

Leroy shook his head. 'No alcohol in their bodies.'

She sat back and scratched the back of her head.

'Anyway, my vic might be a little different.'

'How so?'

'He must have rolled down the hillside. We found him on the freeway shoulder. But not before a thirty foot rig had finished with him.'

'Oh, Christ. What was left of him?'

'He was still intact, if that's what you mean, but there was severe body trauma. And I mean severe. The rig must have been going at over seventy - it was around eleven on a Sunday night – and according to the driver, this figure just appeared on the road. Wandering from the shoulder. The driver wouldn't have had time to react. Just knocked him twenty feet in the air. The body hit the top of the rig as it came down, bounced off the roof and landed back on the shoulder.'

'It was the truck driver who called it in?'

'Yes. He pulled over and called us.'

'Alcohol? The driver I mean.'

She shook her head. 'Dry as a bone. The captain wants us to follow up on his speed. By his own admission, he was over the limit.'

'What is it on the I-5? Seventy?'

'Fifty-five for trucks, so the driver's in deep shit just for that.'

'Wouldn't have made any difference; at fifty-five, the impact would still have killed him.'

'Probably.'

Leroy nodded. 'Probably.'

They both sat for a few seconds in silence until Leroy said, 'So what now? What's your next move?'

'While Connor's not here I thought I'd just finish off all the paperwork. The body's at the ME's so I'll wait for his report.'

'Even with the trauma, Hobson will still be able to establish what was in his system. I'll take book that it's the same cocktail as mine. Clearly cardiac arrest won't apply.'

'No. Where were yours found?'

'Mine was in a parking lot in Century City; Farmer's was off Hollywood Boulevard.'

'Are we treating them as separate cases?' she asked. 'Or one investigation?'

'Had no instructions to say one investigation. I guess that's up to our new lieutenant. I ran into Patterson on the way in: he said Perez starts tomorrow.'

'Swell.'

'Well, in the absence of any such instructions, we'd better get on with our individual cases. Best to keep each other up to date, though.'

'Sure thing, Sam.' Domingo got up and returned to her desk. Leroy turned back to his monitor. His screen had gone into lock-up, so he typed in his password again, clicked *OK* on the password change pop-up again, and returned to the missing persons database. Tabbed down to the last entry he looked at. A comparison of the photographs of the next three missing persons showed they were not his victim.

The next one down, however, was a different story.

The missing person report was for a Lance Riley. White male, aged thirty-one. Lived Vorhees Avenue, Redondo Beach, with partner Michelle Alexander, who filed the report. There was no mention of any children. The photograph was one of the two of them with an ocean as a background, both happy and smiling. Leroy clicked on the photograph, and enlarged it. He carefully studied the larger image and the image from the dead man. Obviously there were slight, cosmetic, differences, but it was clear it was the same man.

Leroy sighed and sat back in his chair. In spite of all the years he had worked in Homicide, and all the cases he had dealt with, he could easily remain detached when it was just a nameless body he was dealing with. But once it gained a name, an address, and family, and a life, this detachment became harder.

The report had been filed around midday Saturday. He

had not been seen since he left for work Friday morning. He scratched his chin. If he was last seen by his partner Friday morning, and his body was discovered late Friday evening, then whatever had happened to him occurred after he left work that day. If he went to work, that is. In any case, he had to visit Michelle Alexander first. He logged off and stood up.

'Success?' Domingo called out from her desk.

He nodded. 'In a way, yes. My John Doe has a name: Lance Riley. His wife - no, girlfriend – filed the report Saturday.'

'You off to see her now?'

Leroy nodded.

'Want me to go with you?'

'It's okay. I'll be okay.'

'She won't be, though. Would save you having to call on uniform.'

'All right. Thanks, Liza.'

'No problem,' she replied, as she got up from her desk. 'I'll drive, and you can eat your sandwich on the way.'

'Oh, yes; I'd forgotten.' He picked up the sandwich as they left.

Once in his car, he passed her the keys and gave her the address. She typed it into the GPS. As they pulled out into Butler, he looked around.

'Thanks for coming with me. I do appreciate it.'

'I told you: no problem.'

'Do you know,' he said as they headed south, 'after all these years, all the times of doing this, it never gets any easier.'

He looked over at her.

'Ever.'

CHAPTER FOURTEEN

'I'LL GO MAKE some tea,' said Domingo, as Leroy sat in
the living room opposite Michelle Alexander.

Michelle looked up. She spoke quietly. 'The tea and the
milk are-'

Domingo smiled. 'Don't worry. I'll find them.'

Leroy leaned back in the armchair and watched her walk
into the kitchen. Then turned back to Michelle. She was
slumped in another armchair, wiping her nose with a
Kleenex. He nodded his head towards her stomach.

'How long do you have to go?' he asked.

She sniffed. 'Another two months.'

'Why don't you try your mother again?' he asked.

She nodded, sniffed again, and reached over to a small
table and picked up a phone.

'Would you like us to call someone?' asked Leroy.

She shook her head. 'It's okay.' She waited a few moments with the phone to her ear, then disconnected. 'Still no answer.'

Domingo returned from the kitchen with a cup of hot tea. She passed it to Michelle. 'Here you are.'

Michelle looked up and took the cup. 'Thanks,' she mouthed.

Domingo sat back down on the sofa.

Leroy looked over to her, then back to Michelle. 'Going back to what I was asking earlier, Michelle,' he said slowly and softly, 'just tell me about the last time you saw Lance.'

She briefly closed her eyes tightly and swallowed. 'It was Friday morning. He just left for work as normal.'

'What time?' asked Leroy.

'About seven fifteen.'

'What does he do? Where does he work?'

'He works in IT. He's a Business Intelligence System Consultant. I don't know exactly what that means. He has explained it to me many times but it always goes over my head.'

'Mine too,' said Domingo reassuringly.

Leroy nodded. 'Same here. Where does he work? Is he based from home, or work from an office?'

'He works out of an office. His firm is called Culver Technologies. They have a suite of offices in Century City. Century Park West.'

'Okay. And he was working in the office on Friday?'

'As far as I know, yes. Normally he spends two or three days a week on the road, visiting clients, but he likes to spend Fridays in the office. You know, clearing up paperwork before the weekend.'

'How did he seem that morning?'

'No different to any other day. Said something about thank God it's Friday, and he would see me home here around six.'

'Six. Is that his normal arrival home time?'

Michelle nodded. 'Normally, yes. Sometimes on a Friday he would try to leave the office earlier, so he got home around five-thirty, but six was the normal time.'

Leroy asked, 'Did you speak to him during the day?'

'I did, yes. He normally phones me around lunchtime. Between twelve and one. Just to ask how my day was going and that he would see me that evening.'

'When he called Friday, did he give any indication of where he was?'

'No. He always used his cell phone, and would say if he was out anywhere. So I guess he was at the office. Why, have they said anything different?'

'Not spoken to them yet. We came here as soon as we identified him.'

'How did you know it was him?'

'I compared the photo we had with the one you provided when you filed the missing person report. He had no ID on him. I'm guessing he always carried ID with him.'

'Of course. In his wallet. His drivers licence and his money. Why? Were they taken?'

Leroy glanced over at Domingo and shifted in his chair. 'When he was found, he wasn't wearing anything. Well, just a pair of red shorts. I take it that was his normal underwear?'

Michelle shook her head, slightly puzzled. 'Well… yes, it was. Why was he only wearing those? What had happened to his clothes?'

'We don't know at this time,' Domingo said.

'Where exactly was he found?' Michelle asked.

'He was discovered in a Century City parking garage. An underground garage,' said Leroy.

'His work garage?'

'Still to be confirmed. We'll be calling on his office later, and will ascertain if that was the garage under his firm's building.'

Michelle nodded and blew her nose.

'Another thing we need to ask you, Michelle,' said Leroy. 'Did either of you - well, maybe I should say just Lance - use recreational drugs?'

'Drugs? No, of course not. Well, not recently.'

'Not recently?'

She rested her hand on her stomach. 'I've not touched anything like that since we started trying,' she said. 'And Lance – well, he's the same.'

'But you used to?'

'Years ago, when we first met. We used to smoke a little dope now and then, and…' She paused a moment, trying to find the right word. 'I forget what they're called. Those little bottles.'

'Poppers?' ventured Domingo.

'Yes, that's it. Poppers.'

'Poppers,' repeated Leroy. 'Amyl nitrite. Used during sex.'

'That's when we had them. But neither of us have touched anything like that for years now. Especially not…' She rubbed the palm of her hand over her belly. 'Why, is that what…?'

'No. Not poppers,' said Leroy. 'But his body did contain a high dose of recreational drugs.'

Michelle put her hand to her mouth. 'Oh, my God. No.'

There was a moment's silence, then Leroy said, 'Look Michelle – this is all the information we need at this time. It's quite likely we will have other questions as the investigation progresses, but we'll contact you at the time. One thing which does remain to be done, however, is for Lance's body to be formally identified. Maybe your mother can bring you when she comes over?'

Michelle nodded.

Leroy and Domingo stood up to leave.

'One more thing,' Leroy said. 'I'm guessing Lance used a laptop for work?'

Michelle nodded again.

'I'm also guessing he took it with him to work.'

'Yes, he always did.'

He looked around. 'Do you have a home computer?'

'Yes we do; it's in one of the bedrooms.'

'Did Lance use it? Or did he stick to his laptop?'

'He never used that. I was the only one. He would always use his own laptop or his tablet, or his phone.'

'Okay,' Leroy said, nodding.

'Do you work, Michelle?' asked Domingo. 'Or have you begun your family leave already?'

'No, I'm still at work. I work as an administrator at a car dealer ten minutes from here. I had a day off today, as I'm due to work tomorrow and Sunday.'

'Would you like us to call them for you?' asked Domingo.

'No, it's all right, thanks. My mother will come over; she'll call them.'

'If you're sure,' Domingo replied.

'You have my card with my contact number,' Leroy said. 'If there's anything you need, or if anything else comes to mind, just call me.'

'I will, yes. Thank you.'

'And you'll get your mother to bring you to identify Lance?'

'I will, yes.'

'Okay. We'll leave you now. And one again: we're both so sorry for your loss.'

Domingo nodded in agreement. 'You stay here, Michelle. We'll show ourselves out.'

Leroy and Domingo left Michelle alone with her thoughts. They walked down the pathway across the lawn which surrounded the modest two-storey house. Got back into the car.

Domingo looked back at the house. 'There's going to be a lot of tears in that house,' she said.

'Yeah,' Leroy said quietly.

'She shouldn't be on her own, Sam.'

'I know, but her mother's going to come over.'

'Sure. Still, all the same…'

'Let's head over to Century City,' Leroy said as he fired up the engine. 'Have a look around before they all go home.'

As they pulled away, Leroy spoke again, 'Before you ask, I didn't think it the right time to mention that he had had sex not long before he died.'

'Didn't know he had. It could have been with her that morning.'

'Could have been. Or could have been someone else. And unless you have midwifery as part of your resumé, I think it's something best left to another time.'

'Fair comment,' said Domingo. 'Jesus, seven months pregnant and to get that news. The poor kid'll never know its father.'

'No. But we need to be asking what was a man with a heavily pregnant girlfriend at home doing to get filled with LSD, roofies and coke.'

'Yeah, I know,' Domingo said, as they headed in the direction of Century City.

'And another thing,' Leroy said. 'Hobson said both victims had had sex not long before death. So tell me: what loving father-to-be goes on a wild drugs and sex binge on a Friday night?'

CHAPTER FIFTEEN

LEROY DID A time check as they turned off Santa Monica Boulevard into Century Park West. It was almost five.

'Dammit,' he said. 'I was hoping to get here earlier. What time do you think they all leave?'

'Five or six, I guess. Should've used the siren.'

'It's not an emergency call.'

'No, but is it the same building?'

'Is what the same building?'

'Over there: there's an underground parking garage. Now, is it the same one as where his body was found?'

'I get you.' Leroy parked at the front of the building. Immediately an elderly uniformed commissionaire appeared. He was just about to remonstrate with them, but stopped when they showed their badges.

'This is 2100,' said Domingo, pointing up at the four large bronze digits high on the wall.

Leroy paused, looking around. '2100? Yeah, I think it is. It all looks so different in the daylight.'

He looked over at the ramp leading underground. A sedan was coming up the ramp. He watched as it paused at the main road, then pulled into the traffic.

'Let's go speak to his workmates,' he said, leading the way up a dozen concrete steps.

Once inside, they could see that Culver Technologies was based on the sixth floor. After showing their badges to another uniformed attendant, they called an elevator and headed up to the sixth.

As the doors slid open at the sixth, they were met by half a dozen office workers who were clearly on their way home. The crowd was about to bustle past the two cops, but Leroy held up his badge and called out, 'LAPD. Could I speak to you all for a moment?'

There was a rumble of disapproval from the crowd until Domingo called out, 'We need literally thirty seconds of your time. Thank you.' With that, the group fell silent.

Leroy asked, 'These are the offices of Culver Technologies, yes?'

All in the group nodded or murmured agreement.

'Does Lance Riley work here?' Domingo asked.

The group all nodded; one voice at the back muttered, 'Jesus, what's Riley done now?'

Leroy ignored this comment, and went on to ask, 'Can you tell me if Lance is at work today?' Domingo reached out and stopped the elevator doors closing.

Some of them looked at each other and shrugged. One woman said she hadn't seen him; the outspoken one at the back called out, 'Give us a break; it's Monday after all. Nobody sees Riley till Tuesdays at the earliest.'

'Was he at work Friday?' asked Leroy.

Again, the same murmuring and looking at each other

for confirmation. This time the consensus was yes.

'One more question,' said Leroy. 'Who's in charge here?'

A small woman at the front of the group spoke up. 'That will be Ms Kennedy. In the office at the far end.'

Leroy looked over and saw a figure sitting at a desk in a glass-walled office. 'Right,' he said. 'Thank you all for your time and co-operation.' He and Domingo stood aside to let the group get into the elevator.

'Lance isn't in any trouble?' asked the small woman as she eased herself in. Fortunately the doors shut before Leroy and Domingo could answer.

They walked up to the office and tapped on the glass door which was hanging ajar. *Emma Kennedy* was stencilled in black on the frosted glass door. She looked up.

'Ms Kennedy?' Leroy asked.

She sat up straight. 'Yes? Can I help you?'

Leroy and Domingo stepped into the room and held out their badges. 'LAPD, ma'am,' said Leroy. 'I wonder if we might ask you some questions.'

'Questions?' Ms Kennedy said, with a puzzled look on her face. 'Of course. Please sit down.' She indicated to the two black chairs facing her desk. The officers sat down and Leroy looked at Ms Kennedy. Even though she was sitting behind a large desk, he could see she was a tall woman. Almost six feet, he guessed, just an inch or so shorter than him. Probably mid-thirties; dark, shoulder-length hair, neatly brushed. A little make up, but nothing excessive. Not what Leroy would call a beautiful woman; more handsome. Something he personally found attractive. An intelligent woman. He noticed the only jewellery on her hands were two dress rings.

Taking all this in caused Leroy to delay asking his first question. Domingo shot him a glance, then asked the first question. 'We're here about Lance Riley. Does he work here?'

'Lance? Yes; he does. Why; what has he done?'

'Why do you ask that?' said Domingo. 'We spoke to some of your staff as they were getting into the elevator, and one of them asked the same question.'

Ms Kennedy shrugged. 'An obvious question, I would have thought. Why else would the police be asking about him?'

Now Leroy spoke. 'Lance was found dead Friday night.'

Ms Kennedy clearly went pale. She stared at him open-mouthed.

'Lance…? Dead? But, how…? What happened?'

'His body was found in the parking garage beneath this building,' said Leroy. 'Late Friday night. There was some kind of office party going on then, and…'

Ms Kennedy frowned. 'Party? No, we had no party then. Wait a minute: one of the other tenants in the building - we share these premises with half a dozen other companies – had something going on Friday. It must have been after that.'

'Must have been,' said Domingo.

'You said he was found in the parking garage,' said Ms Kennedy. 'Was it an accident? Was he run over or something?'

'The cause of death is still being investigated,' replied Leroy, 'but in the meantime, can you confirm if he was at work Friday. His wife - partner, rather - said he likes to use Fridays to catch up with paperwork.'

She put her hand over her mouth.

'Oh my God! Poor Michelle! Whatever can she be going through? Have you met her? She's six months or so pregnant.'

'Seven months,' said Domingo. 'Yes, we just came from there. Her mother's on her way over to the house.'

'You said it's still being investigated. Does that mean he might have been – murdered?'

85

'Like I said, Ms Kennedy, it's still under investigation. So – was he in the office last Friday?'

She sat back and thought. 'Yes. Yes, he-'

'Night, Emma. See you in the morning,' a voice called out. Leroy and Domingo looked round and saw a man standing in the doorway. He was fairly short, dark skin, black hair heavily gelled back. He was wearing a light grey striped suit, blue shirt and a garish yellow tie. 'Excuse me,' he said, 'I didn't realise you were with somebody.'

'That's okay, Rolando. These are...' She looked at Leroy as if to say is it okay; he nodded. 'These are police officers. Something's happened to Lance.'

'Lance Riley? Jeez! What's happened to him?'

Leroy turned round in his chair to face Rolando. 'He was found dead Friday night.'

'Jesus H! What happened?'

'I'll fill you in tomorrow,' Ms Kennedy said. 'If that's okay with you, officers?'

'We're just checking Lance's movements on Friday,' said Leroy, facing Rolando, but addressing both of them. 'He was in here Friday, yes?'

'Correct,' said Ms Kennedy.

'But not today,' added Rolando. Then he slapped his forehead. '*Estúpido!*'

'How did he seem on Friday?' asked Leroy.

'No different from any other day,' said Ms Kennedy. 'Do you agree, Rolando?'

'I agree. Same as any other day.'

'And did he arrive and leave at his normal time? His partner - Michelle – said he sometimes left early on Fridays.'

'I didn't know that,' said Ms Kennedy. 'He always seemed to be around at the end of the day.'

'Do you keep an attendance log?' asked Domingo. 'Or do your staff have to clock in or out?'

'Do you need me any more?' asked Rolando, still

standing in the doorway.

Leroy swung round again. 'No, thanks. If we need to talk to you again, I know where to find you.'

'I'll say goodnight, then.'

'Good night, Rolando,' Ms Kennedy said, as she watched him walk down to the elevator. 'That's Rolando Zinga, one of my analysts. Same as Lance.'

She stared into space for a few seconds, then said, 'We rely on trust here. A lot of the time our staff have to go visit clients, so to log them in or out would be cumbersome. However, I can check to see when he logged on and off our systems here, if you like.'

'Please do,' said Domingo.

'Surely,' she smiled. She turned to her keyboard and typed something. Keyed in a password, and a few more keys.

'Here we are,' she said, reading off a screen. 'Lance Riley. First logged in 08:12AM. Final log out 04:35PM.'

'So not really leaving early,' said Leroy.

'Official finishing time is 5PM, but as you can see...' She tapped her watch.

'Sure. His partner said he normally got home around six, so he must normally leave just after five. Allowing for traffic.'

Domingo nodded. 'Yeah, so Friday wasn't really early.'

'That's right,' said Ms Kennedy. 'And that's just the time he logged off the system. He could have been doing paperwork afterwards.'

'Where's his office?' asked Leroy, sitting up and looking around. 'I'd like to take a look around.'

'Next door to here.' She indicated to the right. 'Help yourself.'

'Thanks.' He stood up. 'How much longer will you be here? We can come back in the morning if -'

'I'll be here till seven at least,' Ms Kennedy smiled.

'Okay.' They both stood up and stepped into the office

next door. It was similarly configured as Ms Kennedy's, only slightly smaller. There was a desk, with PC screen and keyboard, a small bookcase, containing three books, and a small filing cabinet. There was a GANT chart on one wall, and on the corner of his desk was a small portrait of Michelle Alexander, taken before she was pregnant.

'Have a look through the cabinet,' said Leroy. 'I'll check the desk.'

'Are we looking for anything in particular?'

'Not really. See what we can come up with. Although his laptop would be good.'

Leroy checked through the three desk drawers and came up with nothing. Leaving Domingo to rifle through the filing cabinet, he stepped outside and leaned around Ms Kennedy's doorway.

'Ms Kennedy? Sorry to bother you.'

'What can I do for you, Detective?'

'Ms Alexander - Michelle - said Lance used a laptop.'

'He would have done, yes.'

'It's not in his office; I'm guessing he would have taken it with him.'

'Oh, yes; he would always do that. Anything I can help with?'

'No; it's okay, thanks.' He turned to go then stopped. 'There might be, actually. He would have had a company email account, yes?'

'U-huh.'

'Would you have supervisor access to his account? Could you use a password to override the system and get into his account?'

'Yes, I can. Would you like me to try now?'

'Please.' He sat down on one of the chairs.

She pulled out a Filofax from one of her drawers and looked up something, a password Leroy presumed. More keystrokes, then said, 'Here you are, Detective.'

He stood up.

'I need to visit the restroom. Sit here while I'm gone.' She vacated her chair and swung it round to face Leroy.

'Thanks.' He sat in the chair as she left. He moved around in the chair. It was softer than the ones the other side of the desk, and more comfortable. And it smelled of her perfume. Leroy breathed in and turned to the screen.

First of all he checked Lance's email account: the inbox, sent messages, drafts, trash. There were several sub-folders apparently named after Lance's numerous clients: Leroy checked them as well.

'Talk about getting your feet under the table,' said Domingo in the doorway. 'Where's she gone?'

'Restroom. She's logged on as a supervisor for me. I'm looking through his emails and stuff. He would have taken his laptop home. Anything in there?'

'Zip. You found anything?'

'Nothing of interest here.'

'What about his search history? It would only show what he's searched for on there, not the laptop, but it might show something.'

'Yeah, but if he's arranged anything to do with drugs, he would have done it on his laptop, surely?

'Probably, Sam, but it's worth a shot.'

'Yeah, guess so.' Leroy clicked on the search bar, then on Search History. Started to tab down.

'Well,' he said, looking up at Domingo.

'That's interesting.'

CHAPTER SIXTEEN

DOMINGO STEPPED ROUND to the other side of the desk and looked down at the screen. 'What's interesting?' she asked.

'Look at the search history.' Leroy tapped the screen. The search field was blank.

'Nothing there,' Domingo said. 'So what's interesting?'

'The fact that there's nothing there.'

'How so?'

'Think about it, Liza. You type in whatever you're looking for here.' He tapped the blank bar on the screen. 'If you click on this arrowed button here,'- he tapped again - 'you get a list of previous enquiries you've made, previous sites you've visited.'

'Yeah, I know that, Sherlock. You're saying he's

deleted his history. Right?'

'And why would he do that?'

'Hold on, Sam. This isn't his office, is it?'

'What does that have – oh, shit, of course.'

'You need to do this in there, on his PC. Did she give you the password?'

'No, but she's only gone to the bathroom. She'll be back in a moment.'

They both stood up and wandered out into the corridor. Domingo went back into Lance Riley's office and continued her searching. Leroy looked around for Ms Kennedy. There was no sign of her. He wandered down the corridor, past the elevators, until her could hear her voice. Then he came to a small waiting area comprising a low table and three chairs. Ms Kennedy was sitting on the table, holding a paper cup of coffee and talking into a cell phone. She looked up and saw him.

'Hey look; can I call you back?' she said into the phone. 'Okay, bye.'

She pressed a key on the phone and stood up. 'Wanted to give you guys some space,' she said.

'Sure,' said Leroy. 'Look Ms Kennedy -'

'Call me Emma,' she smiled.'

'Emma, he continued. 'What you did with the password and Lance's account back then: could you do the same thing on his computer?'

She nodded. 'For sure.'

She led him back to the little suite of offices. 'I'll just have to log off the one here first,' she said, walking into her office. A minute later she joined them in Lance Riley's.

'Thanks again.' Leroy smiled at her as Lance's screen flickered into life.

'You're welcome.' She smiled back and returned to her own office.

Leroy sat down behind the desk and moved the cursor up to the arrow button. There were three entries in the search history: United Airlines, Catalina Vacations, and Netflix.

'Same again,' said Domingo.

Leroy nodded. 'Yeah. Must have looked at these three Friday afternoon. After he had cleared his history.'

'But why clear the search history? Unless he'd been on a website he didn't want anyone to know about.'

'Like one for wherever he went after work Friday.'

Domingo leaned forward and spoke quietly. 'But the search history had been cleared on that one in there. On hers.'

'That's right.' He got up and went into the office next door.

'Sorry to disturb you, Ms – Emma.'

She looked up. 'How can I help you?'

'We've noticed that Lance had cleared his search history.'

'Right….,' she said slowly.

'But we noticed the same on there.' He pointed down to her screen. 'Does that mean you had done the same thing?'

She sat back in her chair and rubbed her forehead. 'Oh dear,' she said. 'This is so embarrassing.'

Leroy said nothing.

'Is what I tell you – confidential? Between these four walls?'

'As long as it's not illegal and has no bearing on Lance's death.'

'It isn't. It doesn't. I'm – I'm single, and in my late thirties. I – I…oh this is so embarrassing… I – how shall I say – I enjoy the company of younger men. Much younger men.'

'Over the age of eighteen?'

'Early twenties. Twenty-five tops.'

Leroy said nothing.

'There's an agency I use.'

'An escort agency?' he asked.

She swallowed and nodded. 'If any of them out there

found out, I'd be a laughing stock. I sometimes go to their site here and – and search for, for…'

'For a date?'

She nodded. 'If I do, I always clear my search history. Our system is secure, our protocols robust, but just in case…'

Leroy said, 'I get the picture. But do you know of any reason why Lance's search history would be clear also?'

Ms Kennedy shook her head. 'No. No, apart from him not wanting anyone to know where he had been visiting.'

'This is an IT company: is there any way to retrieve what he had deleted? You know, look on the hard drive or something.'

'Er – yes, it is possible. Would you like us to take a look at it for you? See if we can find anything?'

'No thanks, but I appreciate the offer. I'll get our guys in Computer Crime to take a look. I'll just need to take his disc drive.'

She pulled a face. 'I'm not sure if…'

'It would be appreciated. And it would save us having to come back in the morning with a warrant.'

'You don't leave me much choice, Detective.'

Leroy smiled at her. 'We'll give you a receipt, and you should have it back in a day or so. Unless it's needed in evidence.'

'Evidence? Evidence of what?'

'Much appreciated,' Leroy repeated. 'My colleague and I will just disconnect the drive, and be out of your hair.'

Leroy left Ms Kennedy in her office and returned to Lance Riley's.

'Any luck?' he asked Domingo.

'Nah. Nothing here.'

'I've arranged with Ms Kennedy -'

'Emma, you mean?' Domingo said quietly with a smirk on her face.

'Very funny. I've arranged to take the disc drive, or

whatever it's called, back for the CCU to take a look at. Check the hard drive or whatever.'

'Okay.' Domingo leaned down and unplugged the numerous wires. Picked up the black box. Ms Kennedy was talking on her landline as they left; she gave Leroy a wave as he left a small receipt for the processor on her desk.

It was dark by the time Leroy and Domingo got back to Police HQ. A little after seven. They nodded at two groups of uniformed officers who were leaving the building just as they entered. Shift change. Leroy yawned as they walked into Homicide. All desks bar one were empty. A young Indian man in shirtsleeves sat at the desk, working on a keyboard. He looked up.

'Hey, guys.'

'Hey Sudeep,' Leroy and Domingo said in unison.

Leroy slumped into his chair and yawned.

'Overtime?' Domingo asked.

Sudeep turned away from the screen. 'Just finishing off some bits.' He looked at the disc drive. 'That looks interesting.'

'Yeah,' said Leroy. 'It's all to do with the John Doe we had in Century City last week. He has a name now, and we got this from where he works. Only for some reason he cleared his search history. Might be nothing to do with what happened to him but we're going to get the guys in the CCU to have a look at it.'

Sudeep sat up and frowned. 'You don't need them to do that,' he said.

'How do you mean?' asked Leroy. 'I asked the office manager there – and it's an IT company after all – if what he deleted could be retrieved and she said it was possible. Offered to get her boys to take a look for us. See if they can find anything.'

'Bullshit,' said Sudeep. 'Plug it in, Sam. I can do it in

five minutes.'

CHAPTER SEVENTEEN

LEROY STROLLED OUT of the restroom and headed straight for the vending machines. Got himself a coffee and candy bar then returned to the Homicide Desk. The other two had previously declined his offer.

When he got back to his desk, Domingo and Sudeep were hunched over a keyboard. They had attached Lance Riley's processor to Leroy's equipment. Domingo looked up as he arrived.

'Sudeep's just proved it,' she said.

'Proved what?' Leroy asked, sitting down and taking a bite from his candy bar.

'Proved she was bullshitting you,' Domingo said.

'It's quite simple, really,' said Sudeep. He kicked back against the desk so his chair slid back a few feet.

Leroy rolled forward on his chair and sat in front of the screen. 'Show me,' he said.

Sudeep leaned forward and signed out. 'Now log on,' he said. 'Then key in what I tell you.'

'Okay.' Leroy logged on, entered his password and got his Home screen.

'Now click on Internet Explorer,' said Sudeep.

'Okay.'

'See the Tools tab at the top of the screen?'

'Er – no.'

'You don't know much about computers, do you Sam?' Sudeep laughed.

'I get by. Show me Tools. It's okay, I see it.'

'Cool. Click on it. Now: down at the bottom you have Internet Options. See it?'

'U-huh.' Leroy clicked.

'See Browsing History? Click on the Settings button.'

'Okay. Now what?'

'Click on View Files.'

Leroy clicked and a box appeared. The box was empty. 'And?' he said.

'Hmm,' muttered Sudeep. 'This guy's clever.'

'He worked in IT,' Domingo pointed out.

'And he certainly knew how to cover his tracks,' Leroy added.

'We're not done yet,' said Sudeep. 'We just need to go deeper.'

Leroy looked round at him. 'Deeper?'

'Cursor on the Start button. Then right click.'

'Okay.' Leroy right clicked. 'What next?'

Sudeep said, 'Left click on Explore.'

A box headed Start Menu filled the screen.

'Now, scroll down to Cookies. Then left click.'

'What is a cookie, by the way?' Domingo asked. Leroy looked up at her.

Sudeep answered. 'In simple terms, a cookie is a small

piece of data sent from a website when you visit it and is stored in your web browser. When you visit that website again, the data stored in the cookie gets retrieved by the website to notify the site of your previous activity.'

'That makes sense,' said Leroy, with a dead pan expression on his face.

'Sam, do you understand what I just told you?'

'Not a single word, but it doesn't matter. Look: I've clicked on cookies. Nothing there either.'

Sudeep leaned forward and whistled. 'Clever, clever.'

'Well, all this proves one thing,' said Domingo.

'What's that?' asked Leroy.

'This guy had something to hide.'

'Yeah,' agreed Leroy. 'I have to admit, I'm surprised by all this. I really thought we'd draw a blank on here. On the basis that he'd use his laptop.'

'He still might have. Maybe just used this once; still needed to cover his tracks.'

Leroy sat back in his chair.

'Well,' he said as he stretched back and yawned, 'there's nothing on here. Seems there was, but he's deleted it. Deleted it all.'

'There's just one more thing we could try,' said Sudeep. 'Click on Start, then Run.'

'Okay. Now I have c colon slash setup.'

'Good. Now overtype that with regedit.'

'With what?'

Sudeep spelt it.

'What's this?' Leroy asked.

'It's an abbreviation for registry editor,' explained Sudeep. 'It's kind of the soul of the machine where everything that's ever done on it is stored.'

'But he could have deleted stuff from here, also?'

'In theory, yes. But the registry is very sensitive. It doesn't mind you looking but gets cranky if you touch.'

'Like my ex,' said Domingo.

'Like Domingo's ex,' Sudeep repeated. 'If you're going to play around here you need to know what you're doing. If you delete the wrong thing it can make the computer hell to work with and possibly useless. Can be fun, though. I caught my wife and her internet boyfriend this way. Surprise! They never met because I scared him off.'

'There are loads of files here,' said Leroy, getting the subject back on track. 'What now?'

Both Domingo and Sudeep looked at the screen.

'I'm afraid you're going to have to go through every folder and file there,' said Sudeep. 'Then make a list of any of the websites he visited in the days before he disappeared.'

'Jesus. That's going to take days.'

'Never said it was going to be easy, Sam.'

'Will the CCU be able to do it? Quicker than I can, that is?'

'For sure. That's what they're there for.'

'I'll pass it to them in the morning.'

Leroy switched off the computer and rubbed his face. He looked over at Domingo. 'Thanks for your help today, Liza. You'll need to go back to Connor in the morning.'

'You're welcome, Sam. In any case, I could argue that this affects my case. They're obviously connected.'

'Would seem that way, yes. Anyhow, I'm bushed. I'm just going to lock this stuff up and get some sleep. Thanks again, guys.'

'You're welcome. Any time.' Sudeep wheeled his chair back to his original desk.

'What are you going to do about her?' asked Domingo. 'About Ms Kennedy.'

'Not sure yet,' replied Leroy. 'She must have been bullshitting us. She runs an IT office, for Chrissake.'

'And her own history had been deleted,' she said. 'What reason did she give again? Listen to this, Sudeep.' Sudeep looked up.

Leroy laughed. 'She had been visiting sites for male

escort providers. Young male escort providers.'

'A bit of a cougar, was she?' Sudeep grinned.

'Yeah,' said Domingo. 'Sam was too old for her. He's over twenty-one.'

'Very funny,' said Leroy.

'It is possible,' Sudeep cut in, 'that she didn't know about what I've shown you.'

'No way,' said Leroy.

'Way. Possibly. You said she was the office manager. Well, it *is* possible that even though she was managing the office she had no idea of how the technology works. I mean, if she was hired to – to reduce staff numbers, or to fix some customer service issues. She would leave the technical stuff to the others.'

Leroy shook his head. 'Unlikely.'

'But not impossible,' said Domingo. 'Remember that dude who was with the MTA a couple of years back? At the time they were trying to extend the Orange Line up to Chatsworth Reservoir.'

Leroy looked at her blankly. 'Vaguely. So what?'

'He was an accountant. Knew nothing about public transportation. But was hired because he knew about finance, which was what the City wanted.'

Leroy scratched the back of his neck. 'I see what you mean. But I'm still not convinced. I think... I think she offered to get her people to check Riley's computer just in case he hadn't deleted something. And,' – he looked over at Domingo – 'she was quite happy to check the search history on her computer, letting us think it was showing Riley's history. Yes, she will be getting another visit. At some time, but I'm not sure if she's a priority right now.'

'Okay,' said Domingo quietly. 'Fine.' She got up to leave.

'The second thing I'm going to do,' Leroy went on, 'is to compare the missing persons list with the others that were found that night. See if I can get more luck with them. So

I'll be liaising with you and Connor.'

'Cool. What's the first thing?'

'Getting some sleep.'

CHAPTER EIGHTEEN

IT WAS A still night when Leroy arrived home around ten thirty. The Santa Anas which the city had experienced over the last few days had subsided; now there was a gentle, but warm, breeze coming from the ocean. As he turned off Venice Boulevard to make the final hundred yards of his journey, he could see there was a thin layer of mist hanging over the beach. The last few mornings had seen a thick layer of fog - the Santa Ana fog – which had persisted until late morning when the sun burnt it off: a pain to drive in, and Leroy hoped it would not be around the next day.

There was very little parking space around Leroy's building: he had a dedicated space around the side, but tonight somebody had parked an SUV near the entrance. Resisting the temptation to call in, have the vehicle towed and the driver booked for obstruction, he slowly manoeuvred his Taurus between it and the fence. With only an inch to spare, he eventually parked in his allotted space. He looked over the SUV as he walked past it to his building: not a vehicle he recognised; maybe the driver was visiting someone in one of the other apartments. He decided against getting too heavy; after all, he had to live with these people. Instead, he retrieved a letter size sheet of paper from his car, scribbled *you are obstructing a driveway, please take more care in future. lapd* on it and fastened it under one of the wipers with one of his business cards.

As he walked onto 23rd Avenue, he paused and looked around. It was a quiet night. Sometimes, depending on the direction of the wind, he could clearly hear the sound of traffic from Venice Boulevard, or even from LAX, which was seven or eight miles further down the coast. Tonight, however, as the breeze seemed to be coming from the sea, he heard very little. Only a slight breeze, probably not enough to disperse the mist. It was a warm night too, around seventy, he guessed. He looked up into the night sky as he could hear an engine noise: amongst the stars he could make out the white and red lights of an aircraft heading down the coast, about to turn east to begin its approach to the airport.

He swung round as he heard another noise. Faint, but shrill enough to carry on this still night, it sounded like a woman's cry. He looked around, trying to ascertain from which direction the sound had come. Frustrated, he waited a few seconds, then headed in the direction of the beach: it would most likely have come from there.

As he broke into a run, he heard another scream; louder and closer than before. He paused: it was coming from three or four blocks away, from the direction of the marina. He could also make out at least one man's voice. Men's voices, being generally deeper, carried less well.

He turned left on Speedway, and ran down. As he ran on, he could make out the sounds of feet running, then a clatter; maybe a trashcan being knocked over. Then, he could see, two blocks down, a figure run out onto Speedway. In the illumination of the streetlamps, he could pick out the silhouette of a figure. A woman's figure, hair dishevelled and a short skirt. She was wearing only one shoe. She looked back - down 30th, Leroy guessed - and then began to run in the other direction. Leroy ran faster and called out.

'Hey!' he shouted. 'Police!'

The silhouette paused momentarily, and as she did so, two figures appeared from the side street. They paused too, just enough time for her whereabouts to register. Seeing Leroy, one of them put a hand in a back pocket.

'Hey!' Leroy called out again, this time pulling his Glock from its holster. 'Police! Freeze!'

Both figures stopped, looking at Leroy and back to the girl, as if deciding what to do next. As he walked quickly to them, Leroy could make out that they were two men, both Caucasian, early twenties or late teens. Leroy spoke, covering them with his weapon.

'Against the wall, you two. Assume the position. It's all right, miss,' he said to the girl. 'Just wait there, will you?'

Both men leaned against the fence as instructed, and Leroy, still carefully covering them, used his left hand to frisk them. The first was clean; in the other's rear pocket Leroy felt something hard. He pulled out a handkerchief from his own pocket and reached in. Holding the object in his handkerchief, he pulled out a black switchblade. He recognised it as a Magnano. He flicked it, revealing its long blade.

'This looks over two inches,' he said. 'Therefore an illegal weapon, under the California Penal Code.' The owner did not reply.

'You okay?' he asked the woman, who by now was sitting on the kerb. 'What were they trying to do?'

She ran her hand through her hair. 'Rob me, I guess.'

'Rob? You sure that's all?'

She shrugged her shoulders.

Still covering the two men, he unhooked his cuffs from his belt, and cuffed the two men together. Then took out his phone and made a call. Five minutes later a blue and white police vehicle arrived. One of the two uniformed officers recognised Leroy; she and her colleague took off Leroy's cuffs and substituted their own. She then read the two men their rights, and bundled them into the back of the car.

'I heard a commotion and ran down here,' Leroy said. 'The lady says they were trying to rob her.'

'Did they take anything?' the female officer asked the woman.

She shook her head.

'Attempted robbery, then.' She looked down at the woman. The light coloured blouse she was wearing had two buttons torn off. 'Anything else you want to report?'

'You up to making a statement now, ma'am?' the male officer asked the woman. 'Or would you rather call in in the morning?'

The woman looked up. 'Could I come in the morning? I'm so - so tired now.'

'Surely. We'll hold them for tonight, but you must come in tomorrow, otherwise we'll be obliged to release them.'

She nodded. 'Sure. I will.'

Leroy stepped over to the officers. 'What's with tomorrow? You need to take her statement now.'

The female officer shook her head. 'No, Sam; not according to the guidelines from our captain. As long as she files her report by noon tomorrow. We can hold them tonight on suspicion. But if she doesn't come in by then, they're back on the streets. What exactly's your involvement anyway?'

Leroy inclined his head in the direction of 23rd. 'I live only half a dozen blocks away. I had just gotten home, when I heard a scream. I ran up here, and caught those two punks chasing her.'

'That was a piece of luck. For her, I mean; not them. Did they say anything to you after you called it in?'

'Diddly squat. Just stood facing the wall. Here: you'll need this.' He handed her his handkerchief, still containing the Magnano. She took the handkerchief, checked the contents, then showed it to her partner. He reached inside the car and retrieved a small transparent plastic envelope. Dropped the knife inside and sealed it. She held out Leroy's cuffs.

'Here you go, Sam. Fair exchange. You never know when you might need these.' As she spoke, her gaze fixed his. 'At least we can get them on possession of an illegal weapon. Something we can really hold them on. Until something more serious, that is.'

She looked down at the blue and white. In the street lights they could make out the two sitting in the back of the car, silently staring out in front.

'Just a couple of kids. See her top? It has some buttons missing: do you think…?'

'She says only robbery. Maybe she got away before it could develop into anything else. Though she really needs to be checked over. Look: her arm is bleeding. Tonight, I mean; not by noon tomorrow.'

The male officer flashed Leroy a stare, then asked the woman, 'Ma'am, you're bleeding. You need to be checked over by a doctor. Would you like -?'

'It's all right, thank you. I'm okay. Just a little shaken up. I just need to go home. I only live a couple of blocks away.'

'Which street?' Leroy asked.

'Holly Court,' she replied. 'It's only five minutes away.'

'I know Holly Court,' said Leroy. 'I'll walk her home. If that's okay with you, ma'am.'

She looked up from the kerb and, before nodding to

Leroy, glanced over at the female officer.

'It's okay, ma'am; he is a cop, just like us. You wouldn't think so, to look at him.'

The woman smiled weakly at the joke, then stood up. She swayed slightly, unsteady on her feet.

'We'll take these two in then,' said the female officer, 'and leave the lady with you, Sam. Remember to call in tomorrow morning, ma'am. Detective Leroy will give you the address.'

'I will. Thanks.' The woman steadied herself. The uniformed officers got into their car, and left, saying goodbye to Leroy as they turned the car around.

Leroy stepped over to the woman and held her arm. 'You'd better take my arm,' he said. 'You're still a little shaky.' Giving her his arm for support, he led her down 30th Avenue.

'You sure you're okay to walk?' he asked after a hundred yards or so. 'We could have gone back to my place where my car is parked, but I guess that's just as far to walk.'

'Yes, I'm okay to walk,' she replied.

'You live alone?' he asked.

'U-huh.'

'Same here.'

In silence, they crossed Pacific Avenue. 'What exactly happened, then?' he asked, as they took a footbridge which took them over one of the canals.

'I had been out with a couple of girlfriends,' she replied. 'We had been in a restaurant on the 3rd Street Promenade. We shared a cab back home. We dropped one of them off on Lincoln, and me just back on Pacific. Then the cab went on to the other side of the marina.'

'And then what?'

'The car had just gotten round the corner when I saw - or rather heard – those two guys. They were walking on the other side of the road - this side – so I couldn't cross over, but I knew they were following me. I started to walk faster, so did they. Eventually I started to run down one of the side streets, where they caught up with me. And….' She paused; Leroy thought she was about to cry.

'Leave it then,' he said softly. 'Tell the officers in the morning.'

She nodded. 'I guess you think I'm dumb walking in the first place, at this time of night.'

'To be honest, yes. Why didn't you get the cab to go past your place? Hardly out of his way.'

'Don't know. When we go out together, we always go home like that. I've done that walk dozens of times. This is the first time…'

'Sure. Could've been your last. I recommend next time the cab takes you to your door.'

'Don't worry. I will. It's just up there. I'll be okay from here. Thanks Detective…Leroy, was it?'

'Leroy, yes. Detective Leroy. Sam. And I'll take you to your door.'

'Joanna. Joanna Moore. It's here. 2802.'

She led him to a two storey building, attached to which was a shop front. Leroy looked in the window. A sign read *Cutting Edge. Full Service, Hair, Spa, Nails, Foot Massage 310-305-2221.*

'Which floor?' he asked, looking up at the building.

'Second,' she said.

'Stairs or elevator?'

'Stairs only. Why?'

'You're still unsteady. I'll take you up. You've had a shock. You don't know what you might do. And I promised those other officers I'd take you to the door. After all, they need you as a material witness tomorrow.'

'It's okay, Detective. Sam. I'll be fine,' she said.

Then collapsed at Leroy's feet.

CHAPTER NINETEEN

LEROY CAUGHT HER just before she hit the floor. Holding her under her arms, he manoeuvred her over to a corner and lowered her so she was sitting in the corner, slumped against the wall. Then crouched down in front of her. He shook her gently.

'Joanna, wake up. You need to wake up.'

She stirred slightly, muttering something unintelligible.

'Joanna. Where are your keys? Are they in your bag?'

'Sorry,' she whispered. 'I don't know…'

'Excuse me,' Leroy said. He picked up her bag and felt inside. Came across a key ring with three keys on it. He tried one key in the lock of the front entrance door. No joy. The second worked. With the door open, he picked Joanna up and supporting her round the waist, took her inside. The stairs were immediately in front of the entrance door, and he led her up to the second floor. She stumbled a couple of times on the way up. He noticed that each apartment door had a large black letter screwed to it, H, I, J, onwards along the corridor.

'Joanna,' he asked, shaking her slightly to rouse her. 'Which apartment? H? I? J? K? Which?'

'L', she murmured. He led her along to the door to apartment L. There were two locks on the door; he used the two keys he did not use downstairs and opened the door.

As soon as the door opened, he heard a high pitched beeping sound. He looked in the doorway and saw on the wall adjacent to the door was a small keypad from which the sound was emanating. A red light on the device was flashing.

He led her into the apartment and to the keypad. 'Joanna, what's the code?' Slightly more coherent, she reached up and keyed four zeroes. Once she hit a green button, the beeping stopped. Leroy, switched on a light, pushed the door closed with his foot and laid her on a couch. As he stepped back, she began to come to and sat up. She ran her hand through her hair and looked up at him.

'Did I faint or something?' she asked.

'You sure did,' he replied. 'Just downstairs, outside.'

'Oh, how pathetic. I'm so sorry.'

'Don't be. It's delayed shock; quite common. Shall I get you some hot tea?'

'No, something stronger. There's some red wine in the kitchen.'

He could see that the kitchen was one of the doors off the main living room. Above a row of doors, along the length of the kitchen was a granite work surface; once he switched on the light, he could see a half-full bottle of Merlot standing next to a blender. Next to the sink, upside-down draining was a wine glass. He poured her a full glass and took it out to her. She took it and downed half the glass.

'Would you like one yourself, Detective?' she asked. 'It's the least I can do.'

'No thanks. It's late, and I have to be at work early tomorrow.'

She shrugged her shoulders slightly.

'Some other time perhaps,' he added.

She looked into her glass, but said nothing.

'Anyway,' said Leroy. 'You're home safe now and those two guys are locked up. I'll leave you to it. Here's my card.' He handed her one of his business cards. 'Call me if you need anything. Don't worry,' he added as she began to get up, 'I'll let myself out.'

As he put his hand on the door handle, he turned round.

'Don't drink too much of that tonight. You need to be fully alert tomorrow when you make your statement. You won't forget to go in the morning, will you?'

'I'll be fine,' she said, sounding more alert.

'One more thing,' Leroy said. 'You need to change that alarm code. Four zeroes is the factory setting; you need to change it to a proper code. Do you know how to do that?'

'I have instructions somewhere,' she said. 'Don't worry. And thanks for saving me from those guys.'

'No problem.'

'And walking me home.'

'No problem.'

Leroy gave her a brief smile and left the apartment. As he walked down the stairs, he heard Joanna fasten her safety chain and double lock the door. He left the building and started the fifteen minute walk back to his own place. When he got back home, he noticed that the SUV had gone. Feeling satisfied, he let himself in, and walked up to his own apartment.

It was now just after midnight. He groaned as he knew he would have to be up early the next morning. As he lay in bed, his mind drifted back to Joanna Moore's apartment. There was something about it he could not quite put his finger on, an adjective he was seeking. It was relatively small, the door opening directly onto the living room; the kitchen was off the living room. Presumably the other three doors were the bathroom, the bedroom, and a closet. It was very neat and tidy: a plush cream carpet, the furniture was modern and tasteful. The walls were painted a shade of pink, with floral patterns stencilled on in a darker shade. There was a small bookcase containing only a few books, and a couple of framed portraits on the top shelf. On a small table was a television; not a particularly big or sophisticated set. A couple of mirrors and a painting of a landscape on the walls. There was a small glass dining table on which were a closed laptop and a vase of flowers. He noticed another vase of flowers in the kitchen. Although only she sat on the couch, he could tell it was soft and comfortable. Very homey.

No, he thought; homey wasn't the word. Now almost asleep, he finally found the correct word to describe the apartment.

Feminine.

CHAPTER TWENTY

IN SPITE OF the previous day's late night, Leroy was back at his desk by seven-thirty the next morning. Two other detectives, who were working on different cases, were also at their desks. Leroy exchanged greetings with them, and looked around for Domingo, but she had not arrived yet.

As he logged onto his computer, he took a bite from the bagel and a sip from the paper cup of coffee he had bought on the way in. His breakfast. He looked around the almost empty office. For it to be this quiet at this time of the day was unusual. True, some of his colleagues may be out already, but he couldn't help feeling that the pace had slackened since their old lieutenant had moved on. In theory, Captain Patterson was overseeing the department until the new lieutenant took up his post, but he seemed to be doing this at arm's length. Still, Leroy reflected, things would change once Perez took up his post in a few days. He reflected too that things would have been different if... But there was no point dwelling on what might have been; he needed to get on and remain focussed.

His first task was to take Lance Riley's processor to the Computer Crime Unit to get them to check the hard drive. There were more questions to be asked about the circumstances surrounding Riley's death, but seeing what was on his work computer came first. That was why it was so important to get hold of his laptop, but that could be in a ditch somewhere, or already sold on. It was unlikely anyone would be in the CCU till eight, maybe nine, and so for now he would press on with identifying the victim Bill Farmer had in Hollywood. Of course, once he had matched the pictures, he needed to liaise with Farmer. He also needed to get hold of Hobson's report on the guy Domingo had in Griffith Park. Although they were all being treated as separate incidents, Leroy was positive there was a common thread. It was a no-brainer as far as he was concerned.

As he did the previous day, he retrieved the photograph from Hobson's report and compared it with missing persons reports. Back up to the top of page one, and back to some faces he remembered from before.

He got to page eight before he found a match. Guy Robbins, thirty years old, residing in Central Alameda. Reported missing by his wife, Maria, when he failed to return home Friday night after visiting a client. Leroy scratched his chin: a very similar background to Lance Riley.

He got out his phone and called Farmer. To his surprise, it was answered after two rings.

'Farmer.'

'Hey Bill; it's Sam Leroy.'

'Hey Sam, how you doing? I forgot to call you yesterday; you know, to thank you for turning out for me at the weekend. Been so damn busy, you know?'

'Sure, I know. Look, Bill, it's that John Doe I'm calling about. I have a name for you.'

'You do? How so?'

'I was checking down the list of missing persons, and I got a match.'

'Why were you looking?'

'I did the same yesterday with my Century City guy. Got a match and an ID. His girlfriend reported him missing end of last week. I took Liza Domingo down to see his wife yesterday. She said he just never got home from work that night. We went to his workplace, which was the building above the garage where he was found.'

'And...?'

'Not much at this time, but I've taken his office computer away to see if the CCU guys can find anything on it.'

'You think that's connected?'

'Just in case any internet addresses he visited last week are connected to what happened to him.'

'Would he have done that at work?'

'Probably not, Bill, but it's worth a shot. You see, he had wiped all the search history.'

'Sam, you're talking to *me*. What in the hell does that mean? Search history?'

'Basically, it's a record of websites he had been on. Now, there's no reason to clear the search history unless you didn't want anyone to see what he'd been up to. I know it's more likely he'd use his own PC, but that's missing. Probably in some Tijuana café by now, but it's worth checking. Even though he's cleared the search history, it's possible the CCU can find something. Outside shot, but it's all we've got at this time.'

'Is Domingo covering for Quinn then?'

'No. She was here when I found the match. Her own partner was off yesterday. But, Bill - and listen to this – she had her own John Doe last week. Almost exactly the same as ours.'

'Jesus! Where?'

'Off Griffith Park.'

'Sam, this is getting crazy. That's three, all the same circumstances. All the same night.'

'Did you talk to Hobson yesterday? He was trying to get hold of you.'

'Last night. But Sam – he says there's no sign of foul play.'

'Same with mine, and I'll bet he'll say the same about Domingo's. But Bill: this is one mother of a coincidence.'

'What's your theory? One wild party that got out of control? You saw the amount of shit they had in their systems.'

'I know. That's why we need to get whoever's supplying. And fast. Where are you today?'

'I'm in court today, Sam. Or this morning, hopefully.' Farmer paused a moment. 'Sam: can you do me a favour? Could you take a look at this one this morning? I mean, go see the guy's wife. Who knows, it could have a bearing on your case. Would you mind? I'll catch up with you once I'm done here.'

'No worries, Bill. Why are you in court, by the way?'

'It's that frigging McAvoy case. Remember it?'

'Vaguely, Bill.'

'The Defence Attorney's disputing some of the contents of the ME report, so there's lots of legal to-ing and fro-ing. The DA's pulling his hair out.'

'That's not like Hobson to make a mistake.'

'I know. It's all bullshit. Just stalling for time. Trying to get the case thrown out on a technicality.'

'Okay Bill, I'll go visit Mrs Robbins.'

'That the guy's name?'

'Yeah. Literally. Guy Robbins.'

'Okay. Thanks Sam. Catch up with you later. Bye.'

'Bye.'

He hung up and called Domingo. Had to leave a voicemail. He thought he would try his luck at the CCU as it was almost eight. He withdrew the disc drive from secure storage and took it to his car. The nearest outpost of the CCU was in the offices on West Venice Boulevard, a short drive away, then down to Central Alameda to see Guy Robbins's wife.

His widow.

CHAPTER TWENTY-ONE

LEROY HAD ALMOST reached Central Alameda when Domingo called back.

'Got your message Sam; what's up? You taking care of Farmer's vic or something?'

'Kind of. I spoke to him already. He's tied up in court this morning. We discussed the similarities between our vics, and he said it's okay for me to go see this guy's wife.'

'Are they the same, Sam?'

'So identical it's crazy. Must be a connection.'

'You going on your own?'

'That's why I called you. Wondered if you wanted to come down with me, seeing as how you now have your own.'

'Yeah; might be useful. Doesn't need three of us.

There's still a few pieces to mop up with our guy, so I'll get Connor to take care of that while I meet up with you. Give me the address.'

'The guy's name is Guy Robbins. His wife filed the report. They're on Hooper Avenue. 5400 block.'

'Where the hell's that?'

'Over in Central Alameda.'

'What's the ZIP code, Sam?'

'Er – 90011. I should be there in about ten minutes, but I'll wait for you there.'

'I'll be a little longer. Say – twenty minutes.'

'No sweat. See you then.'

Shortly afterwards, Leroy pulled up across the street from the Robbins house. Hooper Avenue was a long, straight road stretching from East 10th Street down to East 92nd. The house was a modest, single storey building with a beige coloured exterior which looked freshly painted. Some of the surrounding houses still had the original chain link fence; here, this had been replaced by a low wall painted to match upon which were black railings. There was a small yard at the front: a lawn which could have used some water and a flower bed in which three cactus plants were growing. Three Herbie Curbies, one black, one blue, one green, were standing, lids open, on the sidewalk outside the house. There was no garage; at the side of the house, there was a short driveway leading to an empty covered carport. Behind the carport was a wooden fence and gate, presumably leading to the back yard. Across the street from the house, on the corner of Hooper and 54th, was a small wooden chapel, painted white with red beams on each corner. Hanging from two windows there was what looked like a white bed sheet. A slogan had been painted on it: being in Spanish, Leroy couldn't understand it, but could make out the words *Centro Evangelista Fuente.*

119

Behind the fencing surrounding the house two doors up, Leroy could see a Hispanic youth of around twelve, dressed in a green tee shirt, nose to the fence, staring at the street. A woman with two small dogs on a leash walked past and said something to the boy, whereupon, he stepped back from the fence and began playing in the yard with a football. On Leroy's side of the street a white haired elderly man with a bright red face and dressed in a sweat suit jogged past, clutching a bottle of water. Leroy watched the jogger in his wing mirror disappear into the distance. Then a black Toyota pulled up behind him. He looked in his mirror and saw Domingo in the driving seat. She got out and joined him in the Taurus.

'That the house over there?' she asked, pointing across the street.

'That's the one.'

'Anybody in?'

'Haven't knocked yet. Waiting for you.'

'I saw some washing out back.'

'Doesn't mean she's in, though.'

'I know that. What's her name?'

'Maria. Maria Robbins.'

'What did she say in the report? Same as yesterday's – not come home from work?'

'Not quite. Says he had to go out that night. Never came back.'

'Go out where?'

'Doesn't say in the report. Just that he had to go out through work. To see a client.'

'A client? What does he do, then?'

'The report doesn't say. Just that he never returned.'

'And we're the first contact since she filed the report?'

'Guess so.'

'Swell.'

Leroy opened his door and stepped out. 'Here we go again,' he said.

'What's happening about the other guy's computer?' Domingo asked as they crossed the street.

'The CCU's looking at it. I took it in this morning. Just come from there.'

'Right.'

They went through the gate and up to the front door. Leroy knocked; Domingo glanced around the yard while they waited.

After a few moments the door opened.

CHAPTER TWENTY-TWO

JERROME CROUCHED LOW behind the silver sedan. He winced as again he felt the pain in his lower back. He had been here for three and a half hours now - since ten – and was considering calling it a day.

He was crouching behind one of the many cars in the 103-space parking lot at the Metro Blue Line station on Florence and Graham. Although there was less of a choice of vehicles here, it was better than a larger parking garage, where there were cameras at every corner, and a guy couldn't walk from one end to the other without appearing on someone's television set. Here, although the lot was not without security, maybe because it was in the open air, it was easier to avoid the cameras. Especially if you had been there many times and knew exactly where the cameras faced.

And its location was ideal. There was no need for Jerrome to get up too early. If he rose just after nine, he had time for breakfast and a five-minute walk to the 103rd Street/Watts Towers station – two stops away. The parking lot at his own stop had room for only sixty-three cars; less choice and as his long since deceased father used to say, 'never shit on your own doorstep'.

So it was quite simple really. A quick trip up here and take up position on the red metal bench on Graham Avenue with a prime view of the parking lot. There he would wait for a vehicle driven by an appropriate driver to park. Appropriate meant preferably female, although a man with a small build or elderly, and with no passengers would be okay too. A guy he knew didn't bother to check the back seats and to his horror there were two kids strapped in back. So he was nailed for child abduction as well when they caught him.

Quite simple, but Jerrome had to get it right. Once he had picked out the right type of driver, he would watch for her to return. Once they were no less than a hundred yards from the car, he would quickly, keeping low to avoid the security cameras, make his way to the reverse of the vehicle, where he had previously tied onto the tailpipe a chain on which was attached a handful of metal tools. A file, and three screwdrivers: tools which would make a loud sound when scraped along the surface of the parking lot. They would pull away but stop after six feet or so to investigate the scraping sound. Nine times out of ten they would keep the keys in the ignition and the engine running. Once they were attempting to get the chain off the tailpipe, he would leap up, get into the car, and then he was off. Down to Compton and into the garage before she had time to even get through to the cops. Next day he would call the guy he normally called and he would come over and check the car out. Agree a price and Jerrome would have the cash for his

123

next supply.

Also, the beauty of this location was that the station here was used by a combination of commuters and shoppers. The commuters would arrive early and take the train up to their downtown offices; those arriving later were generally shoppers.

As was the case today. At ten thirty, he observed the sedan parking. A woman, young-looking, dark hair tied into a pony-tail got out, bought a parking ticket, then walked over to the Blue Line station. She was wearing white pants and a bright yellow top. Jerrome watched as she headed for the platform. Within minutes a Downtown-bound train arrived; when it left she was no longer there.

Jerrome wandered around for the next hour, even across the tracks to the McDonalds. Took a free newspaper from a dispenser outside the station, then back to his bench. Each time a train arrived for Long Beach arrived, he would sit up, watching out for her.

At one-twenty he heard the siren from the crossing, signalling that a train was on its way. He looked up and saw it was a southbound headed to Long Beach. As the last car pulled away, he could see her beginning to make her was back to the parking lot.

Jerrome leapt off his seat and ran across Graham Avenue to the lot. As soon as he reached the sidewalk he dove through a gap in the bushes, bushes which has the effect of hiding his supine form from passers-by. He crept over to the vehicle parked next to her sedan. He had no idea the make or model of this or her car: he could only identify a vehicle by its colour: was it red, was it black, was it silver. He crouched behind a black vehicle, larger than hers.

He heard the click and the flash of the side lamps as she unlocked the door. Heard her climb in and start the engine. Heard and watched her pull away with the expected scraping of the tools. Watched as the car stopped after three feet. Heard the driver door open. Got ready to make his move.

Then…

'You got a problem, dear?' came a woman's voice from the other side of the car. Jerrome sat back down in disbelief.

'I heard a noise as I pulled away,' the driver said. He could tell she was walking to the back of the car, so quickly scuttled around the side of the black car.

'Something loose, I guess. What the fuck -?'

'What is it?'

Jerrome could hear as she was untying the chain.

'Look at this. Some asshole tied this to my tailpipe.' Jerrome could hear the chain rattling.

'My God.' It sounded like an older woman. 'Kids, I guess.'

'I'll give them kids, goddam it.'

Jerrome heard her toss the chain so it landed on the verge of the lot, just under the bushes which formed a perimeter around the lot. Then the sedan door slammed as she got back into the car and pulled away. There was a squeal of brakes as the woman drove around the lot to the exit. Jerrome moved on all fours to the bushes again and waited. He would probably call it a day now; just a matter of waiting until the older woman had left.

He sat for a while, waiting for the sound of another car starting and leaving. This was made difficult by the sound of the traffic on Graham Avenue.

Jerrome was just about to leave when he heard another vehicle pull up, in front of the cars behind which he was crouching. He could hear a door opening, the sound of shoes on the ground, then the door shut and the vehicle left. He frowned, puzzled. What the hell was that about?

Then two cars away, he heard a groan, then a splattering noise. Something wet had hit the ground. Then the smell of vomit hit him. He looked under the cars, in the direction of the noise. He could make out a puddle of something on the ground, and somebody moving. Jesus, he thought, what a day: first he loses a car, then some dude pukes up next to me.

He heard a groan, then another splash. Jerrome thought he had better do something. He stood up and walked round to where the sound was coming from.

'You okay there, dude?' he asked, only to open his eyes wide at what he saw. There was a large pool of vomit on the ground, and a man wearing only a dress shirt and shorts. His hair was unkempt and his face was deathly pale, almost a light shade of green. His eyes were bloodshot, and the skin around them was dark. He looked at Jerrome, and held one arm out to him.

'Help me,' he said weakly, then collapsed on the ground at Jerrome's feet.

CHAPTER TWENTY-THREE

THIS TIME IT was Leroy's turn to make tea. He left Domingo sitting at the small wooden dining table with Maria Robbins. The living area and kitchen comprised one large room: the kitchen area was separated from the rest of the room by a breakfast bar. As he turned on the gas to boil the water, Leroy looked back: he could see the two women talking softly and Domingo reach out and touch Maria's arm. Of all the various duties he had to perform in his job, this was the one he disliked the most. Armed standoffs he could deal with; high speed car chase he could deal with; but giving bad news to a recently bereaved never got any easier, especially where tears were involved, which there normally were. Waiting for the kettle to boil he looked out of the small window into the back yard. Today, he was so glad Domingo was with him.

As he waited, a small grey-haired woman in her sixties shuffled over and joined him at the stove. She was short and of slight build, grey hair neatly cut. Her arms were folded as she came over. Her eyes were red.

It was she who had opened the door earlier. Expecting a woman in her thirties, Leroy and Domingo were slightly taken aback when they first saw her.

'Mrs Robbins?' Leroy had said.

'No, I'm her mother,' she had replied. 'Maria is my daughter.'

They both held up their identifications. 'Detective Leroy, and this is Detective Domingo. Is Mrs Robbins at home? We need to speak with her.'

Her face turned ashen. 'Oh my God, is this about Guy?'

Leroy nodded.

'You'd better come in, then.' She held the door open and the two detectives stepped inside.

As the kettle whistled, Leroy looked around for cups.

'The cups are here,' she said quietly, opening a cabinet door. Took out four cups. 'They keep tea bags and sugar in there. And the milk in the refrigerator. I'll take coffee, I think: I will need it.'

Leroy smiled down at her. 'Thanks.'

As she helped him make the four drinks, she looked up to him and said, 'Thank you so much for coming over to tell us.'

He looked down at her.

'For telling my daughter in person,' she added. 'I was expecting a phone call. To come in person is so much more…respectful.'

'You were expecting a call?' Leroy asked quietly.

'I'm not a fool. I've lost two husbands myself. Guy's been missing since Friday night. Maria called me Saturday afternoon and I've been here ever since. She's tried his cell phone again and again, but it always goes to voicemail.'

'Does it ring first, or go straight to voicemail?'

She frowned. 'I think it went immediately. Why? Does that mean something?'

'Possibly. Can I have his number?'

She picked up a phone which was lying by the sink and checked it. 'Here it is,' she said, and jotted it down on a scrap of paper. 'When it got to Saturday night Sunday morning,' she continued, 'it became a case of hope for the best and prepare for the worst.'

They both looked over as Maria Robbins burst into tears for the third time.

'What am I going to do with her?' she asked Leroy. 'And what can I tell her boys?'

'They have children?' Leroy asked. 'They weren't mentioned in the report.'

'Two. One five, the other seven. They're both at school right now.'

'What have they been told so far?'

'Just that their father had to go away on business.' She picked up two cups and took them over to her daughter and Domingo. Leroy followed her with the other two. Domingo looked over to him as she sat down.

'Maria said that Guy went out around eight o'clock Friday night. To see a client.'

'A client? What's his job?' Leroy asked.

Maria Robbins replied slowly, her response punctuated by sniffs. 'He's….he was an accountant. This was a potential client, he said; otherwise he wouldn't have had to go out on a Friday night in such bad weather.'

Domingo frowned. 'Bad weather?'

Maria nodded, looking down at the table. 'Yes, there was heavy rain. It didn't last for long. I said to Guy can't it wait; it's really bad weather. I didn't want him to have an acc…..' She began sobbing again. While her mother sought to comfort her, Domingo spoke quietly to Leroy.

'Don't remember any rain Friday.'

'There were some isolated cloudbursts that night. I got caught by one on the way to Century City. Short and sharp.'

Maria had composed herself by now, so Leroy asked, 'I am guessing that Guy was self-employed. Did he keep his business records on a computer? A laptop?'

She looked up, over at a desk the opposite side of the room. 'Yes, he did. He used a laptop; it should be in that bag over there.' They all looked over, and a small black bag was resting under the desk. Domingo walked over and picked up the bag. She unzipped it, looked inside, and nodded to Leroy.

'Why are you asking about his computer?' Maria's mother asked. 'I thought Guy was in a road accident.'

Leroy and Domingo exchanged glances. 'Excuse me, why did you think that?' Leroy asked.

She shrugged. 'I just assumed that. Bad weather, he would be in a car wreck. Are you telling me that wasn't the case?'

'It wasn't the case,' he answered. He turned to Maria. 'Maria, can you think of any reason why your husband would be in Hollywood that night?'

'Hollywood?' she said. 'No. Not unless his client lived there.'

'Detective Leroy, how was Guy found?' the old lady asked.

'He was found,' replied Leroy, 'in a parking lot just away from Hollywood Boulevard.'

Maria flashed a glance to her mother, then back to Leroy. 'I…I don't understand. Was he in an accident? Hit by a car? Was he mugged? Please…just tell me how he died.'

'He was found lying in a small parking lot. A vehicle did run over him, but that was not the cause of death. He was dead already.'

Maria put one hand to her mouth and reached for her mother with the other.

'How did he die?' her mother asked.

'We're not a hundred percent certain,' Leroy said slowly.

'Not certain?'

'Let me rephrase that. Guy was filled with a massive dose of narcotics.'

Maria's eyes opened wide. 'No. No way.'

Leroy continued, 'It was a cocktail of three different drugs. Recreational drugs. In a nutshell, that's what killed him. But we need to know how and where he got hold of the drugs, and who he got them from.'

Domingo added, 'Maria: as far as you know, did Guy use recreational drugs?'

'No. Never. He was dead set against that. We have two boys and….oh my God!' She looked at her mother, a look of panic on her face. 'What am I going to tell them?'

'What are *we* going to tell them, darling,' he mother said softly. 'For now, just think about what these officers said. Guy didn't use drugs, did he?'

'No,' Maria repeated. 'Never.'

'Is that why you were asking about his work computer?' Maria's mother asked. 'Might it tell you where he got the drugs from?'

'Ideally, yes,' said Leroy. 'But that might be too much to wish for. I'm hoping, though, that it might give details of that appointment he went to that night.'

'Where was the car found?' Maria asked.

'It hasn't. Again, once we find it, we're hoping that might give some clues on what happened.'

'What car did Guy drive?' Domingo asked. 'It's in the report you filed, isn't it?'

'It's a Lotus. I never liked it – too….what's the word – showy…for me. But he said he needed it to give the right impression to clients. Silver. He bought it last fall.'

'Your finances,' said Leroy. 'Were all your accounts in joint names?'

'Y-yes,' answered Maria slowly.

'So, your joint checking account – Guy's pay went in, and all the bills and other outgoings went out. Is that right?'

Marie nodded. 'Yes, but why?'

'It's to do with those drugs,' Leroy explained. 'I hear what you said about Guy being clean, but he was filled with…you know. I was just seeing if there were any large sums going out that you couldn't account for.'

'We're talking many hundreds of dollars,' added Domingo.

'No,' Maria repeated, shaking her head.

'Okay,' Leroy said, nodding his head. He looked over at Domingo. 'I think we've asked all we need to ask for now.' He turned back to Maria and her mother. 'One last thing, though, Maria. We need you to formally identify your husband.'

'Where is he?' she asked.

'He's at the city morgue. It's not that far - it's adjacent to the California State University.' He checked his watch. 'What time do your sons finish school?'

'Three pm.'

'If you are happy to go now, Detective Domingo can drive you there.' He checked with Domingo. 'And back. You'll be back in time to collect your sons.'

Maria seemed unsure of what to say. Her mother patted her on her hand and put an arm round her shoulder. 'It's better this way, darling. Get it over with.'

'Okay,' Maria mouthed. They all stood up.

'Is that okay, Liza?' Leroy asked. 'Once you've brought them back here, then you can join me back at HQ.'

'Sure. No problem, Sam.'

Leroy turned to Maria and her mother. 'Well, thank you for your time, Mrs Robbins, Mrs…?'

Maria's mother replied, 'Turner. Katy Turner.'

'Mrs Turner,' he repeated, then turned directly to Maria. 'And Maria, once again, I am so sorry for your loss.'

'I'll leave you these,' said Domingo, leaving two business cards on the table. One has my contact details; the other is the toll-free number of a bereavement counsellor. If you feel like…'

Mrs Turner nodded her thanks. Leroy and Domingo said they would wait in the cars, and went outside. Leroy picked up the laptop bag on his way out. As they stood by the cars, Leroy said, 'I'll phone Russ Hobson; get him to have her husband's body ready for identification. Make it as quick as possible for her. So they're back here for the kids. Use your siren if you need to.'

'Right you are, Sam. You going straight back to the station house with that?' She pointed down at the laptop.

'Yeah. See if we can have any more luck than with Lance Riley.'

'You'll need the password.'

'Shit, of course I will. Ask her on the way up to the morgue, then text it to me, will you? Oh, it's okay; here they are.' Led by her mother, Maria came out of the house. As the two women paused by the cars, he asked, 'Sorry, Maria, but I need to ask one more thing: do you know the password Guy used?'

She paused. 'It's DREWJACK. The names of our two boys.'

'Okay. Thank you very much. Now Detective Domingo here will take drive you there, and bring you home also. Please don't hesitate to call either one of us if you have any more questions, or if any other details about last Friday night spring to mind.'

He watched as they climbed in the back of Domingo's car. 'See you later,' he said to her as she climbed in the driver's seat. Then got into his own car, putting the laptop on the passenger seat.

Domingo headed off for the Forensic Science Center; Leroy started the Taurus and began the drive to Police HQ. His hand rested on the black bag. Hopefully there would be something on the laptop which would tell them what did happen that night to Guy Robbins.

And to the others.

CHAPTER TWENTY-FOUR

BACK AT POLICE Headquarters, Leroy parked and walked to the building entrance, clutching the laptop under his arm. As he made his way down the corridor to Homicide, he could hear Captain Patterson's voice. The captain was on the phone, and sounded as if he was trying to end a conversation. The call was clearly with one of his superiors, maybe the Deputy Chief, as the conversation was punctuated with a number of 'yessirs'. The door to the captain's office was slightly ajar, and as he passed Leroy could just make out some movement as Patterson put down the phone.

'Asshole,' he heard Patterson mutter, then, 'Is that you, Sam?'

Damn.

'Yes sir, it's me.' Leroy turned back slightly and looked round Patterson's half-open door. The captain's desk was cluttered with files and sheets of paper, and the captain was in shirtsleeves, looking very flustered. 'Everything all right, sir?' Leroy asked.

'Yes, yes, yes,' Patterson snapped. 'It's....oh, never mind. How are your enquiries going? What's that?' he pointed at Guy Robbins' laptop.

'I've just come back from seeing Guy Robbins' wife,' Leroy replied, holding up the laptop.

'Guy Robbins?'

'He's the guy they found back of Hollywood Boulevard the other night.'

'But that's not even your case. Not even our Division.'

'I know sir, but there are many similarities between this one and mine that we feel there has to be a connection -'

'Connection? Who's *we*?'

'Bill Farmer and I, sir. We spoke earlier this morning. Farmer's in court, at least for part of the day, and we figured it would help to progress both investigations if I went to see the widow now, rather than wait.'

'What does that have to do with it?' Patterson pointed again to the laptop.

'If we can identify any websites Robbins or Riley - my guy - visited just before they died, it might give a clue as to their last movements. We drew a blank with Riley's: it seemed he had deleted all his search history, and I've had to take it to the CCU.'

'What makes you think this one will be any different?

At that point, Leroy's phone rang. He checked the display. Not recognising the number, he let it go to voicemail. He looked up at Patterson. 'I don't, sir. I've just brought it back. Going to check it out now, if that's all.'

'That's all, that's all,' said Patterson, waving Leroy away. 'Just keep me up to date.'

'I will, sir.' Leroy pulled the captain's door closed and

walked over to his own desk. Poured some coffee into a paper cup, pulled a face when he tasted it, and sat down with the laptop. He sat back in his chair as the laptop booted up.

While he was waiting, he checked his phone for voicemail. There was one message. 'Detective Leroy - Sam, isn't it? This is Joanna Moore. From last night, hope you remember. When you are free, could you call me back please?' She gave her number.

He frowned as the Desktop appeared on the laptop screen. He keyed in the password Maria Robbins had given him. It worked. As the Home screen came on, he returned Joanna Moore's call. She answered after three rings.

'Ms Moore? Detective Leroy here. Sam. Is everything okay?'

'Yes, everything's fine. Thank you so much for calling me back. I hope I'm not disturbing you. I just wanted to thank you for what you did for me last night.'

'It's what I'm paid to do, Ms Moore. Joanna.'

'I know that. But I'm still very grateful.'

'No problem.'

'I was just wondering - as you seem to live so close - if you would let me cook dinner for you tonight. Just my way of saying thank you.'

'Joanna, there's no need.'

'You wouldn't be infringing some code of police ethics if you accepted, would you?'

'No, nothing like that; it's just -'

'You know where I live. Please say yes. It's just my way of saying thank you.'

Leroy paused a moment then said, 'Okay then, you've talked me into it. My shift ends around six.'

'Eight-thirty, then?' she asked. 'You know the address.'

'Yes, I do. See you eight-thirty, then.'

'Bye,' she said and hung up.

Leroy pressed the end call button, put the phone down on the desk and looked up at Guy Robbins' Home screen.

First of all, he checked the email account, all boxes, but found nothing of any significance there. Then he went to the browser search history.

'Hmm. Well, lookie here,' he muttered, as he went through the last few sites Guy Robbins had visited.

'Stop yawning, Leroy!'

Leroy looked up. Liza Domingo stood in the doorway. He laughed and stretched. 'How long have you been there?'

'Just got back.'

'How were things?'

She shrugged and sat on a chair by the next desk. 'As much as I expected. She ID'd the body okay. We were only there fifteen minutes. Then drove them back.'

'How was she?'

'Seemed pretty calm. Quiet.'

Leroy looked over to her. 'No telling what she's like behind closed doors. Lucky her mother's there. In my experience, telling any kids is always the worst.'

'I can imagine. Is that his laptop?' She took a mouthful of his coffee, and pulled a face.

'Didn't taste any better when it was hot,' Leroy quipped. 'Hey, Liza, take a look at all this.' He tapped the screen.

'Don't tell me he'd deleted everything as well,' Domingo said.

'No, he hadn't.'

'Sweet. So, what did you find?'

'There's only about twenty addresses here. I can't tell how far back chronologically it goes, but look at where he's been.'

'What kind of places?' Domingo asked, wheeling her chair to get closer.

'Well, to start with,' Leroy said, as he moved the cursor, 'he had visited two airlines' sites: Spirit and American…'

'Looking for what? Maybe he was booking a vacation for them all.'

'Don't think so. He was looking for prices for LAX to McCarran.'

She frowned. 'McCarran?'

'Vegas. Two adults. Tuesday to Thursday.'

'So clearly not a family trip.'

'Anything booked?'

'Not so's I could tell. We'll have a look at the bank accounts in due course, although if he was up to something, he wouldn't have used the family credit card.'

'What else?'

'Just stuff here. Amazon.com, Home Depot, Staples Center, Nickelodeon...'

'For the kids, I guess.'

'Yeah. But then we get to these. Look: Between9and5.com.' He opened the page.

'Dirty bastard,' she said. 'He wanted a hotel room daytime, yes?'

'I think so. Then there's this.' He clicked again. It opened on www.arrangeadate.com. The Home page was filled with thumbnail portraits of young women.

'Arrange a date dot com,' Domingo read out loud. 'Bastard. So that's what he was up to. Son of a bitch.'

'Seems like it was. I looked through all five hundred twenty four pages -'

'Five hundred....? No way.'

'Way. And that was just the women looking for men section. There were other categories, but I thought this was the best place to start.'

'And?'

'See each thumbnail has a link underneath? Well, two of the links are coloured purple.'

'Meaning the link was used recently?'

'Yeah. Not sure how recently; a week, I think,' Leroy said. 'So we know which ones he responded to, maybe arranged a meeting with.'

'Hang on a minute, Sam,' said Domingo. 'He could quite easily have made the contacts on his cell phone, or Blackberry, or whatever.'

'Oh yes, of course he could. But remember, he - and the other guys - were found bare assed naked. Or virtually. So this is all we have to go on at this time.'

Domingo nodded and scratched her ear. 'Yeah, I forgot. So, what do we do now? Get the owners of arrange a date dot com to give us the details?'

Leroy shook his head. 'They won't know. All they will have is an email address, which could be remote. Our best bet is to answer the posting, and arrange to meet one of them.'

Domingo slowly nodded. 'Any other places he visited?'

'No. That was it.' He stood up. 'Tell you what, Liza. I need the bathroom. Can you send replies to those two; try and set up a daytime meet. Either this afternoon or tomorrow.'

'Sure thing.' She moved over to his chair. 'Get me a decent cup of coffee while you're away, Sam? And a sandwich?'

'Okay,' he said, stretching. 'Any preference?'

'Whatever,' she replied from behind the laptop screen. She started typing, then looked up when she noticed he was still standing in the Homicide room.

'What?' she asked.

'Nothing,' he said, grinning. 'Nothing.'

'Then why the smug grin on your face?'

'Oh,' he grinned, taking his phone off the desk and tossing it from one hand to the other. 'Just a call I took earlier.'

'And…?'

He swung round to leave and looked back over his shoulder. 'I have a date tonight.'

CHAPTER TWENTY-FIVE

'I'LL BET YOU my next year's pay checks,' said Leroy, as he and Domingo sat in the Taurus, having just pulled up outside an apartment block on Sepulveda Boulevard, 'that she's a hooker.'

'Well, there's a newsflash,' replied Domingo, looking over at him.

'What do you mean?' he asked.

'You serious?'

'It's just residential here. Nobody on the streets. And we're not in a red light district.'

'Look around you, Sam. Apartment buildings. There's a Best Western over there, a Comfort Inn across the street, and over the other side of Burbank there's a Hampton Inn. And we are in a red light district.'

'No, we aren't.'

'Yes we are. Mainly from Burbank down to Ventura. Up and coming, you might say, if you excuse the pun. When they began cleaning up Hollywood a few years back, some of the trade moved out here.'

'Oh, I forgot: you spent some time in Vice, didn't you?'

She nodded. 'Only six months. Covering a maternity break, would you believe? But I got to know plenty of the hot spots.'

'And this is one of them?'

'When you've got a number of budget hotels and places like this,' - she looked out at the apartment building they were stopped outside - 'well, it's ideal, isn't it? You wait till it gets really dark. It's only twilight now.'

Leroy agreed. 'Guess so.'

'Anyway, I told you back at the station house she was, didn't I?'

'You did.'

Earlier in the day, Domingo had visited the pages of the two girls it appeared Guy Robbins had contacted. The first, a redhead named Alexandra, had not replied by the time she and Leroy had to leave to meet Tanya, who was blonde and looked around sixteen.

'She's probably around thirty,' Domingo had said. 'This is an old photo, or even one of somebody else.'

'What has she said?' Leroy asked, as he drained his coffee cup.

'Just that she'd like to meet. Meet you, I should say.'

'Where and when?'

'She suggests in the lobby of the Denny's on Sepulveda and Burbank.'

'Classy. What time?'

'Six. Should just be getting dark by then. What time's your date?'

'Eight thirty. So we should have plenty of time. What's her name?'

'Tanya. Though that's probably not her real name.'

'Don't really care what her real name is. As long as she knows what happened to Robbins.'

'It's ten of six. Let's go.' Leroy started the engine, manoeuvred into the northbound traffic and moved off. Once they had crossed Burbank, he made a left and drove into the parking lot. He reversed into a space, and switched off his lights. 'Just a matter of waiting,' he said, sitting back in his seat.

A few minutes later, a station wagon pulled in and parked. Leroy and Domingo sat up, only to relax when the occupants, a family of four, got out and walked into the restaurant. Two men left at the same time, walked to another car, and left the lot.

Five after six, and no further activity. Then, a figure got out of a Beetle parked in the corner of the lot. The car was already parked when Leroy and Domingo arrived: it was in darkness, so they assumed it was empty.

'Sam…?' Domingo nudged Leroy's arm.

'I see her,' he replied. The figure, petite, hair tied up into a bun, miniskirt, and a jacket, was in silhouette so they could not see if the face matched the thumbnail on the arrangeadate website. She was headed for the restaurant doors. Leroy opened the car door and stepped out. He too headed for the restaurant.

She must have heard his footsteps behind her so stopped and turned round, one foot on the entrance steps. As she turned, her face was caught by the light from the restaurant lobby, and he could see this was the same person as that in the thumbnail.

'Tanya?' he asked. 'I'm Sam.'

She held out her hand to shake his. 'Nice to meet you,

Sam.' She looked around. 'We could have a drink here first, if you'd like. Do you have a car? You could leave it here; I have a room at the Best Western.'

'We won't need that,' Leroy said, holding up his shield and identification card.

'Shit!' Tanya spat, angrily looking around.

'Don't worry, I'm not here to bust you. I just want to ask you a few questions.'

'Questions?'

'About one of your johns. My car's over there.' He took Tanya's arm and led her back to the Taurus. 'Get in the back,' he said.

She climbed in the back seat, giving a look of surprise as Domingo turned round to face her.

'This is Detective Domingo,' said Leroy as he sat back down in the driver's seat. 'Detective Domingo, this is Tanya. You might recognize her, Tanya: she used to be in Vice.'

Tanya stared at Domingo's face, then shook her head.

''I don't think we've met before, Sam,' Domingo said.

'It's not important. Tanya,' said Leroy as he took a photograph of Guy Robbins from the dashboard and held it up, 'have you ever seen this guy?' He turned on the interior light.

She looked at the photograph. 'No. Never seen him before.'

'You sure?'

'Yeah. What's his name?'

'Robbins. Guy Robbins.'

'Never heard of him.'

'They why did you react when I told you his name?'

'I didn't.'

'Look, Tanya – I don't have time to jerk around all night. Answer the damn question. Who is this guy?'

'I don't know.'

Leroy said nothing.

'But he did contact me.'

'He did? Through your website?'

'My web….?'

'Arrange a date dot com,' Domingo said.

'Oh, that. Yes, it was through there.'

'And? Did you arrange to meet him?'

'We arranged to meet, yes.'

'Where?'

'Here.'

'Here?' Domingo repeated.

Leroy turned to her. 'Not a million miles away from home. Two freeways a few blocks away.' He turned back to Tanya. 'When was this?'

'End of last week. About this time. Maybe later.'

'And?' he asked.

She shrugged. 'Just didn't show.'

'And that's it? What did you do, then?'

'I waited about thirty minutes, then went home.'

'Home? No other clients?' Domingo asked.

Tanya looked over at her. 'I ain't no hooker. Don't ask for money. Just want some company, that's all.'

Domingo nodded. 'Company. Sure you do.'

'Listen, when all you have to go back to is a ten by ten, one tiny window, you'll want some company.'

Domingo was about to reply when Leroy cut in. 'Okay, Tanya, if that's all you can tell us, we'll let you go. Here,' - he reached into his pocket and passed her a thin wad - 'take this. Have dinner on me.'

Tanya took the cash, bundled it in her bag, and stepped out of the car. Leroy and Domingo watched as she walked back to the Beetle, get in and drive off.

'Told you she was a hooker,' Domingo said. 'How much did you give her?'

Leroy shook his head. 'Fifty.'

She whistled. 'You know what I think?' she said. 'He didn't show here because he was seeing the other one.

Alexandra, wasn't it?'

Leroy nodded. 'Could be. We'll check in the morning if she's gotten back to us.'

'Sure.' She checked her watch. 'Six thirty. Plenty of time for you to get home, put on gallons of aftershave, get ready for your date.'

'What plans do you have?' Leroy asked as they left the parking lot.

'Just takeout and a DVD, I guess.'

'Sorry.'

'No need to be sorry. *I* wouldn't be. I'll just expect a full report next morning, that's all.'

'Report?'

She looked over at him. 'On whether your date makes a good breakfast.'

CHAPTER TWENTY-SIX

LEROY WAS ON his phone when Domingo arrived at Police HQ the next morning. She mouthed 'Coffee?' to him: he nodded as he spoke on the phone so she went to the vending machine. He had finished when she returned.

'Thanks,' he said as he took a mouthful. 'Just come off the phone with Bill Farmer,' he said, swirling the black liquid around in the paper cup.

'He wants his body back?' she asked. 'Or is he still in court?'

'Neither. He's back in the office, but asked if I'd mind if we saw this thread through to completion. Says he has other fish to fry.'

'And you said...?'

'I said fine. Suits me. As far as I'm concerned, this will

help solve one of my cases. What about you?'

She scratched her head. 'Well, I guess as Connor's back today, we'd better get on with our own stuff.'

'Okay,' Leroy replied reluctantly. 'Guess so. Thanks for your help anyway. In any case, the Guy Robbins thread might be a blind alley anyway, if Tanya last night was anything to go by.'

'Did the other one reply yet?'

'Haven't checked yet. Let's have a look. He logged on, and waited for the Inbox to come up. 'Sweet Jesus, she's replied,' he said, reading from the screen. 'She'd love to meet me. Is free today, and she's even given a cell number.'

Domingo snorted. 'Yeah, her work number. Call it.'

'I'll text, I think.'

'Whatever,' said Domingo as Leroy typed and sent the message.

'Just a matter of waiting until she replies,' he said, tossing the phone down on the desk and leaning back in the chair.

'Sure,' she said, staring at him for a moment. 'Look, Connor'll be in soon, so I'd better get back to our own case.'

Leroy nodded. 'In any case, Liza, our paths will cross again soon, as they say. You can bet your ass your Griffith Park guy is connected to mine.'

'Probably. I think that's going to be our first line of enquiry: you know, check for any similarities. When's Quinn back from honeymoon, by the way?'

Leroy looked over at a chart on the wall. 'Not for another few days yet.'

'Well, I'll see you around,' she said, walking back to her own desk.

'Oh shit!' exclaimed Leroy.

'What is it?' she asked, looking up from her PC screen.

'All that talk about Connor and Quinn coming back to work, I'd forgotten Perez is due back today.'

She looked around. 'No sign of him around. Would

have thought he'd be in early; first day in a new job.'

Leroy shrugged. 'Probably out playing golf with Patterson. I'd like to be out of here before he gets in.'

'Why?'

'Because he's a prick.'

'Fair enough.'

Just then, a text message came through on Leroy's phone. He snatched it off the desk. 'It's her!' he said. Domingo sat up.

'What does she say?' she asked.

He frowned as he read the message. 'Not much. "Can you make The Groves Overlook at 11:30?"'

'Groves Overlook? I've heard of that. Somewhere along Mulholland Drive, I think. Do you know where it is?'

'Rings a bell with me.' He touched his phone for the Maps app, then entered the name. 'Yes, I thought so.' He looked up at her. 'It's one of those scenic view places along Mulholland.'

'A bit deserted.'

'Ideal if you're a hooker meeting a john.'

Domingo checked her watch. 'It's early. When are you going to leave? I'll come with you.'

He stood up, putting on his jacket. 'I'm going to leave now. Partly to avoid Perez when he gets here, partly to make sure I'm there before she arrives. You don't need to come.'

'I'm coming as back up, Sam. I'll call Connor on the way. He can start work on Griffith Park while we're out.'

They both left the station house and walked swiftly to Leroy's Taurus. Leroy started up and they pulled into the rush hour traffic on Iowa. As Leroy turned into Butler and headed towards Mulholland, Domingo rang Detective Connor, and asked him to review the details of the Griffith Park body and compare them with those of the victims in Hollywood and Century City. After she ended the call, she said, 'We just missed him. He arrived a minute or two after we left.'

'We were in early,' replied Leroy.

'Yeah, and he said Patterson and Perez just got in too.'

'Damn. Was hoping to catch them,' Leroy quipped.

'I'm sure we will get the chance.'

'Yeah. I'm hoping to make some progress on this thread before we do,' said Leroy. 'Last time I spoke to Patterson, he told me the CODs had to be natural causes, weren't connected, and I would make better use of my time following up older unsolveds.'

'That's bullshit, Sam. They're obviously connected.'

'I know that, you know that, Bill Farmer knows that. But Patterson thinks otherwise. And if Patterson thinks otherwise, you just know Perez will think otherwise too.'

'Well, let's hope this one – what's her name? Alexandra?'

'Alexandra,' Leroy confirmed.

'Alexandra. Let's hope she gives us more to go on than the one last night.'

'Yeah. Let's hope so.'

She swung round in the passenger seat and looked at Leroy. 'Talking about last night,' she said. 'How was your date?'

Leroy grinned. 'I was wondering how long it would take you to ask.'

'Well? Tell me about it, then. Who is she?'

'Her name's Joanna. Joanna Moore. And it wasn't really a date. I met her the other night.'

'Met her? How did you get time to meet anyone?'

'I had just gotten home, late. I could hear some screaming - it was a very still night - so I ran in the direction of the noise, and found her fighting off a pair of muggers. So I cuffed them, got a local car to pick them up, and walked her home.'

'She didn't live far, then?'

'In Venice, also. An apartment near the canals.'

'That's sweet. Near neighbours.'

'Anyway, I took her home, made sure she was okay. No injuries, just a bit shaken up. Next morning, she called to invite me for dinner just to say thank you.'

'And how was dinner, then?'

'Dinner was very nice, thank you.'

'And breakfast?'

Just as Leroy opened his mouth, Domingo's phone rang. 'It's Connor,' she said as she glanced at the screen. As she took the call, Leroy could infer why her partner had called, and she confirmed it. 'He just called to tell me Patterson and the Lieutenant Perez just arrived,' she said. 'Wanted to know why we were pooling scarce police resources into a pointless case. Perez wants to see you the second you get back.'

'Just to see *me*?'

She sat back in the seat. 'You're the senior officer, Detective. I'm just following orders.'

'We'll soon be on Mulholland,' Leroy said, as they joined the exit ramp from the I-405. 'Then the location isn't far.'

Sure enough, five minutes later, just after the road took a sharp bend, they came across the Groves Outlook. On their left was a small row of buildings. Not houses, but some light industrial buildings. One seemed to be closed: the gates were shut, and the small parking lot was empty. Next to it appeared to be selling RVs, but again, apart from a couple of battered vehicles and three equally maintained cars in the parking lot, there was no activity. To the right was a small parking lot, not paved, more of a dirt turnout. It was empty. Leroy pulled in.

It was 10:50. As they sat and waited, now and again, a car would pass by on Mulholland.

Leroy wound down his window. 'It's quiet here,' he muttered. 'Pretty deserted.'

'Wrong time of year for visitors. This is actually the Mulholland Scenic Parkway,' she said. 'Gets really busy in the summer. Did you know that, Sam?'

'No, I didn't know that.'

'I don't know – you New York City boys. You are from New York, aren't you?'

He nodded. 'Queens.'

'Thought so. Why did you move out here, Sam?'

He paused, then said, 'Long story.'

'We've almost half and hour to wait.'

'It's complicated.'

'I can do complicated.'

He glanced at her. 'I came here for the skiing.'

'Skiing? Sam, LA's in the middle of a desert.'

'I was misinformed.' He smirked. He had the feeling he was misquoting a movie somewhere. 'Let's take a look round,' he said as he climbed out of the Taurus. She followed, and they walked from the parking lot towards the overlook. They were soon walking along a dirt track, climbing a slight hill, through a grove of eucalyptus trees, from where the location got its name.

'Man,' said Leroy as they reached the summit. 'That's some view.' They now had a commanding view of the San Fernando valley: immediately below them was a large private house with swimming pool; further in the distance they could see the traffic moving along the twisting and winding road that was Sepulveda Boulevard, and to the west Leroy could just make out the Encino Reservoir.

'Impressed?' asked Domingo, as she stood beside him. 'Bet you've never done the tourist thing here, have you?'

He shook his head.

'Well, you ought to.' She looked around. 'Look, even though Mulholland is only a hundred yards away, and is quite a busy thoroughfare, we could be in the middle of nowhere here. Lots of places to take a girl, or a guy.'

'Or a hooker. Or a john,' Leroy said, turning to walk back to the car. 'Come on, she'll be here soon.' They walked back through the eucalyptus groves. 'Of course, she might not have come alone,' he said.

'Another reason for you to need back-up.'

'Point taken.'

'Eleven twenty,' said Leroy as they arrived back at the car. They climbed back in and began to wait.

'Eleven forty,' said Domingo, a little later. 'Where is she, I wonder?'

'I'm going to wait over there,' said Leroy, pointing at an outbuilding on the edge of the lot. You stay in the car. I'll be in plain sight.' He wandered over to the building, which turned out to be a long since closed restroom. He looked back at Domingo, who was now sitting low in the driver's seat. Over the next few minutes, five cars went past; Leroy looked up and down the street. Shit, he thought, this is going to be abortive. Patterson will love this. Then, just as he was about to turn back, another vehicle came around the sharp bend. Leroy could see it was slowing down; then it began to indicate left. He watched as it turned into the lot. It was an old car: a Ford, but he was unable to make out the model. The colour caught his eye: it seemed to be still painted in grey undercoat. He could just make out the figure driving.

The Ford parked some twenty feet away from where he had parked the Taurus. A figure climbed out. She was tall, maybe slightly over six feet, with a sturdy figure, and long thin legs, accentuated by the micro dress she was wearing. She also wore a tiny pink cardigan. Her hair was dark, and long. She walked towards him, taking careful; steps in her high heeled shoes. Two things flashed through his mind: one was relief that she had come alone, even though he had back up in the form of Domingo. Secondly, how incongruous her attire was for this location.

As she approached him, she looked around. When it was apparent Leroy was on his own, she smiled. 'You must be Sam,' she said. 'I'm Alexandra.'

CHAPTER TWENTY-SEVEN

SHE HELD OUT her hand to shake his.

'Hi, Alexandra,' he smiled back. 'Yes, I'm Sam.' He looked around, pretending to be nervous. 'Look, I'm sorry, but this is my first time. What...what happens next? Do we do it here?'

She gave him a reassuring smile. 'Don't worry, honey. Everyone has to have a first time. It's down to you really: where you want to go; what you want to do.'

'Okay...' he said, hesitantly. 'How much are we talking? Money-wise, I mean.'

'Like I say, honey, that depends on you. Your choice. We can drive somewhere. We can get a room not far from here. Or we can use your automobile.' She nodded over to the Taurus. 'Or if you like nature, there's plenty of spots we could use in the groves.'

'Okay,' Leroy said, looking around, pretending to consider all this.

'As far as the money is concerned,' she went on. 'If you only want oral, that's a hundred. If you want to whole *tamale*, it's three hundred. If we go get a room, that's another hundred on top. So, what's it to be, honey?'

Leroy reached into his pocket and fished out his badge and card. 'Not what you had in mind, honey.'

She took a step back. 'You fuck! You can't do this; it's entrapment. You called me.'

'Possibly. But we're not here to book you.'

'We?'

'My partner's over there in the car.' He waved for Domingo to join them. 'I just need some information.'

'Yeah, what?' she growled.

'Do you know this man?' he asked, showing her a picture of Guy Robbins. 'He's dead, as you can see.'

'No. Never seen him before.'

In spite of her denial, Leroy noticed a flicker of recognition in her face. 'Are you sure, Alexandra? He's left a wife and two kids. Why not help us find who made her a widow?'

She shuffled around a few times. 'Well, yeah, I might have seen him.'

'Was he a regular, or was it a one-off?' Domingo asked.

Alexandra shook her head. 'I – I can't remember. A one-off, I think.'

'Where did you meet him?' asked Leroy. 'Here?'

She paused a moment, then replied, 'Yeah, that's right. Here.'

'And what did he get?'

She paused again, running her hand through her hair. 'I don't remember.'

Leroy said nothing.

'I told you. I don't remember.'

Leroy said nothing.

'Okay,' she finally said. 'I just gave him oral. The cheap son of a bitch wouldn't pay any more.'

'So, you met him here, he paid you a hundred, got himself a blow job, and then you both left. Is that right?'

'U-huh,' she mumbled. 'That's it.'

'Separately? You left separately. Separate cars?'

'Of course. Why, is that important?'

Leroy said nothing.

Finally, Alexandra impatiently asked, 'Is that it? Can I go now? Or are you going to book me after all?'

'One more question,' Leroy asked. 'How did he get hold of you? Through an ad?'

She shuffled again, a look of resentment on her face. 'Same way you did.'

'The arrange a date dot com website?' Domingo asked.

'Yeah, that's the one.' She replied to Domingo but kept her gaze on Leroy. 'So can I go *now*?'

'Okay,' Leroy replied, putting Guy Robbins' picture back in his pocket. 'But make sure I don't see you again.'

With a snort, she swung round on her high heels, and stomped back to her car. As she turned the car round on the dirt, a cloud of dust rose in the air. Leroy and Domingo took a few steps back to avoid the cloud.

'Well?' Domingo asked, as they watched her get back onto Mulholland and head back the way she came. 'Do you believe her?'

'Not really,' Leroy replied. 'Come on, let's see where she's headed.'

CHAPTER TWENTY-EIGHT

'WHAT PART OF her story don't you believe?' Domingo asked, as Leroy took the Taurus east under the San Diego Freeway.

'Most of it, really,' Leroy replied.

'Okay,' she said, peering ahead at the traffic on Mulholland. She could make out the grey Ford five vehicles in front.

'First of all,' Leroy continued, 'she lied right at the beginning about knowing Robbins. Then…well, let's just say I'm sceptical. I think she's hiding something. I'll take book that she already knew he was dead.'

'You think she killed him?'

'No, not really. But his death might be something to do with whatever they did, or wherever they did it. Look at the way she was dressed and what she was charging. No way would she just do the business in the middle of a eucalyptus grove. She's too upmarket for that.'

It was hardly a high-speed police chase. Whilst not particularly busy, being an undivided highway the traffic moved at the speed of the slowest vehicle, and the school bus ten or so ahead was going at thirty; the amount of traffic heading in the opposite direction prevented any overtaking. In any case, Alexandra appeared to have no idea Leroy and Domingo were following her.

They continued their almost leisurely pursuit along the winding and meandering highway, past the intersections with Beverly Glen Boulevard and Benedict Canyon Drive.

'You were telling me about your date,' said Domingo as they waited at the stop lights at the Coldwater Canyon Avenue. Fortunately, Alexandra had also been stopped at the light.

'No, you were asking,' replied Leroy, as they began to move again.

'You planning on seeing her again?'

'Maybe.'

'Only maybe?'

'Only maybe.' He paused. 'Only maybe Saturday night. She's coming to mine.'

'Sweet. Plenty of places in Venice to go for breakfast.'

'Domingo, you need to get out more.'

'Well, at least you've admitted something. 'You're going to see her again, right? So it *was* a date.'

Leroy said nothing; just shook his head in resignation.

After a particularly sharp bend, the traffic slowed momentarily. 'Can you see what's happening?' Leroy asked.

Domingo leaned to the right and looked ahead. 'I think she's made a right. Into a side street.' Leroy slowed down to around fifteen and indicated. He slowly turned the Taurus right and came off Mulholland onto a dirt road which went up a slight hill. The road was in fact a dead end. Three gated residences either side up the hill; at the summit, the road widened, and a larger gated building at the end of the road. As they drove up to where the road widened, they could see the gates to all seven residences were closed. Leroy pulled up at the end of the road and looked around.

'She must have gone in one of these places,' he said. 'There's nowhere else for her to go. It's a dead end.'

'Yeah, but which one? All the gates are shut.'

Leroy looked around too. 'We need to check these places out. But we can't just blunder in. Any ideas?'

CHAPTER TWENTY-NINE

THE IDEA THAT they eventually came up with was that a police helicopter pursuing a suspect from a store robbery had observed the suspect leave his vehicle on Mulholland, and scurry through the substantial gardens of the properties in this street. The helicopter had lost the suspect now; he had probably gotten another vehicle, but they would still like to check the grounds.

All the seven properties in the street had gated entrances, each with intercoms by the side of the gate. They were given access to the first house using this ploy and were allowed by a housekeeper, a tiny Spanish lady, to look round the exterior of the house and the gardens. The same went for the third property, except on this occasion they were greeted by the owner's wife, a woman in her sixties, who clearly by the way she was dressed and made up, had a fantasy that she was thirty years younger. While Leroy and Domingo checked round the back of the house where the three Porsches were garaged, she joined them to ask how long they would be as she had a lunch appointment on Sunset. In neither of these places did they locate the fugitive, or in real terms, the grey Ford.

There was no answer when they called the intercom at the second property. Leroy retrieved a pair of binoculars from the Taurus to get a closer look at the house: all the windows and doors at the front were closed, and there was no sign of life. Domingo checked the dirt track as it led up to the gate and could see that the gravel had not been disturbed recently.

They returned to the Taurus and drove to the fourth set of gates, those at the entrance to the house and the end of the street. Leroy leaned out and pressed the *Call* button on the intercom. After a moment there was a crackle from the speaker, and a voice said, 'Yes, who is it? What do you want?'

'Police,' Leroy said unnecessarily, noticing a small camera lens above the speaker. 'We believe a fugitive from a store robbery may have gotten into your grounds.'

'No, the gates are locked as you can see. Nobody has gained access to these premises. But thank you for your concern.'

Leroy glanced over to Domingo, then back to the intercom. 'I appreciate that, sir; however, we do need to check. So please unlock the gates. It will only take us a few minutes to carry out the search, assuming the fugitive is not on your property.'

'As I said, officers, thank you for your -'

'There is also the possibility that the man is armed, so it is in your interests to let us in. Unless *you* are the owner, please speak with your employer now. It would be far easier if you opened the gate now; those in the house could potentially be in danger.'

'Please wait there.' The intercom clicked silent.

'"Please wait there"?' muttered Domingo. 'Where the

hell does he think we're going to go?'

Leroy said nothing; just rubbed his chin and stared at the intercom.

After a couple of minutes the intercom crackled again. 'Thank you for your patience, officers. Please follow the road up to the house.' There was a click from the gates, and they swung open. Leroy drove through the gateway and along a short road to a large house. As they pulled up outside, one of a set of large double doors opened, and a white-haired man dressed in a black suit came out. He walked up to the Taurus and opened Leroy's door. 'Please come this way, sir. Madam,' he added as Domingo got out of the passenger seat.

'Thank you very much,' Leroy said as they followed the man inside. Leroy turned back to look at Domingo, who was trying to suppress a grin.

'Please wait in here,' the man said, having led the two police officers into the first room off the large hallway, the centrepiece of which was a grand staircase.

He turned to face them in the doorway. 'Mr Mason will see you shortly, officers,' he announced, then turned and left.

As he and Domingo waited, Leroy looked around the room. It reminded him of photograph he had seen of rooms in the thirties or forties. The only concession to contemporary living was a large flat screen television set in one corner. Domingo looked around too, giving Leroy a *this is weird* look.

'Do you have your identification, officers?'

They both spun round to see in the doorway, a man dressed smartly in a business suit. He was short, around five feet, with blond hair cut in a traditional way, with a heavy fringe which he had to brush back with his right hand as he spoke.

Leroy held out his. 'Detective Leroy, LAPD. And this is Detective Domingo.' She held out hers. Rather than just giving the credentials a perfunctory glance as most people tended to do, he took the identification and carefully studied each one. He did not wear any glasses, but held the items about six inches from his face as he checked them.

Eventually he returned them. 'Thank you very much, officers,' he said, giving an insincere smile. 'They appear to be in order. My name is Mason, Dwight Mason. How can I help you?'

'As I said on the intercom, sir,' replied Leroy, 'an LAPD helicopter in pursuit of a vehicle used in a store robbery saw the vehicle being left down on Mulholland. The suspect then fled on foot, climbing over the walls of the neighbouring properties.'

'And where is your suspect now?' Mason asked, stooping over slightly, inclining his head and grinning. By now, Leroy had taken a dislike to him.

'Unfortunately, the copter crew lost sight of him. We are assuming he is hiding somewhere in the grounds of the houses around here.'

'In the grounds? So you don't need to search inside?'

'With your permission, we need to firstly search the grounds, including any outbuildings. Then we'll check the first floor doors and windows for any break-ins.'

Mason grinned again, and straightened up. 'Well, I'm sure that will be satisfactory, officers, although I am sure you will find nothing.'

Leroy said nothing.

After an uncomfortable pause, Mason spoke again. 'In that case, officers, I will lead you outside.' He did so, pausing and turning to them outside the large front doors. 'The grounds, officers, are not as extensive as you might think.' He gesticulated slowly, showing Leroy and Domingo where the gardens were, as if they were unable to see them.

'And round the sides and back of the house?' Leroy asked.

Mason gesticulated again, this time with his left arm. 'As you can see, you can walk right round the house. It is all open.'

'Are there any outbuildings?' Domingo asked. 'Garages, summer houses, and the like?'

'Yes, there are. All out back.' He stood back and smiled, as if to say *anything else, or have you finished wasting my time?*

'Thank you very much, sir,' said Leroy. 'You can leave us to it. If we have any questions, we'll call you. If we do find the suspect, as he may be armed, we may need to call in back-up.'

'I'm sure that won't be necessary,' Mason smirked. 'I don't think your quarry is here.' With that, he turned and went back inside the house.

'Jerk,' muttered Domingo, as the door closed behind him.

'Come on,' said Leroy. 'Let's get on with it. We'll make a show of checking the undergrowth over there; then we'll head out back. If she drove here, the car's most likely there.'

'Why are we being so ostentatious?' Domingo asked as she and Leroy looked behind bushes.

'Because I have a hunch we're being watched. And I wouldn't be surprised if that jerk as you so rightly called him calls in to validate why we're here. So we'd better move swiftly. Let's go out back.'

They walked round the side of the house and came across a large garage, a pool and a pool house. The only person they saw was the pool cleaner, using a cleaning device on a telescopic pole. He looked up at them inquisitively, only to go back to his pool after Leroy held up his badge. The two officers walked first to the garage building. The garage seemed wide enough to hold three vehicles side by side. The roller doors were shut, but at the side there was a small window and a small glass door. Leroy tried the door: it was locked, so he peered in the window.

Even though it was only around two feet square, the window was very clean, and afforded a view of the entire garage. Inside the place looked whitewashed, both walls and floor. It was empty apart from a large black RV, and a motorcycle. Both looked either brand new, or highly polished.

'Nothing in there,' Leroy said, and he and Domingo made their way over to the pool house. The door to the pool house was open. Domingo stepped inside and looked around. Inside the house was a suite of furniture: sofa and two armchairs and a bar. Leroy stood outside and looked around, strolling casually around the lawn adjacent to the pool house. 'Liza,' he called out.

Domingo stepped out of the pool house to see what her partner wanted, then saw Dwight Mason coming out of the main house. 'I take it you've found nothing, officers?' he said, folding his arms and giving them another lopsided grin.

'No, it appears to be all clear, sir.' Leroy started to walk to the side of the house as he spoke. He stopped after a few feet and turned around. 'Just one question, though, Mr Mason. You have garage space for – what, six vehicles? But I can only see an RV and a bike. Are these the only vehicles you have here?'

Mason paused, frowning slightly. Then the obsequious grin. 'My employer owns a sedan, but he is away on a business trip at this time, so in answer to your question, those are the only vehicles here.'

'It's quite a large house,' Domingo said, looking up at the second floor windows. 'What about domestic staff? Where do they park?'

Mason folded his arms again. 'I'm sorry, officers – I understood from what you said earlier that your suspect - *if* he was on these grounds – would have come here on foot.'

'You are quite right, Mr Mason. Things appear to be clear here. Sorry to have troubled you. We'll try the next house.'

'No trouble at all. Always happy to help.' Mason leaned again and put a hand on Leroy's shoulder, their difference in height making him lean even further. Leroy had the impression he was being ushered off the premises. Mason led them through the house: in through the back double doors, along a cream painted corridor to the hall they had seen earlier, and out the front door. He even opened Leroy's car door for him.

'Once again, thanks for your time, Mr Mason,' Leroy said after winding down his window.

'And once again, always happy to help.' Mason knocked on the Taurus roof as if giving the two police officers a signal to leave, then turned and walked back into the house. Leroy took the Taurus back down to the gated entrance, slowing down to allow the gates to swing open.

'That was one oily fucker,' said Domingo as they drove through the gates. 'Next house, then?'

'No need,' said Leroy, as they headed down the hill, back to Mulholland Drive. 'I've seen all I need to see.'

'How so?'

'While you were checking the inside of the pool house, I had a look round the outside.'

'And?'

'I noticed some tyre tracks on the grass, so I quickly followed them. Just in time as it happened, as Mason came out just then.'

'Go on.'

'Behind the pool house. The grey Ford she was driving.'

CHAPTER THIRTY

'WHY DIDN'T YOU say something?' Domingo asked.

Leroy turned the Taurus into Mulholland Avenue. 'What could I say? "Oh, I am sorry, Mr Mason. I've just remembered we're not looking for a fugitive from a robbery, but a battered old sedan driven by a hooker called Alexandra." I don't think so.'

'What do you think's going on there, then? Is the house a whorehouse, you think?'

'Could be, if Alexandra was working out of there.'

'She must be; why else would she head back there? Surely she hadn't arranged to see you at eleven-thirty, and someone there at eleven fifty. She's a hooker, not a dentist. And why park the car hidden behind some pool house?'

'Why indeed? Another thing: that looked a pretty fine

house, inside and out. Not quite the sort of place you'd expect a hooker doing tricks for three hundred bucks to work out of. Place like that, you'd expect to pay five, ten times that. And then there's that Mason guy…'

'Dwight Mason,' Domingo said slowly and carefully.

'Yeah. I can't quite make him out. There was something about him that didn't quite seem right.'

'Tell me about it.'

'No, I don't mean that. Who is he? He talked about his employer, so he isn't the owner of the place.' Leroy shook his head. Turned the car left at a junction. 'He seemed….seemed strangely familiar to me. His face, I mean.'

'Really?'

'Yeah, but I can't put my finger on what. Once we get back to the Desk I'll find out who owns that place. Might help place him.'

'You could try Google,' Domingo suggested.

Leroy looked over. 'What? Google him?'

'Why not? You never know: he could be someone famous whose face you can't place.'

He nodded. 'Okay, let's do that.'

'You never know -' Domingo started to say, only to be interrupted by her cell phone. 'It's Connor,' she said, picking up. She listened to what her partner had to say, replied, 'Okay, we're on our way,' and then looked over at Leroy.

'What did he have to say?' Leroy asked.

'He was relaying a message from Lieutenant Perez. We have to get our asses back to the station house. He wants to see you like yesterday.'

'So he has started today,' Leroy said. 'Swell. We were going back anyway.'

*****

168

Once back at HQ Leroy and Domingo walked back to the Homicide Desk. They had to pass the office of Lieutenant Perez, a smaller version of the room Captain Patterson used. Perez's door was shut.

'Let's get it over with.' Leroy paused at the door. 'You make a start on Mason and that house. See you in a bit.'

'Sure thing, Sam,' Domingo nodded and went to her desk.

Leroy knocked on the door. A voice from inside called out, 'Come in.' Inside, Lieutenant Perez was sitting behind a desk covered with case folders. Leroy reflected that it was a similar picture to the captain's desk. Clearly the rumours were true: Perez was Patterson's protégé.

'Be right with you, Sam.' Perez fished around the desk and picked up a folder. A thin folder. 'Take a seat.'

Leroy grunted his thanks and sat down. 'I guess congratulations are in order – Lieutenant.'

Perez looked up and smiled. 'I appreciate that, Sam.' He paused, as if in thought, then said, 'You know, strange isn't it? Two weeks ago you were calling me Roman: now it's Lieutenant.'

Leroy smiled insincerely. 'Yeah. Strange.'

'They say a week is a long time in police work, but two…' His voice tailed off. 'Look, I want to get one thing out in the open first.'

Leroy's eyes widened. 'Oh, yes?' he asked inquisitively.

Perez continued, 'I mean it's no secret you were up for this job. I would say sorry you didn't get it, but…'

Leroy shrugged. 'May the best man win, as they say.'

'That's not what I meant. I just wanted to say, I hope there's no hard feelings…'

Leroy shook his head. 'Not here, there aren't.'

Perez went on, 'And we can carry on working together.'

'I hope so too. I can't see any reason why not.'

'Great. That's really great.'

Leroy said nothing.

'So, I've been looking through the files on these recent John Does.'

'Not all John Does now. We have identified two of them: Guy Robbins and Lance Riley.'

Perez slowly nodded his head. 'Really? I didn't know that. That's good, but it doesn't change the fact that you have been spending - that you and Detective Domingo have been spending – one hell of a lot of time driving the streets of LA investigating two or three cases - similar cases, I'll grant you - of deaths by misadventure.'

'We're not sure they were misadventure.'

'What have you found then? I understand one of the victim's laptops has been sent to the CCU: have they come back to you?'

'No, not yet. We haven't found a lot yet, I admit, but it's still early days.'

'I think you're wasting your time.'

'Excuse me?'

'And Detective Domingo's time.'

'Oh?' Leroy sat up. 'How so?'

'You're wasting time on non suspicious deaths. There were no signs of foul play, were there?'

'No, but -'

'You know what I think? They were all of a similar socio-economic status, weren't they? I think they all got involved in some sex and drugs orgy thing, which went too far. Not pleasant, I agree, especially for them.'

'But the drugs came from somewhere, Lieutenant.'

'I agree, but you want to know how many homicides took place in this jurisdiction in the last twenty-four hours? Eleven, eight of which were drug related. So, you tell me: which should get our priority? Eleven shootings, a gang rape, five muggings, or three possible suspicious deaths.'

Leroy stood up. 'It's all a question of money, isn't it?'

'Of course it is. We both know that. But we have to

prioritise. And your John Does, which I and the captain are certain were not suspicious are way, way down the food chain. Do you get me?'

Leroy nodded.

'I agree it's not been easy, running without a lieutenant, but now I've taken up my post, you and your fellow detectives can get the guidance and support you all need. Yes?'

Leroy said nothing.

'So,' Perez continued, 'just clear up the paperwork on the John Does by,' - he checked his watch - 'two, then both you and Domingo have deaths worthy of investigation to look into. She has Detective Connor to look after; when's Quinn back from vacation?'

'Day after tomorrow,' replied Leroy.

'Well, do what you can on your own. But any situations when you feel you need backup, call me straightaway. Okay?'

'Okay, Lieutenant.'

'Well, don't let me keep you. Update me at the end of the shift.' Perez closed the thin file and picked up another, much fatter one. He leaned back in his chair, reading the file.

Meeting over, Leroy thought.

He left Perez to his file, and slowly walked back to his desk. Sure enough, there was a small pile of brown folders waiting for him. He looked over at Domingo's workstation: she was standing talking to Connor. They were both about to go out. She looked over to Leroy, said something to Connor, who left the room, and stepped over to Leroy.

'What did he tell you, Sam? She asked. 'Drop the John Does?'

He nodded. 'That's right. Gave me until two o'clock to finish the paperwork. Says he and the captain believe they are a waste of resources.'

'So what are you going to do?'

Leroy shrugged. 'What I'm told I guess. Where are you two headed off to?'

'The Rape Crisis Centre.'

'Okay. Well, thanks for all you did, Liza.'

'You're welcome. See you around. Good luck with that lot.' She indicated to the pile of files on his desk. 'But check your emails first.'

With that she left him alone at his desk. He sat down and logged on his computer. Went to his emails. Trawled down to one Domingo sent ten minutes earlier. Clicked to open it. There was one short line of text: *nothing on google re mason*, and an attachment, which he opened right away.

It opened to details of the house they visited earlier that day. It looked as if Domingo had highlighted the name of the owner.

'Oh. My. God,' Leroy whispered.

CHAPTER THIRTY-ONE

LEROY REACHED ACROSS the desk for his cell phone. He was just about to dial when Perez appeared at his desk, clutching a sheet of paper. He put the phone down and looked up at the lieutenant.

'Sorry, Sam,' said Perez. 'I know I said write up the John Does by two but something has come up, and everybody else is out. It appears quite straightforward; don't think you'll need backup for now.'

'For now?' asked Leroy.

'This is the deal,' explained Perez. 'A report's come in of a stabbing over at Grand Central Market. It was reported about forty minutes ago. Uniform are there and have sealed off the area and one of the CSIs is there.'

Leroy raised his eyebrows. 'Already?'

'Apparently. Anyway, the sooner they can get started on the scene the sooner they can hand it over to you. Just get down there and co-ordinate the non-science stuff. The two patrolmen have already started talking to witnesses: I need you to wrap things up there. If it turns out you do need any backup, then call in. I'll partner you myself if need be.' Perez handed Leroy the call-in sheet, and returned to his office. Leroy read through it: it was just as the lieutenant had said. He picked up his phone, put on his coat and left, in a hurry. The call to Domingo could wait.

In the minds of many Angelenos, what you eat is as important as what you drive, in terms of sophistication, and concern over what other people think. The Grand Central Market on South Broadway is a refreshing taste of simpler times and cuisine. First and foremost, it is a collection of outlets for LA's many varied ethnic groups, but is also popular for celebrity chefs and the artists of all kinds. Always busy, when Leroy arrived, it was deserted. A small crowd of passers-by and would-be shoppers was gathered in the main entrance. Yellow tape prevented entry, and a uniformed officer was chatting to some of them.

Leroy stepped over the tape, waved his identification to the officer, and stepped inside. As he walked through the market, it was eerily quiet. He had been here many times, through work and as a shopper, and never failed to be amazed at the variety of produce that could be found here. As he walked down the first aisle, past a tortilleria, past a stall selling apples of varying sizes and shades of red, yellow and green. The next stall sold peppers, types of which he had never heard of. Another uniformed officer was standing at an aisle intersection, below a green neon sign reading *La Casa Verde*.

The officer recognized him. 'Ah, Detective Leroy. I thought it was you. Good to see you again, sir.'

'Officer Blake; good to see you again, too.' Leroy looked around. 'Where is everybody? Where's the crime scene?'

Officer Blake pointed over to his right. 'Downstairs in the restrooms, Detective. A guy from the CSI office is there already.'

'Downstairs? Then why's the whole market closed?'

'No idea, Detective. Sorry.'

'Who's the senior officer here?'

'That'll be Sergeant Jackson. He's down there at the crime scene.'

'All right. Thanks.' Leroy went past a few more stalls then down the stairs to the restrooms. The door to the men's room was wedged open, and five uniformed officers were milling around. A figure with white epaulettes whom Leroy recognised as Jackson looked up, finished the conversation he was having with another officer, and met Leroy at the foot of the steps.

'Hey there, Sam,' said Jackson.

'How you doing, Jacko?'

'Same old, same old. You know the story.'

'Sure. Where's the body? Men's room, I guess.'

'No. He's in the ER over at the Medical Center.'

Leroy sounded surprised. 'He's not dead, then?'

'Wasn't when he left here. Lost a lot of blood, though. Took a knife just here...' Jackson indicated to just above his left thigh.

'Where did it happen? In there?' Leroy and Jackson stepped over to the men's room.

'That's right,' replied Jackson. 'Take a look.'

Leroy stepped inside. He was met by a large red viscous pool. The other side of the pool stood a figure wearing a light blue tyvek jumpsuit, rubber gloves, and matching shoe and head covers. He was busy taking photographs of the scene. When he saw Leroy enter, he stopped and gave a small wave.

'Detective Leroy,' he said across the pool.

'Hey there,' Leroy replied, recognising the CSI but not being able to recall the name. He thought the guy was new. 'Any idea what happened?'

'Pretty cut and dried, for lack of a better expression. The guy was standing at the urinal over there, was finishing off, and another guy stabbed him. On his left side.'

'Who put the call in?'

'Not sure. Have a word with Jackson.'

'Okay. Thanks.' He wandered outside to where Jackson was standing. 'So what happened exactly, Jacko? And do we really need have the whole market closed? Surely we only need this floor isolated.'

Jackson nodded. 'That was a first precaution. I've just ordered them to open up again, just keep down here secure. As far as what happened: it seems he was in there taking a whiz when another guy stabbed him.'

'Guy?'

'We're assuming that for now, yes. He must have been lying on the floor there for a while going by the amount of blood on the floor. Someone else came in, saw him, and called 911.'

'Where is he? Whoever made the call.'

Jackson shrugged. 'No idea. Left the scene. Disappeared after he called it in.'

'I see. So he could be the suspect also. Why else would he leave the scene?'

'Lots of reasons, Sam. Especially in this part of town. We need to keep an open mind here.'

'I hear you. And now the vic's over at the MC.'

'That's right.'

'No other witnesses, I guess.'

'None that we can establish at this time. There's no CCTV in there of course, but there is a camera up there.' He pointed to a camera, red light flashing up in the corner.

'Anyone looked at the footage yet?'

'Not yet. Thought we'd leave it to you guys. Where's your partner, by the way?'

'On honeymoon. Back in a couple of days. Where does the market manager hang out?'

'Office on second floor, I think.'

'Okay, I'll need to get over to the MC before…'

'Before the guy dies, you mean?'

'Something like that. See what he can tell me. Jacko, can you get one of your guys to get a hold of whatever the camera picked up? Once I'm done at the hospital, I'll come back and pick up the disc, or whatever it's stored on.'

'Sure thing, Sam. See you.'

As he climbed up the stairs and walked back through the market to his car, Leroy tried Domingo's number. She answered after two rings.

'Hey Sam, how you doing?'

'Good, I guess. Am just down at the Grand Central Market. A stabbing.'

'Swell.'

'Well, this one's not dead. I'm off to see him at the hospital now. You still at the rape centre?'

'Just winding up here. Now, Sam: did you get to read my email?'

'I did, yes.'

'And the attachment?'

'I saw that too.'

'What do you think?'

'I think…. I'm not sure what to think yet.'

'What are you going to do?'

'I'll have to think about it. Perez *and* the captain have both told me to close down the John Doe cases.'

'What about Bill Farmer?'

'Not spoken to him yet. What about your Griffith Park vic?

'Connor and I have been told the same thing too.'

'I wonder if Farmer has too.'

177

'He has. According to the lieutenant anyway.'

Leroy reached his car. Got in and turned the ignition.

'Sam, you still there?'

'Still here. Am in the car now.'

'What do you think we should do?'

'*We* should do?'

'Yes, we. As soon as I saw who owned the house, I knew we can't just let it drop.'

'I agree. Yes.'

'So what do you want to do?'

'When does your shift finish, Liza?'

'Six. Why?'

'Let's get together over a drink, or over a coffee. Agree on what to do.'

'Sounds a plan. Look, Sam, I have to go. We got a call coming in. Have a good day, what's left of it. See you at six. Right?'

'See you.'

Leroy took the short drive down to the California Hospital Medical Center. The stabbing victim was still in the ER undergoing emergency surgery. Leroy chatted briefly with one of the doctors.

'How is he, doc?'

'He lost a lot of blood, but the surgery went as expected.'

'Can I talk to him?'

'Sorry, Detective, not right now. He's sleeping now.'

'Will he be in a position to talk later?'

'Oh, I would think so. Will it keep till the morning?'

'Will have to, I guess.' He shook hands with the doctor. 'Well, thanks, doc. Here's my number. If anything changes…. You know, call me, yes?'

'Sure thing, detective. You have a good day, now.'

His unproductive trip to the hospital over, Leroy made his way back to the market. Now it had re-opened, it was full of shoppers, making up for lost time. He fought his way through the crowds back to the basement floor. Jackson was at the foot of the stairs again. Through the open men's room door, Leroy could see somebody inside, cleaning up.

'The camera footage is on its way to you, Sam,' Jackson said.

'Excuse me?'

'It's stored digitally, apparently. Not on disc or tape. The manager said he will email a file with the footage for so far today to you.'

'So I can view it back at the station house?'

'That's right,' Jackson replied.

'Wow, isn't technology wonderful,' said Leroy.

'How would you know?' laughed Jackson.

Leroy laughed. 'Did anybody get a chance to view it already?'

'None of my guys. The manager might have done.'

'No problem. I'll check it out at the office. Take it easy, Jacko.'

'You too, Sam.'

Back at the HQ, Leroy managed to avoid getting waylaid by his lieutenant and his captain, and logged on. Checked his email inbox. He briefly re-read the one from Domingo, then went on to the only other unread one: from the Grand Central Market manager. Then clicked on the attachment, which was a video file of eight hours footage of market customers going in and out of the restrooms. He fast forwarded to the approximate time of the stabbing. He saw a man walk in, only to run out a few seconds later, clutching a phone. Running, he soon left the camera's POV.

Leroy reversed the video slowly. The man ran in backwards, walked out backwards. There was a short gap, then another figure stepped in backwards. Leroy clicked to a frame by frame view and peered closely at the screen to study the image. The figure was of slight build, a dark complexion, but most of his features were hidden by the hood he was wearing. Leroy checked his watch: it was almost five. He kept thinking about what he and Domingo should agree to do, then brought his thoughts back to the present, and whether this person was the stabber.

He kept the video in reverse frame by frame, and saw the hooded figure back into the men's room, again a short interval, before he reversed out. Three other men did the same: one of these, Leroy reflected, must have been the victim. But who carried out the stabbing? Was it the figure wearing the hood? Or was it the guy running out?

He had a craving for caffeine. He visited the restroom and returned to his desk via a vending machine. Carrying a strong black coffee he wandered back to his desk, but was distracted by the sound coming from the end of the corridor, where the lockers were positioned. Or rather, the lack of sound. Frowning, he wandered down to see what was going: it was never this quiet. Around the bank of lockers stood half a dozen of his colleagues, four in uniform. They were talking quietly, and stopped to look up when Leroy arrived. One of the uniformed officers, a woman in her early twenties, looked pale and her eyes were red.

'What's going on?' asked Leroy.

'You obviously haven't heard,' one of the uniformed men replied.

'Heard what?'

'The call's just come through,' the officer said. 'It's Detectives Domingo and Connor.'

'What about them?'

He swallowed. 'They've both been shot. Both killed.'

CHAPTER THIRTY-TWO

LEROY FELT HIS legs go weak, almost buckle under him. He put his hand on the wall for support. 'But I was only.... What happened?' he asked.

Another male officer spoke. 'It was this afternoon, Sam. A patrol car noticed their vehicle in a side street, parked with its hood right up against a dead end. They figured everything was okay – you know, that they were handling something. There had been no call for back-up or anything. They passed by the same street an hour or so later. The car was still there, so they decided to check it out.'

'And found what?' asked Leroy, straightening up.

The officer swallowed first, then replied. 'They found both Detectives Domingo and Connor in the front seats, each with a gunshot wound to the head.'

'Both dead on the scene?' Leroy asked. 'You know, sometimes in the heat of the moment, you make an assumption -'

'The officers checked for vital signs, Sam. There were none.'

Leroy looked around. 'Where's Perez?'

'The lieutenant's gone down to the crime scene,' replied the officer, 'with the captain.'

'What about the officers who found them?' Leroy asked.

'I'm not sure,' the officer replied. 'I think they might still be at the scene. The captain and lieutenant will want to speak with them.'

I'm sure they will.' Leroy ran his hand through his hair as he spoke. 'Somebody else will, I'm sure.'

'What do you mean, Sam?' asked the officer.

'For a start, I will. Then the investigation will be passed to another Division. Standard procedure.' Leroy sat down on a desk and paused a moment. Then asked, 'Where did it happen?'

'I'm not sure... I don't...,' the officer stammered. He looked around at his colleagues. Anybody know?'

'Anybody know?' repeated Leroy, addressing the half dozen officers milling around.

'I know,' a female officer called from the back. She stepped nearer to Leroy as she spoke. 'It was a side street off Erwin.'

Leroy frowned. 'Erwin? Where's that?'

Another officer spoke. 'It's North Hollywood. Just off Lankershim before it hits Victory Boulevard.'

'What in the hell were they doing up there?' Leroy asked, posing the question out loud to himself more than the other officers.

There was a general mumbling and shaking of heads. Nobody could answer him.

Leroy spoke again. 'When we spoke around midday,

they were off to the Rape Crisis Center. Where's that? UCLA isn't it?' The female officer nodded. 'So,' Leroy went on, 'they must have either not gone to the RCC, or headed up there as soon as they were done. Let's give the Center a call – see if they actually showed.'

'We would have heard if they hadn't, Sam,' said the first officer. 'They wouldn't leave a victim just waiting indefinitely.'

'No, you're right. I just can't -'

Leroy was interrupted as the doors opened and Lieutenant Perez walked in, some two steps behind Captain Patterson. The captain just walked through the room, not speaking to the officers. His eyes darted to Leroy's as he passed, but he said nothing. With a grim expression on his face, he went straight into his office, and closed the door. Perez, however, stopped and addressed the officers.

'Guys: just a few words. By now, you all know about the tragic circumstances concerning Detectives Domingo and Connor.' He paused. 'The investigation into their slayings is being carried out by officers from the Major Crimes Division, and I'm sure you are as confident as the captain and I are that they will leave no stone unturned until they bring the perpetrators to book.' He paused again. 'Once the necessary, er – arrangements have been made, I will update you all. Now please return to your duties, as I'm sure Detectives Domingo and Connor would have done.'

The officers started to make their way out. Perez turned to Leroy. 'I'm glad you're here. Come in, will you.' He stepped into his office; Leroy followed. 'Close the door, Sam, will you.'

Leroy gently closed the glass door and turned to the lieutenant.

Perez collapsed into his chair and leaned forward onto the desk. 'Great start to my first day.'

'Not so great for Domingo and Connor,' replied Leroy as he sat down.

Perez looked up. 'I didn't mean it like that. It's just… I don't know.'

Leroy spoke softly. 'What exactly happened, Roman? What the hell were they doing up in North Hollywood? I spoke to Liza around midday and she said she was off to see someone at the Rape Crisis Center. And that's in UCLA.'

Perez shook his head slowly. 'I don't know at this time, Sam. They went to the Center. Liza spoke to a rape victim there. That took about an hour, according to the Center manager.'

'Any record of a call they might have received? What about the GPS record for their car?'

There was a weary tone in Perez's voice. 'It's all been passed to the Major Crimes Division. Captain's orders.'

Leroy shrugged. 'Standard procedure.'

'That's right. So they will be looking at those questions. The captain wants us to focus on our own enquiries and let the MCD guys do their job.'

'What about the officers who found them?'

'The captain and I spoke to them. They've made statements. The captain sent them home; they were both pretty shaken up.'

'Did you…?'

Perez nodded. 'Nothing had been moved when the captain and I arrived, though the crime scene guy was there. They were both sitting upright in the car, though Domingo had leaned slightly to the left so she was almost resting her head on Connor's shoulder.'

'Connor was driving?'

'Mm. He had entry and exit wounds on either temple; she had one right here.' He pointed to the centre of his forehead.

'Almost like an execution.'

'Possibly. That'll be part of the investigation. One line of enquiry out of many.'

'Any idea who's going to be dealing with it? From the

Major Crimes Division, I mean.'

'Not yet. But, I repeat: the captain wants us all to let them do their job without any assistance from us. He was quite insistent. You won't be playing out of the box on this, will you?'

'Don't worry. I get the message.' Leroy stood up to go. 'You'll let us know about the funeral, any memorial, won't you?'

'Of course I will, Sam. Liza was Catholic, so I guess there'll be a wake, a big affair. She was single, wasn't she?'

'She was, as far as I know. But Connor – Jesus, Roman: he had a family.'

'I know. I'm just off to see his wife.'

Leroy said nothing. The expression on his face said it all.

Perez stood up and walked round the desk. He touched Leroy's arm. 'You go home, Sam. Get some rest. See you in the morning.' He opened his office door and slowly walked out. Leroy watched him walk down the corridor.

Deep down, now he was glad he didn't get that promotion after all.

CHAPTER THIRTY-THREE

FOR EVERY POLICE Headquarters building, somewhere within a two block radius, there will be a bar, used almost exclusively by the men and women from the Area.

Martha's was no exception. Situated on Iowa Avenue, between Colby and Butler, Martha's had been an established watering hole since the early eighties. Martha herself, the granddaughter of an émigré from Germany between the two World Wars, had retired to Palm Springs seven years back and the bar was now run by her son Kenny. Since Martha had left, nothing had changed: Kenny had retained his mother's name for the bar, the food was just as bad, and the same clientele visited.

Kenny passed another beer to Sam Leroy, who leaned forward and took a mouthful. Once Lieutenant Perez had told him to go home, Leroy did not need telling twice. He cleared up his desk, logged off, and walked down to the bar. Always mindful of how much he could drink without going DUI, he planned on only staying half an hour or so. Then he would drive home and get really smashed. Hold that thought – he had arranged to see Joanna that night. He contemplated calling her and cancelling, but decided not to. He felt he needed to talk.

Kenny noticed Leroy deep in contemplation, and stepped over. Kenny could always be seen with a red dish towel over his left shoulder. He leaned forward and wiped the bar top in front of Leroy. 'Penny for them, Sam?'

Leroy looked up. 'Huh?'

'You were deep in thought. Bad day at the office?' This was Kenny's stock phrase if one of his customers had had a rough day.

'Yeah, you could say that.' He looked up at Kenny. 'Liza Domingo got hit today.'

Eyes wide open, Kenny stopped wiping. 'No way. You mean…?'

'Her and her partner.'

'Who was her partner again?'

'Guy called Connor.'

'They both…?'

Leroy nodded.

'Jesus, man,' said Kenny. 'I'm so sorry, Sam. How did it happen?'

Leroy shook his head. 'Not sure yet. Seems to be a professional job. By that I mean a clean hit. They were both still in their car. Pop pop.'

'I didn't know Connor,' said Kenny.

'He had only been with her a short while. Had a wife and family.'

'Fuck me. Make sure you get the sons of bitches, Sam.'

Leroy finished his beer. 'Don't worry, Kenny. We will.' He stood up to leave.

'You going already, Sam? Want something to eat?'

'Nah. Need to get home. Meeting up with a lady friend. Having a bite to eat with her, then have a few more of these.'

'Alrighty. Take care then, buddy. See you soon.'

'You too, Kenny.'

Leroy straightened up and left the bar. As he got out onto the street, turning left to walk back to the parking lot, he bumped into Captain Patterson. The captain had finished his shift; now wearing an open-necked shirt, he was on his way into Martha's. He and Leroy stopped and faced each other.

'Sam,' said Patterson.

'Captain,' Leroy replied.

'I take it you heard about Detectives Domingo and Connor,' said the captain.

Leroy said nothing, just nodded.

'Terrible business. Terrible,' muttered the captain, almost as if he was talking to himself.

'Lieutenant Perez says it's being investigated by the MCD. Is that right?'

'Yes, it is.' Patterson seemed taken slightly aback by the fact that Leroy knew this. 'I think it's best. A complete and objective enquiry.'

'Objective?'

'To avoid the danger of some of their former colleagues being out for revenge.'

'You're not saying…?'

'No, I'm not. I am merely ensuring that we can get a conviction. Don't want them to get off on a technicality. Do you agree, Detective?'

Leroy nodded. 'Do you know who at the MCD is dealing?'

'No, not as yet. Why? Do you know anybody there?'

Leroy shook his head. 'No. Just curious, that's all.'

Patterson paused a moment, then said, 'Well, goodnight, Sam. See you tomorrow.'

Patterson pushed open the bar door and Leroy resumed his walk back to the car. He rubbed his temple as he walked back: maybe it was him, but recently all of his conversations with the captain tended to have a surreal feel.

Once back at HQ, he stepped inside for a restroom stop. Inside, the atmosphere was still subdued. Leroy had no wish to linger; he went straight back out to the car.

He checked his watch as he got back home: despite the detour to Martha's, he still had plenty of time to freshen up and get over to Joanna's. Their plan was to head for the Third Street Promenade in Santa Monica, have a meal, and take in a movie. He stepped in and out of the shower, put on a fresh set of clothes, and got back into his car. The journey to Joanna's place took just over five minutes; he parked in one of the spaces in front of her building, and briskly walked to the intercom. Pressed her buzzer and waited for her voice.

'Hello?'

'It's me.'

'Hey, Sam. I'm nearly ready. Come on up.'

There was a click from the entrance doors; Leroy pushed them open, and climbed up to Joanna's door. She was standing in the doorway, her auburn hair down, and wearing a short black dress. She was barefoot.

'Come on in,' she said, holding the door open. She reached up and kissed him as he stepped in. 'I'm almost there,' she called out from the bedroom as he wandered into her kitchen. 'How was your day?'

Leroy got himself a glass of water and stood in the kitchen. He looked over at Joanna as she stood in the doorway, now also wearing a pair of black shoes. 'Well?' she asked.

He put the glass down. 'Very nice.'

She smoothed down her dress. 'Thanks. But I meant how was your day?'

He wiped his mouth. 'You don't want to know.'

'Oh, that bad?'

'Worse,' he said.

Joanna raised her eyebrows. 'Mm?'

'I lost a partner today.'

'Lost? You mean…?'

Leroy nodded.

She put her hand to her mouth. 'Oh my God, Sam. I'm so sorry, Sam. What happened?'

Leroy proceeded to relate to her what had happened; as he did so she stood in the kitchen doorway, nodding, still with a shocked look on her face. 'I'm so sorry,' she said again, when he had finished.

'Thing is,' he continued, 'I've lost partners and fellow officers before - not that many, but it still doesn't get any easier.'

'Nor should it. God, it's awful. I don't know how you can deal with it. How long had you known them for?'

'I'd only met Connor a few times, didn't know him that well. He was fairly new. Had a family.'

'Oh, no,' said Joanna.

'But Liza, I'd known for a few years. We were partners for a time a while back, and she was partnering me temporarily until this morning when we got pulled off the enquiry. Connor was her actual partner.'

'Oh, that's right; you told me the other night. Your partner's on vacation.'

'Honeymoon. Due back any time now.' He paused a moment, then stood up. 'Come on, we won't have time for the movie.'

Joanna stood up too. 'Be honest, Sam; do you really feel like going out? I can fix us something.'

Leroy took a deep breath. 'Okay,' he said, putting his hands in his pockets.

Joanna took two steps forward and looked up at him. 'You shouldn't be alone tonight,' she said, reaching up and putting her hand on his cheek.

CHAPTER THIRTY-FOUR

SAM LEROY LAY back, his head resting on a soft pillow. He noticed that an image of a teddy bear was embroidered on the edge of the pillow case. He looked around the bedroom; all of the furnishings: two small chairs, a dressing table and a closet, even the pictures hung on the wall, spelt feminine. So did the smell of the room, of the bedclothes, of Joanna herself. He leaned over and picked up the watch he had left on the small bedside table forty minutes ago and squinted to pick out the time in the moonlight coming through the drapes. 12:20AM.

He looked up at Joanna as she returned from the bathroom. They had left a light on in the lounge, and her naked body was silhouetted in the doorway. 'I thought you had gone to sleep,' she said quietly, as she returned to the bed.

He shook his head. 'No. Just lying here.'

Rather than walking round the bed to get to her side, she climbed over him, stopping and lying on top of him. 'You're not going to go home, are you?' she asked, running her hand through his hair.

'Hadn't planned to,' he replied. 'I'll bet you make a nice breakfast.' He smiled briefly, the smile leaving his face as the mention of breakfast reminded him of Domingo.

'What's the matter?' she asked.

'Just a flashback from yesterday. I'm okay.' He ran his hand down her hair, he shoulders and arm.

She kissed him tenderly on his lips. 'Anything I can do?' she asked.

'Not really, other than what you're doing now.'

'Pleased to be of service,' she said, as she began to brush her lips against his chin, then down his neck and his chest, pausing to run her tongue over his nipples. Then down his chest, sweeping her mouth through the vertical line of hair on his stomach. Soon he was ready for her once more. Her gaze remained fixed on his as she sat up, reached over to the drawer her side of the bed. Momentarily, she was manoeuvring herself onto him, slowly sliding down until her butt cheeks were resting on his legs. For a moment she remained still, then began to move up and down slowly, leaning forward to rest her hands on his shoulders. He raised his head slightly to kiss her.

She sat back up again and rocked and rocked back and forth. Leroy lay back and looked up at the ceiling. Then he suddenly gasped, putting one hand to his temple.

Joanna stopped. 'What is it?'

'I just had a thought.'

'And…?'

'It's nothing. Sorry. Carry on. God, that sounded so dumb.'

'You said it, Detective,' Joanna said, and resumed

rocking, this time also pushing down with her hands on his stomach.

Once again, Leroy lay back on Joanna's scented pillow, looking up at the ceiling. Totally spent, she collapsed beside him. She wriggled down and lay on her side, one leg across his, and one arm across his chest. She kissed him on the shoulder. 'What was up earlier?'

He looked down at her face. 'It was nothing. Sorry.'

'Okay.'

'A thought just flashed through my head. About work. Sorry, bad timing.'

She lifted her head up and rested her chin on his shoulder. 'Maybe you have a point about the timing, but it's not wrong to think during sex.'

'Yeah, but...'

'If I wanted to have sex with someone who doesn't think, I'd have gone to the stores and bought a cucumber.'

He looked down at her and laughed.

'A slicing one, of course,' she added.

'Of course,' he repeated.

She lifted herself up so she was resting on his chest. 'That's the first time you've laughed tonight.'

'Is it?' he replied, sounding surprised.

'It's okay to laugh, even when something bad's happened.'

Leroy nodded, thinking. Then asked her, 'Do you have a laptop here?'

'Why, yes. Do you need to use it? *Now*?'

He sat up slightly, gently easing her off his chest. 'If I can, if that's okay with you.'

She climbed out of bed, and went into the living room, returning momentarily with a black case. She sat back down on the bed, and pulled a laptop out of the bag. Leroy, in the meantime, had switched on a bedside light, and sat up in bed. She switched on the laptop, logged on, and passed it to him.

'Do you do this often?' she asked.

He gave her a puzzled look.

'I mean get flashes of inspiration during sex, with an urgent need to go online?'

He laughed. 'Sorry, Joanna, but the answer's yes. To the second part, that is. Not a problem normally, living alone. I had this thought, and if I don't do this now, I'll never get back to sleep. It won't take long.'

'Don't worry. Happens to me sometimes. Normally concerning unruly kids. Want a drink? Tea or something?'

'No, I'll be okay, thanks.'

'I'm going to have one.'

'Well, if you're boiling the kettle, yes, I'll have one.' He feverishly typed into the laptop.

'Cream? Sugar?'

'Hmm?'

'Your tea. Cream or sugar? Same as your coffee?'

'Oh, milk, please.'

Joanna left him to it, as he started to search Google. When she returned ten minutes later, she found him sitting up in bed, his head resting against the wall, with a satisfied look on his face. 'Finished?' she asked, handing him his cup. She walked round to the other side of the bed and joined him.

'Yes. Much appreciated.' He sipped the tea. 'As is this.'

'No problem.' She sipped hers. 'Did you find what you were looking for?'

'I think so. Assuming I know what I'm looking for.'

'Sam, in English, please.'

He sat back again, his gaze fixed across the room, where the wall met the ceiling. 'You remember Donald Rumsfeld?'

'The former Secretary of State for Defence?' She looked puzzled.

'Yeah. He was famous for weird quotes he used to come out with.'

'A bit like Bush?'

'That sort of thing, yeah. But the one which sticks in my mind is one which goes something like, "There are known knowns. There are known unknowns. But there are also unknown unknowns." Something like that.'

Joanna said slowly, 'I *think* I know where you're coming from.'

'What I mean is, in my line of work, we have to dig around and around in the course of an investigation, but we don't really know what we're looking for. But when we find it, we know we've found it.' He looked across at her and saw she was smirking. 'I'm not making much sense, am I?'

She laughed. 'I think you're just verbalising it badly. I know what you mean.'

'How would you verbalise it then? You're the school teacher.'

'Sam, believe it or not, the life and sayings of Donald Rumsfeld isn't in the curriculum of the average fourth grader.' She finished her tea. 'So what does all this have to do with what you were looking for?' She checked the time. 'At one in the morning?'

'At this time, the feeling is that Domingo and Connor were killed because of one of their cases.'

'The feeling? That's a bit vague, isn't it?'

'Bad verbalising again. Basically, as far as my department's concerned, the prime suspect would be someone who they had put away. Or someone connected with a felon they had dealt with.'

'I get it. You mean like a relative who's doing time after they arrested them?'

'Yes, although, it could be that only one of them was the intended victim, the other taken out because they were there at the time.'

'I see. Take out one cop, you might as well take out

two?'

'Yeah. Also, we must be talking some major crime. After all, you wouldn't risk killing a cop in revenge for booking you for jaywalking. Not normally anyway.'

'So, have you just been checking their old cases?'

'No, can't on here.' He paused. 'Look, Joanna – what I'm telling you is totally confidential, yes?'

'Of course it is, Sam. You can trust me.' She kissed him on his left breastbone.

'If that theory's correct, it might not be one of their old cases.'

'One they're working on at the time, you mean?'

'Connor had been away, so Liza was partnering me as my own partner's been on vacation.'

'What were you investigating with her?'

'Have you read, or seen on TV, about a number of men found at various spots in the city, cause of death unknown?'

She thought a moment. 'Yes, I think I have. A couple of weekends ago, wasn't it?'

'End of last week. They all died in the same night. All filled with a drug cocktail. We were investigating that. The case is closed now, as it's felt - in some quarters - that the deaths were accidental, and we have more urgent cases to follow. Anyway, before we were taken off the investigation, Domingo and I found that one of the victims had met with a hooker he found on an online dating site.'

'Hence the drug cocktail?'

'Maybe. We managed to get hold of one of the hookers and met with her. She gave us a load of bullshit, naturally, but we followed her back to a big house off Mulholland Drive.'

'And?'

'We were met by a creepy little guy who denied all knowledge of her. Said his employer was out of town.'

'Who did he work for?'

'I'll come to that. We knew he was bullshitting us too

when I saw her car hidden out back.'

'What did he say?'

'He doesn't know we found it yet.'

'More known unknowns?'

'Kind of. Sometimes it's best to dig around a bit before making a challenge. Now, this creepy guy: I couldn't place where, but his face kind of seemed familiar.'

'Go on.'

'Back at the office, one of the last things Liza did was email me that she had found out who actually does own the house. Earlier - while we were, you know, I could make a connection between the house and what happened to them. A thin one, but nevertheless a connection. So I tried Google.'

'Show me.'

'Take a look.' He passed the laptop to her, still switched on and at the appropriate page.

She started to read, then looked up at him. 'The owner of the house?'

'The very same.'

She carried on reading until she finished the article. Then looked up at him again.

'Sam, what are you going to do?'

CHAPTER THIRTY-FIVE

THE ATMOSPHERE AT the station house the next morning was tense. Since Leroy had gone home the previous night, another shift had arrived and departed and more of Domingo and Connor's workmates had heard the news. Where there was normally the hum of numerous conversations taking place, this morning there was silence. Officers were going about their business quietly; those that were on the phone were speaking quietly. As he walked to his desk, Leroy noticed others were red eyed; a couple of female officers were walking around clutching a Kleenex. Already, there were two large bunches of flowers lying on Domingo's desk. He noticed Lieutenant Perez standing by a vending machine, talking on a cell phone. The lieutenant was wearing the same clothes he had on the previous day, and had a deep five o'clock shadow. He looked as if he had not made it home last night.

Leroy sat down at his desk and fired up the computer. Then stared at the Home screen, pondering what to do next. Should he return to the Grand Central Market case, or stay with the John Does? Normally at this time case files would be given out: he was sure Perez would be doing so soon, as there would have been a dozen incidents reported last night; but as he was still without a partner, he was hoping he would be able to remain under the lieutenant's radar.

He was wrong.

'Morning, Sam,' came Perez's voice from across his screen. Leroy looked up at the dishevelled lieutenant.

'Morning, Lieutenant. Man, you look like shit.'

'Thanks. Feel like shit. I've been here all night. First, Connor's widow, and then....'

'I can imagine. The guys from the MCD here yet?'

'Not yet. They'll be over later this morning.'

'I'm glad to see they're treating the case as urgent, then.'

'Give me a break, Sam.'

Leroy sat back, arms folded. He nodded.

'How did you get on at the Market yesterday?' Perez continued.

'The vic was taken to the LA Medical Center. He lost a lot of blood, but he'll be okay. He was still sleeping yesterday afternoon, so I'll go see him later. See what he has to say; see if he knew his attacker.'

'CCTV?'

'Yeah, there was some. Not much, though: the attack took place in the men's john.'

'*In* the john? So we have CCTV of people going in and out?'

'That's about it. I was checking it out when the news came through about Domingo.'

Perez nodded, a serious look on his face. 'Any use?'

Leroy pulled a face. 'A guy wearing a hood, and another. Want to see?'

Perez gave a *I'm really too tired to, but I guess I'd better* look. 'Sure,' he said, stepping round to stand next to Leroy. Leroy returned to the email the market manager had sent, and opened the file. He fast forwarded to the time in question. Perez leaned closer. 'His face is completely hidden,' he said of the hooded figure. 'Ah, that's better,' he said when the second man came running out.

Leroy froze the footage.

'Can you enlarge?' asked Perez. 'Enhance?'

Leroy manoeuvred the mouse to crop, then enlarge, but lost a lot of definition.

'Damn,' Perez muttered. 'I was hoping for better.'

'It might help,' said Leroy.

'May do. However,' Perez dropped a manila folder down on the desk, 'as the victim's still alive, it's not a homicide, and moves further down the line. This one, though, is higher up the food chain.'

Leroy picked up the folder and began to leaf through it as Perez continued. 'It's another stabbing, although this one was fatal. Took place in your neck of the woods, Sam.'

Leroy ran his eyes down the front sheet. The location was Palisades Beach Road. 'I see,' he replied.

'The victim was a young woman in her twenties,' the lieutenant went on. 'She and a friend - another girl - were walking along the edge of the park and saw a group of transients on the grass. A few of them were begging for money, holding up some signs with obscenities written on them.'

'Like what?' asked Leroy, still scanning the paperwork.

'It's all there.'

Leroy found a photograph containing the signs. They were crudely made of thick cardboard and had been hand painted. 'Go on,' he said.

'A couple of these guys approached the girls asking for

money and they refused.'

'So they followed them?'

'Began to, but one of the girls - the one who died - turned round and began taking pictures of them with her cellphone.'

'Jesus.'

'So they attacked her. Stabbed her three or four times. As luck would have it, a patrol car was at the end of…. Montana Avenue, I think it was, and noticed the disturbance. She was taken to the Nethercutt ER but died a few hours later.'

'And the other one?'

'She was taken there also, but only sustained injuries to her arms.'

'She's still there, then?'

'Good. I'll go talk to her. Any witnesses?'

'Better than that. The attackers have already been booked on suspicion of murder. The patrol car brought them in.'

Leroy looked up at the lieutenant. 'It seems pretty cut and dried, then.'

'I just need you to tie up any loose ends. Make sure there were only two attackers, that kind of thing. I'll arrange for a patrol car to meet you at the scene, just in case you need any back up.'

'Okay,' said Leroy. 'Listen, Lieutenant, I need to talk to you about the John Does Domingo and I were -'

'No, Sam. Those cases are closed. Accidental death. You know that.'

'Just listen, will you? For a start, they're not John Does: we have names, for two of them at least.'

'Makes no difference. For all of them, at a senior level, and that includes the DA, the verdict is death by misadventure. Case - or cases, to be precise, closed. *Terminado*.'

'Okay, okay, but just let me ask you this. One of them

201

had been using an online dating agency -'

'So?'

'To get hookers, I mean.'

'Jesus, Sam. Is that all you got?'

'Domingo and I managed to track down two of the hookers he had seen.'

'And what did *they* tell you?'

'Not much, I admit. But we followed one of them back to a house off Mulholland Drive.'

'Cat house?'

'Don't think so. No signs of that, at any rate. We were met by this really weird guy who denied all knowledge of the hooker, even though I saw her car parked out back. But this is the clincher: he said his employer was away on business.' He pressed the mouse key a few times to get to the email Domingo had sent him. 'Now look at this,' he said, pointing to the screen. 'This must change things. Now tell me the cases are closed!'

CHAPTER THIRTY-SIX

PEREZ LOOKED DOWN at the screen. '*Carajo!*' he exclaimed, eyes wide open.

'Well? Does that change anything?' Leroy asked.

The lieutenant straightened up, scratched his stubbly chin, and looked round, in the direction of Captain Patterson's office. 'Don't see how it can, Sam. At the end of the day, there's no real evidence of it being anything other than death by misadventure, in all three cases.'

Leroy's voice went down to almost a whisper. 'Roman, you gotta be kidding .'

Perez put his hand up, palm towards Leroy. 'Just accept it, Sam. And move on. That's the decision by the DA, and people on a much bigger pay grade than you or me.'

Leroy looked back at the screen, then back up at Perez.

'Jesus Christ,' he persisted. 'The house is owned by the fucking United States Secretary of Defence. How can you say -?'

'Listen.' Perez was beginning to get impatient. He was already dog tired. 'This is the last time we will discuss this. Sure, Secretary Davison owns the place, but he probably owns several. Was he there at the time? No, of course he wasn't. The fact that you and Domingo followed some two bit hooker there means squat. Who's to say the guy you spoke to there even knew about the car? And who was this guy anyway? Dwight Mason: he's the Secretary's General Counsel for Christ's sake. Are you telling me that the Secretary of Defence is somehow pumping half naked men with drugs then leaving them on Hollywood Boulevard?'

'Has happened before.'

Perez impatiently shook his head and waved his hand dismissively. 'I don't care about before. The Secretary has nothing to do with it. Maybe he was banging that hooker, but that hardly connects him, does it? How many johns did she see that night, anyway? She could have been on her way to see Mason.'

'No, not Mason. I've read his biography.' Leroy pointed to the screen.

'Whatever. Case closed. Case closed. Understand?'

Leroy said nothing.

'Do you understand, Detective?'

Leroy nodded his head. 'Understood.' He slowly leaned forward and exited Domingo's email.

'Good. Now get the hell down to the hospital and talk to that Palisades Beach survivor.' Angrily, the lieutenant spun on his heels and walked back to his own office.

Leroy watched him leave, right till he could see his silhouette through the hammered glass walls return to his office and close the door. Took a deep breath and read through the folder the lieutenant had given him.

Santa Monica's first hospital was founded in 1926 by two local physicians, Dr William S Mortensen and Dr August B Hromadka. In 1955 the hospital became part of UCLA Health, and today is part of the massive UCLA Medical Center. Specialising in Orthopaedic medicine, a limited amount of surgery, the Center also houses a small emergency room. The survivor of the attack was occupying one of the twenty-two beds here in the ER.

Leroy parked outside the main entrance, next to an LAPD patrol car. Immediately a figure in a blue and gold uniform appeared and asked for his car keys. Leroy had not noticed that there was valet parking here. He held up his badge and the valet backed off. Just at that moment, another vehicle pulled up, and the young man ran off to park that.

Slightly puzzled as to why a patrol car should be here, Leroy walked inside and made his way to the reception desk. A uniformed guard directed him to take a left and make his way to the Southwest wing, where the ER was situated. As he turned the last corner, he saw waiting by the elevators outside the ER door, a uniformed officer. She stood up on seeing him.

'Detective Leroy?' she asked.

He briefly held out his ID. 'You were expecting me?'

'Officer Lin. Yes, we had a message from a Lieutenant Perez asking for some back-up for you.'

He looked at her. 'And you're my back up?'

'That's right, Detective.'

'Son of a bitch,' Leroy muttered, looking around.

'Excuse me, Detective?'

'Nothing, er – Lin. Kind of a misunderstanding between the lieutenant and me.' He nodded over to the ER doors. 'She in there still?'

'Yes, she's asleep now, though. Should I get one of the staff to wake her?'

'Best not. Not yet anyway. Did you get to talk to her?'

'A little, yes.'

205

'I've read the initial report. What did she tell you?'

Lin put her hands on her hips and took a deep breath. 'Well, she says she and her friend -'

'Are they from around here? Or from out of town?'

'Very out of town. They're both from Hamburg, Germany.'

'Great. You speak German, then?'

'No, Detective; she speaks English.'

'Well, that helps. What did she tell you?'

'They're both booked in at the Holiday Inn in Hollywood, and came here as part of a city tour. She said they had a half hour to spare before they had to be back at the bus, so took a walk through Palisades Park.'

'Nice.'

'They saw five or six transients standing around with some homemade signs saying something like *fuck me for $5 no change given*. She said two of them approached them and asked for five dollars. They said no, and walked off. At first the men stayed where they were, but then her friend turned and began to take pictures of them with their cells.'

'Why on earth…?'

Lin shrugged. 'They thought it was amusing. Part of Southern California life, maybe.'

'Well, they got that right. Go on; what happened next?'

'The two men began chasing them, soon caught up, and had them on the ground. There was a lot of screaming; there were other people in the park at the time, and by coincidence a black and white was passing along the beach road. When they heard the siren, the two men got up and tried to run off, but the officers from the black and white got them pretty soon. But when the girls got up, they were both covered in blood, just from cuts on the arms in this case, but the other had already lost a lot of blood from chest wounds. They brought them both here, but she died just after arrival in the ER.'

'All right, Lin; thanks.' He peered in the small windows

of the ER door. 'There's no need to wake her, especially if she's not in any danger. Take my number; give me a call on my cell when she wakes, and I'll come back. That okay?'

'Sure thing, Detective,' Lin said, pocketing Leroy's card. 'You going to the crime scene now?'

'I'll have a brief look, then speak to the two suspects.'

'I'll come with you, shall I?'

'No, it's all right.' Leroy moved his jacket slightly so she could see the butt of his service pistol. 'You stay here with her; let me know when she wakes. I'll see you later.'

'Okay, Detective.' Lin sat back down as Leroy walked back to the main entrance hall, and then to his car. As he got to the car, he looked around, thinking. There was not enough time to go home, so he pulled into 16th Street, then did a right onto Santa Monica Avenue. A ten block ride took him to the main public library. The small street level parking lot was full; a sign did direct him to a subterranean garage, but he decided to park on the red kerbed section of street right outside the library. He ran up the steps to the glass entrance doors, then took the elevator to the second floor, and the seventy public access internet stations. He showed his identification to the white haired lady behind a semi-circular desk, and she gave him a temporary identification number and password.

Leroy found a vacant place, sat down and logged on. Checked his watch. Once he got to the welcome screen, he moved the cursor to Google, and clicked. Once the next screen appeared, he typed in the name, and sat back and waited.

There were a lot of entries for Secretary George Davison.

CHAPTER THIRTY-SEVEN

LEROY CLICKED ON the first entry. There were only three lines of sketchy biography. The second entry had far more. He got himself a cup of water from the cooler nearby and sat down to read.

Personal Details
Born – George Henry Davison
August 1st, 1950
Flagstaff, Arizona
Political party – Democrat
Spouse – Barbara LaHood (m. 1975)
Alma mater – Northern Arizona University
Trinity College, Oxford, England
Profession – Attorney
Religion – Roman Catholic
Siblings - One

Political Offices
Chairman of Senate Indian Affairs
Chairman of Senate Aging Committee
US Secretary of Defense

Early Life and education
Davison was born in Flagstaff, Arizona, one of four sons. His mother, Alice (née Adams), was of Catholic Irish ancestry, and his father, Henry Davison managed a restaurant.

While in high school, Davison was a basketball player and was named to the Arizona all-state high school team.

Legal, academic, and early political life
After graduating, Davison returned to Flagstaff and earned partnership in a local law firm. He became assistant county attorney for Coconino County. He was elected to Flagstaff City Council and served as Flagstaff mayor for one year.

Leroy stretched and nodded slightly. He knew a little about Secretary Davison from the media. This was nothing new. He continued reading.

House of Representatives and Senate
After serving one term as Mayor, Davison won a seat in the US House of Representatives, succeeding fellow Democrat Alan Clay, who was elected to the US Senate.

During his time in Congress, Davison was one of the first to break with his party, and voted for the impeachment of President Bill Clinton.

After two terms in the House, Davison was elected to the US Senate, defeating Alan Clay in his first bid for re-election. He was re-elected himself twice, and served a total of 15 years in the Senate.

While in the Senate, he served on the Senate Armed Services Committee. During the Iraq War, he was highly critical of President Bush but was hesitant to call for an immediate and complete pull-out. He announced that he favored withdrawing most of the US forces from Iraq and leaving a small force in the Northern region for a limited period. While acknowledging that a withdrawal would lead to more violence, he felt that it would be the only way for the Iraqi government to take control of their country.

After retiring from the Senate, Davison was appointed by the President to the position of Secretary of Defense. One of his first major duties as Secretary of Defense was to present to Congress the Fiscal Year Defense budget, which had been prepared under Secretary Bryant. Davison requested a budget of $255.2 billion, which represented 3 percent of the nation's estimated domestic product. Davison stressed three top budget priorities: people (recruiting.....

Leroy stretched again, and rubbed the back of his neck. All this was very interesting, but was not really relevant to what he was looking for.

International relations and situations
As he settled into office, Davison faced the question of the expansion of the North Atlantic Treaty Organization, which he supported, and its relationship to Russia. At a summit meeting between the President and Russian President Putin, Putin acknowledged the inevitability of broader NATO membership. Two months later he agreed, after negotiations with NATO officials, to sign an accord providing for a new permanent council, to include Russia, the NATO secretary general, and a representative of the other NATO nations, to function as a forum in which Russia could air a wide range of security issues that concerned that country

Social issues
Finally, Davison had to address social issues that engaged the widest public interest. These issues included the status and treatment of lesbian and gays in the military, the role of woman in combat as well as in other jobs in the services, racism, and sexual harassment.

He had read enough. He was not sure exactly what he was expecting to find, but all this information was public domain stuff, and didn't help. But it gave him a better understanding of what Davison was about.

But not why a hooker would be rushing back to a house he owned in California. In fact, from the biographical detail, there was no California connection. His entire life seemed to be centred around three locations: Flagstaff, Arizona; Oxford, England; Washington, DC.

He leaned back in his chair and scratched his chin. Why would a politician working on the East Coast own a mansion here? Maybe if it was a beach property: somewhere in Malibu maybe, looking out to the ocean – that he could understand, but a secluded property off Mulholland Drive: he failed to see the attraction.

He checked the time at the corner of the screen: time to get back to work. This would have to be homework. He logged off, made a quick restroom stop, and returned to his car.

Five minutes later, he pulled up on Ocean Avenue behind a patrol car. He watched as an articulated bus slowly made a left from Washington Avenue, holding up traffic in the process. In the park, an area of grass about thirty yards square was still taped off, and two officers were standing by the tape. Leroy walked over the grass to join them. He recognised both officers.

'Guys,' he greeted them.

'Detective,' they both responded.

'I take it the forensic guys have finished here?'

The first officer nodded. 'Yes; they both left twenty minutes ago.'

'Why the tape then?'

'They said you were coming over, and to leave the tape until you'd had the chance to look.'

'I see,' said Leroy, amused. 'As if I would find anything else.' He stepped under the tape. 'Where exactly did it happen?'

'In the centre here,' said one of the officers, joining him inside the tape. There was very little sign of anything, apart from the flattening of the grass where people had been standing.

Leroy knelt down. 'No sign of blood,' he said, looking

up at the officer.

'Apparently most of it got soaked up by the victim's clothes. She was lying on her back and the wound was in her front.'

'Are you two the ones who were here at the time?'

'No; they took the suspects back for questioning.'

Leroy looked around, then stood up. 'Do you know about any other witnesses?'

'As far as I know, just the woman the victim was with. There were some passers-by, but they had all moved on by the time anyone realised she had been stabbed.'

'The other transients? I take it there were more than two here.'

'Sorry, Detective, I don't know. It was all over by the time we arrived. We were just ordered to stay here until you had cleared the scene.'

'I'll ask when I go talk to the suspects.' Leroy turned and looked out to the ocean. The sun was high in the sky now, its light being reflected off the water. He squinted, and put on a pair of sun glasses. Through the shades, he could make out some boats on the water. A helicopter was flying north, parallel with the coast. It seemed peaceful, apart from the sound of traffic travelling along the Pacific Coast Highway underpass.

He turned back to the officer. 'You can remove the tape now,' he said. 'I'm done here.'

'Sure thing, Detective,' the officer replied, and began winding up the tape. Leroy walked back to his car, looking around the park. Whilst not particularly busy, there were still several people wandering around the park. In spite of the traffic sound, it still seemed peaceful; after all these years, Leroy still found violent crime incongruous with such a location. Across the street was a branch of Wells Fargo bank: Leroy remembered having to attend the bank after a robbery homicide eighteen months or so back. Three masked raiders, heavily armed, forced the staff and customers in a corner at gunpoint, and proceeded to empty the safe. One customer foolishly tried to tackle one of the raiders, and was hit in the chest almost at point blank range. In the commotion afterwards, the security guard tried the same thing, and was killed as well, this time with the addition of a single shot to the back of his head, execution style. It was always the same with robbery homicide: once one person was down, the raiders would have nothing to lose.

Leroy turned back to the car; just as he opened the door, his phone rang. It was Medical Examiner Hobson.

'Hey there, Russell,' said Leroy, as he climbed back into his car.

'Hey, Sam. Where are you right now?' Russell asked.

'Over at Santa Monica. A stabbing.'

'Ah, yes; the two women. Look, Sam: I need you to get over here.'

'Why? What's happened?'

'Nothing had happened. Not today, anyway. I just need to show you something. It has a bearing on the John Does.'

'Can't really right now, Russell. For one thing, I have two suspects to interview; and for another, all the John Doe cases have been closed.'

'Yes, I know they've been closed, but something's come to light.'

'Come to light? What do you mean?'

'I was just finishing up one of the bodies, when I noticed something. I went back to the others, and found the same thing.'

'And that was?'

'On each of them, on the left foot, between two of the toes, was a needle mark.'

Leroy sat up. 'A needle mark?'

'Yes, so tiny, so hidden between the toes, that they got missed.'

'So where does that leave us?'

'Maybe not much, maybe a lot. But the angle of the mark would make it difficult for someone to self inject. They seem to come up from below the foot. Something like a forty-five degree angle.' There was a pause. 'You there, Sam?'

'Yes, Russ, still here. Was just thinking. That must be the way the drug cocktail got into their systems.'

'Probably, yes.'

'And there was no way they could have injected themselves?'

'Not no way, but unlikely, in my opinion. So before you ask: I think these men didn't die as a result of misadventure. I think they were murdered.'

CHAPTER THIRTY-EIGHT

RED LIGHT FLASHING and siren wailing, Leroy hit the 10 Freeway at sixty-five. It was just over twenty-five miles to the Forensic Science Center, so he should be with Hobson within thirty minutes.

The ME had offered to send photographs of the puncture marks to Leroy's phone, but he wanted to see them in person. After he had hung up on Hobson, he considered whether to speak to Perez, hopefully get him to say, 'Okay, Sam; you get yourself up to the ME's and take a look for yourself. Don't worry about the suspects and witnesses you have to interview,' but hell would freeze over before the lieutenant departed from the official line. Leroy wondered what he would have done had he gotten the lieutenant post: he was sure he would have reopened the cases. No, he would never have closed them. Maybe that was why Perez was the lieutenant now.

As soon as Hobson told him about the needle marks, he knew he had been on to something all along. Thing was, he still was not sure exactly what he was on to.

Thirty minutes to get to the ME, thirty minutes there, and another thirty minutes back to Santa Monica; the two suspects in the cells and the victim's companion could wait another hour and a half.

The eastbound traffic was heavy, but moving steadily, and vehicles moved over without any hesitation to let him pass. As he finally left the freeway, he had to drop his speed: negotiating the sharp bend as the road approached Eastern Avenue, he had to drop to forty-five, even though the sign specified a maximum ten miles per hour lower. Even with the windows closed and the AC on, he could smell the rubber of his tyres burning as he negotiated the bend.

Once on Eastern Avenue, he easily negotiated the traffic leading up to the University Campus, and was soon at the Forensic Science Center. Moments later, a breathless Detective Leroy burst in to Hobson's laboratory. The ME was sitting at a desk, typing on a keyboard. He looked up and laughed.

'You took your time, didn't you?' he joked.

Leroy laughed and sat down on a chair opposite, still out of breath from running from the car and up four flights of stairs.

'Surely you didn't run all the way,' Hobson laughed as he hit his return key and pushed the keyboard back.

'No, just up the stairs.' Leroy took a deep breath and sat back. 'That's better.'

'I guess you want to see these guys' feet,' said Hobson, standing up. 'Let's go take a look.'

Hobson led Leroy out of his lab and down the corridor into another room. On the way, they stood to one side as a white-coated man pushed a gurney on which there was a green plastic sheet, covering whoever was on it. Hobson nodded to the man.

At the end of the corridor they went through a set of double doors to a room where on all three other sides of the room were banks of drawers, four high. Hobson led Leroy over to the far end and pulled open a drawer.

'I was just preparing the bodies for release back to the families,' Hobson said, 'and thought I would give them one more look over. Then I found the marks. Here's the first one,' he said, pulling out the drawer. 'This is the one they found in the parking garage in Century City.'

'Lance Riley,' said Leroy.

Hobson picked up the single sheet form which was resting on Lance Riley's shrouded legs. 'Yes, that's right.' He lifted up the lower part of the green sheet covering the body and lifted up one foot. 'Look, Sam; here. Between the big toe and the next.'

Leroy bent down and checked between the toes. Hobson said, 'You will need to move the toes apart slightly.' He did so, and just as Hobson had said, between the two toes, was a tiny puncture mark. Still bent over, he looked up at the ME. 'And the others were like this also?'

'Yes. You want to see them?'

'Go on, then.'

Hobson replaced the proforma and pushed the drawer closed, then took Leroy over to another drawer. Opened it, and checked the paperwork. 'Guy Robbins,' he read.

'Found behind Hollywood Boulevard.'

'That's him. Check the foot.'

Leroy did so, and found a puncture mark in exactly the same spot. Hobson closed the drawer, and asked, 'Now, you want to see Ted Parker?'

'Ted Parker?' asked Leroy. Then he realised. 'Was this the one from Griffith Park?'

'Yes, that's right. Oh, I forgot that wasn't yours. It

was…'

'Domingo's. That's right.'

'Shit, Sam. That was awful, wasn't it? Any news yet?'

Leroy shook his head. 'Not to my knowledge. It's all been handed over to Major Crimes.'

'Mm,' said Hobson, reflecting. 'From what I heard, they were both in their patrol car.'

'They were. Up in North Hollywood. Both with one shot to the head.'

Hobson slowly shook his head, as if in disbelief. 'Look, here's the last one.' He pulled open this drawer, and Leroy checked the toes. Same as before.

'Now, as you know,' explained Hobson, holding the foot up, 'this spot here is a common place for drug users to inject themselves.'

'If they don't want to show any marks,' added Leroy. 'Not like in the arm, or wrist.'

'Correct. Now, there are two points of interest here. First: if I'd had one body in here with marks like that, I'd think nothing of it. Business as usual, you know: outwardly respectable guy a secret user. Two - maybe the same. But *three* - and all brought in on the same night. No way.'

'There *has* to be a connection,' Leroy agreed.

'The second point is this,' continued Hobson. 'If you're injecting yourself there, you'd be sitting down, and the point of entry would be straight on - I mean level with the base of the foot, or at a slight angle upwards, up to twenty, maybe thirty degrees. But if you look here,' - he put one index finger on the mark - 'you'll see it's at an angle, but in the opposite direction to what you'd expect. It would be very difficult to inject yourself at that angle. It's not impossible, but for three out of three people to have the same puncture wounds on the same night - well, go figure.'

Leroy stood silently for a moment, staring at the foot.

'What are you going to do now, Sam?' asked Hobson.

'I'm going back to the station house. I'm going to talk

to Perez. This is all too much of a coincidence. There has to be another party involved. And Domingo and I came up with some other angles.'

'You did? What?'

'Tell you another time. I must get back. They *have* to re-open the cases now.'

CHAPTER THIRTY-NINE

LEROY STARED AT Lieutenant Perez in disbelief. He knew he should not have been surprised; after all, he had known the lieutenant for years, and the conversation they had earlier would have dispelled any doubts.

After his meeting with Russell Hobson, Leroy left the Forensic Science Center and headed back to the freeway to return to Police HQ. He had only been driving ten minutes, when Perez rang.

'Sam, where are you? I thought you were going to see the two suspects.'

'I've been to see Russell Hobson.'

'The ME? You've been up to the Science Center? What the hell for?'

'It's about those John Does, Lieutenant -'

'I'd better be hearing things, Detective. Didn't we talk about this before?'

'He's uncovered some new evidence.'

'What new evidence?'

'Some puncture wounds. Injection marks.'

'What? Injection marks? They were all full of drugs, and you're telling me they had needle marks?'

'It's more that that. Look, I'll stop off at HQ and fill you in. On my way back to Santa Monica, that is.'

There was a moment's pause, and then, 'All right. I'll give you ten minutes. Take it out of your lunch hour. And it'd better be good.' Then Perez hung up.

Now, the lieutenant was sitting behind his desk, shaking his head in disbelief. 'I don't fucking believe this, I really don't,' he said. 'This is nothing. It's bullshit.'

'Just think about it, Roman,' Leroy replied, getting as heated as the lieutenant. 'In all three -'

'I could hear raised voices,' said Captain Patterson, leaning round the half opened door. 'Any problem?'

Perez sat back in his chair and answered the captain. 'Detective Leroy here has uncovered new evidence in the cases of those three John Does.'

Patterson briefly closed his eyes as if in thought. 'Ah yes, I recall: the three accidental deaths due to drug overdoses.' He looked down at Perez. 'Those cases are closed, aren't they, Lieutenant?'

Leroy answered. 'Sir: yes, they have been closed, but new evidence has come to light.'

'New evidence?' asked Patterson, surprised. 'What new evidence could there be?'

'Medical Examiner Hobson has found needle marks on one foot of each man,' Leroy replied. 'Between two of the toes.'

Patterson frowned. 'I don't understand. First of all, the bodies came in last Friday, did they not? Why is he only reporting them now?'

Leroy started to answer. 'He said -'

'Secondly,' the captain cut in, 'I think I'm right in saying that hidden between two toes is a common place to inject. So what's the beef?'

'I am aware about why people inject between the toes,' said Leroy calmly and slowly. 'But Russ... Hobson's point was the angle of the mark. They were all at such an angle that would have rendered it unlikely they were all self-inflicted.'

'But not impossible.' The captain smiled and puffed up his chest.

'No, not impossible,' said Leroy. 'Just unlikely.'

Captain Patterson directed his next sentence to Perez. 'Lieutenant, did you explain to Detective Leroy that the decision to close the cases was taken at the highest level?'

'I did, sir,' said Perez. Leroy looked down at the lieutenant, and noticed the odd look on his face, as if his mind was elsewhere.

'Where the amount of work Detective Leroy had put into the cases has not gone unnoticed?'

Leroy and Perez just looked at each other.

The captain continued, 'So, let's move on. The cases are closed. There are a lot of homicides going on out there, and we mustn't be distracted by Medical Examiner Hobson playing at Sherlock Holmes again. I must have a word with Sheriff Welch.' He looked over at Leroy and Perez, said, 'Well, good day gentlemen,' turned and returned to his own office.

Perez looked up at Leroy. 'See? My hands are tied. Cases closed. Move on. There's plenty of other work to do out there, and doesn't Quinn get back tomorrow?'

'I think so,' mumbled Leroy. 'But despite what the captain says, there are still uninvestigated threads here.'

Perez leaned on his desk, resting his forehead in one hand. He sighed, and pressed some keys on the keyboard on his desk. Still looking at the screen, he spoke. 'It says here you have a week's vacation owed.'

'What?'

'I said you have five days' vacation to use. Don't worry; when Quinn gets back, we'll find him something to do.'

'Vacation? What are you talking about, Lieutenant? I can't take a vacation in the middle of all this.'

'Take some R and R. Do whatever you want to do. Go wherever you want to go, within reason. Of course, while you are on vacation, you are just a private citizen. Do you understand what I'm saying, Sam?'

Leroy nodded. 'Yes, Lieutenant. I think I do.'

'Good. Now, clear up your desk. I'll send someone else over to Santa Monica; it might be your partner tomorrow.'

'Right, I will.' Leroy backed away from the desk.

'And Detective?' Perez called out as Leroy reached the door.

'Yes, Lieutenant?'

'Enjoy your vacation.'

CHAPTER FORTY

LEROY HAD GOTTEN the lieutenant's message, although couldn't quite understand the motivation. Sure, he had a week's vacation time owing - more in fact - but was taken aback when Perez told him to take it, and take it immediately. The Area was busy, so there was the question of whether they could afford to be a man down. Then again, there was never a good time to take vacation. So what was Perez up to? Did he, deep down, and despite outward appearances, believe what Leroy was saying? Was that his way of continuing the investigation even though a decision had been made *at the highest level* to close the cases? And what exactly was *the highest level*? And by warning Leroy that he was a private citizen for the next seven days, was there a hidden message there too?

On the other hand, Perez could be so pissed off with Leroy banging on about the cases, that he just wanted him out of his hair for a few days. No more than that.

Leroy leaned back in the booth in Martha's. He had finished a turkey and ham sandwich, washed down by two cups of black coffee, then gratefully accepted the offer of a refill. Whatever Perez's reasoning, he decided, this was his chance to make some progress, to prove that these were no deaths by misadventure. Surely, others - apart from him and Hobson - could see this was no coincidence. Still, Quinn was back tomorrow, and having his partner on the inside as it were would help, provided he would not get into trouble.

Leroy leaned back in the booth and closed his eyes. He went through the facts of these cases. On one night, three men, all of a similar socio-economic profile, are found dead in disparate parts of the city, all with the same COD, all with that tiny entry wound hidden between two toes; entry wounds which Russell Hobson says are unlikely to have been self-inflicted. Two of the men had laptops which the CCU are analyzing - or were, now the cases were closed - where the search history had been wiped, but they did find that one of the victims used a dating site to get hookers. They speak to one of the hookers, who then flees to a house owned by a major politician, where one of his staff denies all knowledge of her, even though her car is hidden out back. And the clincher: Domingo and her partner are murdered, their slayings may or may not be related to all this.

So where, in his capacity as a private citizen, could Leroy start? It seemed the last person to see one of the victims alive was the hooker Alexandra. He needed to get hold of her first. He could park outside the house and wait, but there may be a quicker way.

He stood up and walked over to the bar. Kenny was chatting to another customer at the end of the bar, saw Leroy and sauntered over.

'What can I get you, Sam?' Kenny asked. 'More coffee?'

'I'm okay for now, Kenny, but I need a favour. I take it you have internet access here?'

'Sure, we have free Wi-Fi.' He pointed to a sign on the wall.

'Fine, but I don't have a computer with me.'

'We have one in the office out back. You want to use it?'

'If you don't mind. Could I?'

'Sure, Sam; come this way.'

Kenny led Leroy behind the bar and into a small office. A really old monitor was perched on a desk, amongst the clutter of glasses, cups and magazines.

'Don't worry about all that,' Leroy said as Kenny began to clear the desk. He looked up as he could hear the sound of people coming into the bar. The end of a shift, he guessed. 'I'll be okay, thanks, Kenny,' he said, sitting down. 'Do me a favour though: if they are from the station house, don't let them know I'm here. Okay?'

'Sure, Sam. Why, what's up?'

'Long story. Tell you another time.'

'All righty.' Kenny left Leroy alone in the tiny office. He typed in www.arrangeadate.com into the search bar, and waited. After a couple of seconds the site Home page appeared. In the area box, he clicked on Los Angeles, then had to choose which district. He had a choice of Westside-Southbay, San Fernando Valley, San Gabriel Valley, Long Beach, Antelope Valley, and Central LA. He chose the latter, then had to select he was a man looking for a woman. Once he clicked, then the familiar thumbnails appeared on the screen. He trawled though eleven pages until he found a picture which caught his eye. He paused, clicked on the thumbnail to enlarge, and stared at the image. It was a different picture than the one he and Domingo had seen the other day, but it was definitely her.

But the name was not Alexandra.
It was Marisol.

CHAPTER FORTY-ONE

IN SPITE OF everything else that was going on, Leroy laughed. So Alexandra was now Marisol. He would take book that neither was her real name. He clicked on the Contact button, and typed in a brief message that he liked her picture and was she free later today. Sent the message and sat back.

And waited.

He could hear the sounds of laughter coming from the bar outside. He looked at the screen. No reply.

The door opened and Kenny came in with a cup. 'Thought you could use some more coffee, Sam,' he said.

'My hero, 'said Leroy, gratefully taking the cup.

'Any food?' Kenny asked.

'No. Coffee's good for me, thanks.'

Kenny left Leroy alone again. Still no reply. Leroy shrugged: maybe she was with a client. He called up the page for the *Los Angeles Times*, read a few pages, then searched for the *Santa Monica Observer*. He read some of that, until the monitor bleeped. Returning to the site, he saw a pop up announcing a message for him. He clicked on there and saw that Alexandra/Marisol had replied. She was so thrilled to hear from him, and was he free at six o'clock today? She could meet him at either The Groves Overlook, just off Mulholland Drive, or, if he preferred a more intimate meeting, she had a luxury apartment not far. He thought her luxury apartment might be preferable to an outdoor location, so replied that he would prefer her apartment. Once he sent his reply, he picked up the coffee, and had two mouthfuls before her reply came through. She would meet him in the parking lot at Denny's on Sepulveda and Burbank.

He laughed. Firstly, he doubted if Denny's knew that their parking lot was being used in this way; secondly, how could she think here was not far from the overlook? He checked the two locations on Google Maps: the 405 Freeway passed by both locations. Only around five miles, but at that time of day, the time taken to make the five mile journey could be anybody's guess. He arranged to meet her at six in the parking lot.

He arrived at the location just after five thirty. It was still daylight, and would be so for at least an hour and a half. The last thing he wanted was for her to recognise him and run again. He walked into Denny's, showed his identification to one of the servers, and took a seat in the window, but where he could have a good view of the parking lot.

Five minutes before six, he recognised the battered, undercoated Ford pull in, and reverse into a space. He saw Alexandra/Marisol climb out. She looked around, then went to stand by one of the small conifer trees which stood either side of the pathway to the door, and lit a cigarette.

Leroy stood up, thanked the server as he walked past her, and went outside to meet the hooker. 'Marisol?' he asked.

She turned round and smiled at him. 'Sure is, hun. You didn't give me your name before.'

'Sam.'

'Nice to meet you, Sam. Hey, have I met you before. Your face seems kind of familiar.'

Leroy said nothing. Then the penny dropped.

'You're that fucking cop, aren't you. I thought I -'

Leroy grabbed her by the arm and led her to his car. A couple with two young children were coming up the path. The man looked at Marisol, a slightly worried look on his face. Leroy showed him his badge, and let the family go inside. 'Shut up, and get in my car,' he snapped.

'Get your hands off me, you son of a bitch,' Marisol protested as Leroy bundled her into his car.

'I told you: shut your mouth,' he spat back, as he climbed in next to her. 'Now, your choice: do you want me to cuff you, or are you going to talk to me like a normal person?'

She calmed down, looking out of the windshield, a look of resignation on her face. 'What you want to know this time?'

'The guy I asked about before: Guy Robbins.'

'Yeah? What about him?'

'You told me he paid a hundred for a blow job. Is that right?'

'Guess so. If that's what I said.'

'Answer the question. You met him at the overlook, and that's all that happened?'

'For a hundred bucks, that's all that's going to happen.'

'No drugs?'

She turned round in her seat and looked at him. This was the first time he had been able to look at her close up. He hadn't realised how young she looked - around twenty, maybe. Behind the thick make-up and tired, world-weary expression on her face, her eyes were a vivid blue. 'I told you. No drugs, no nothing. We arranged to meet there. He was very nervous, kept looking out to the main street. I told him how much I charged and for what. He said he only had a hundred bucks on him, so I told him what he'd get for that.'

'Which was?'

'Which was a hand job or some oral. His choice. He chose oral. He only lasted a couple of minutes, then he paid me.'

'Then?'

'Then I got back into my car, and left.'

'Left him at the overlook.'

'Yeah. Why, was I expected to take him home?'

'Do you get much work from that site?' Leroy asked. 'I mean, a hundred can get a guy much more other places.'

'Honey, I'm high class.'

'Oh yes, I forgot; you have a luxury apartment. Where's that?'

She shook her head and pointed down Sepulveda Boulevard. 'Motel room two blocks down.'

'Hm. Very high class.'

'Whatever. Look, are we going to be long? If this is all you want, I can be earning some cash somewhere else.'

Leroy reached into his pocket and pulled out some bills. He passed them to her, and she flicked through them greedily.

'There's two hundred here! Man, I can give you a really good time now!'

'Take the night off. On me.'

'Night off? I don't get it. Don't you even want to -?'

'No, I don't. Go home, wash all that shit off your face and be… How old are you anyway?'

'Nineteen. Why?'

'Just wondered. And is your name Marisol? Or is it Alexandra?'

'It's Alexandra. Why?'

'Why did you call yourself Marisol on the site? And change the picture?'

She began to get defensive. 'Just decided to. Okay? Is there a law against that?'

'Not against changing your picture or name, no.'

She grabbed the door handle. 'Anything else you want, pig?'

'Just one more question. When we spoke last, once we'd done, you went to a house off Mulholland Drive.'

'Y-yes,' she said slowly, suspiciously. 'You followed me?'

'Do you know who owns that house?'

'Don't know anything about no house,' she snapped. She pulled open the car door and made to run off. However, the high heels she was wearing prevented her from running too fast, so Leroy was easily able to leap out of his door and chase after her. As she ran through the bushes which separated the lot from the street, one of her heels broke and she tumbled to the ground. Leroy caught up with her, and leaned over her to help her get up. He could not have seen the rock she had picked up while both palms were on the ground: she swung round to her left, holding the rock with her right hand, and caught Leroy on his left temple. With a cry, he fell to the ground, clutching the side of his head. With one broken heel, she staggered out on to the sidewalk, then into the street. Into the rush hour traffic.

As he got up, dazed, Leroy heard a horn blare, a scream, a dull thud, then a screech of brakes. As he got through the bushes and into the street, a small crowd had already gathered around. The sound he had heard was of a bus braking. Behind the front wheel of the bus a trickle of blood was running into the gutter.

The bus doors hissed open and the driver leapt out,

hysterical. 'I couldn't stop!' he cried. 'I couldn't stop! She ran right in front!'

Leroy crouched down in front of the bus. The fender was dented and he could make out a shape lying still underneath the bus. He turned, looked around and noticed something lying on its side in the road.

A shoe, its heel broken.

CHAPTER FORTY-TWO

SAM LEROY PERCHED himself on the edge of the table. It was eight fifteen, and he was in the emergency room of the Ronald Reagan Medical Center. The doctor attending to him had just left the room, saying he needed a couple of stitches, and she would be back shortly. As he sat alone in the room, with its white floor and walls, Spartan furnishings and decorations, he watched the silhouetted figures pass the shaded windows. He put his hand up to the wound on his temple and winced as he ran his fingertips across the wound. Although the brick with which Marisol had hit him was not particularly large, it had a jagged edge on one side, and it was with this side that she caused a wound an inch long.

It needed a couple of stitches, Dr Lee had said. Not something Leroy was looking forward to. He had undergone numerous such repairs over the years, but having stitches always seemed to be something he dreaded.

Dr Lee returned to the room. She was a petite Chinese woman in her early thirties, and no more than five feet tall. Her black hair was cut into a neat bob. 'Ready for your stitches, Detective?' she asked, with more than a hint of amusement at his dread of the needle.

'Ready as I'll ever be, I guess, Doctor,' Leroy replied.

'Well, you'll be relieved to know the wound's not big enough to require conventional stitching,' Dr Lee said, unwrapping a plastic container. 'I'm only going to need some steri-strips this time, so I guess you've gotten away with it today. Hold still now.'

'That's some good news, at least.' Leroy inclined his head slightly to the right, while the doctor applied four strips, one along the length of the wound, and three across, at each and in the centre

'They will need to stay in place for five to seven days,' Dr Lee said as she applied the strips, 'and try not to get them too wet.'

'Not too wet?'

'A shower should be okay, provided you minimise how much water touches them, but don't go swimming with them on. Do you own a shower cap?'

Leroy looked at her, saying nothing.

'I'll take that as a no. So just make sure they don't get too wet.'

'Five to seven days? How will I know?'

'You'll know. When the wound clearly hasn't bled for a few days. Check it daily, but don't take them off prematurely. They will come off of their own accord after seven days.'

'That's great. Thanks, Doc. I just -'

The door opened and in walked Lieutenant Perez. 'Mind if I come in, Doctor?'

Dr Lee looked over her shoulder. 'Sure. I'm done here.

There you go, Detective. Remember: keep the steri-strips dry.'

Leroy nodded and felt the strips. 'Thanks, Doc. I will.' He gave here an awkward smile as she packed up her instruments and left.

Perez watched as she left the room and closed the door behind her. 'So, you want to tell me what's going on?' he asked.

Leroy touched his temple again and winced. 'I got hit on the head.'

'I know that.' Perez stepped over and took a closer look. 'It hurt?'

'A bit, yes.'

'Good.'

'Excuse me?'

'You know perfectly well what I'm talking about.'

Leroy said nothing.

'It wouldn't have anything to do with that dead hooker down the hall, would it? The one that got hit by a 206 bus?'

'How did you know to come here?'

'I overheard the call come in, and thought, "This has got Sam Leroy written all over it."'

Leroy said nothing. Perez leaned up against the opposite wall and folded his arms. 'So: you going to tell me?'

'I managed to get back in touch with one of the hookers Liza Domingo and I saw the other day. It was the one we followed back to the house off Mulholland.'

Perez raised his eyes to the ceiling. 'Go on. How did you get in touch with her?'

'Through the same dating website we used the other day. The same one Guy Robbins used. Before he showed up behind Hollywood Boulevard.'

'Have you spoken to Bill Farmer about it? After all, it was his case, wasn't it?'

'No. I figured, the cases are officially closed. Farmer's a company man, so he will just accept and move on.'

'Unlike you.'

'Lieutenant, they must be -'

'Connected? Don't want to know. Cases closed. You are on vacation. So what did this hooker tell you?'

'Well, firstly, I had trouble picking up on her picture. Her thumbnail on the website was different.'

'Different?'

'The picture was different. Same face, obviously – though made up differently, and her hair was styled differently. Same colour – I think. And she was under a different name. Not Alexandra, but Marisol.'

'So what?'

'Don't you think it strange that the day after she gets questioned by the police, she changes her picture and name?'

Perez thought a moment. 'No, not really. She's - was – a hooker after all. Probably changed it every day or so. Like a box of cereal changes its design, or a company changes its logo. Rebranding, they call it.'

Leroy shrugged.

'So,' asked Perez, 'when you spoke to her, what did you discuss?'

'It was only a short conversation.'

'Before she made you, you mean?'

'Yeah. Just tried to give me the same story as before, until…'

'Until?'

'Until I asked her about the house. That's when she tried to get away. Said she knew nothing about any house, was out of the car like a bat out of hell, and ran across the parking lot.'

'Denny's?'

'Yeah. She was wearing stilettos and one broke as she was running. She was making for a gap in that row of bushes which separates the lot from the sidewalk. She fell, hit the dirt with both hands. Must have found the stone she did this with.' He touched his temple again, and winced.

Perez looked around. 'Jesus, Sam: I thought if you went on vacation, things would have gotten quieter. But it seems…' He finished mid-sentence.

'So now what?' asked Leroy.

'Now what?' Perez repeated, standing up from the wall. Well, the hooker's not going anywhere. Clearly an 11-79. There'll be an inquest, I expect, and let's hope you're not called to explain why you were chasing her out of some bushes. As for you: I believe I said you were on vacation.' He took three steps forward so he was a foot away from Leroy. 'Look,' he went on, 'let's not pussy around. You know why I put you on vacation; I know what you're going to do with your vacation time. So all I can say is: if you want to waste your time, go ahead. But take care: anything you do is in the capacity of a private citizen. *Entender*?'

Leroy nodded and stood up.

'So where are you going now?' asked Perez.

'I'm going home, to take a long bath, catch up with some sleep.'

'First bit of sense I've heard from you all day,' said Perez, turning to leave. 'See you in a week.'

'See you,' Leroy replied. Then, after Perez had left, 'And it wasn't the 206.'

He looked at the door, as if his eyes were still on the lieutenant's back.

'And I'm not wasting my time,' he added.

CHAPTER FORTY-THREE

LEROY PONDERED AS he drove home. His few days as a private citizen had not gotten off to a good start. The first witness he spoke to told him zip, and was now lying in the City Morgue. He decided to take a leisurely drive home, through the residential streets, rather than the freeways: pulling into the gas station on Cloverfield, after filling up parked in a small bay away from the pumps, and ate a burrito he had bought when paying for his gas. Hardly healthy, he thought, but he was starving. Then he called Joanna. They had made no plans to get together that night, but he had promised to get in touch. He told her briefly about his day, saying he would fill in the blanks when he saw her next. For her part, she was sitting on the floor watching *Downton Abbey* on PBS while marking her students' test papers. They arranged to get together the next evening: this time he would be cooking for her; as he agreed, something inside him told Leroy that it was a bad idea. Cooking was not his strongest skill.

They wished each other good night, and he put the phone down on the seat, finished his burrito, started the car, reversed out of the bay, and rejoined the late evening traffic.

He hit a red light just as he was about to make a right into Venice Boulevard. While he waited, he looked up at the clear night sky. He could make out the lights of two aircraft in the direction of the ocean: both seemed to be heading north from LAX. As he speculated on where they were headed, a thought came to him that Marisol may not have told him zip. He cursed himself for being so dumb: with his experience as a detective he should have realised that she had told him quite a bit. Not intentionally, of course; but her reaction when he asked her about the house off Mulholland. 'Don't know anything about no house,' she had said, then ran off. The cocky attitude was in a second replaced by a look of fear and panic. And she was prepared to risk charges of assaulting a police officer to get away. There was some connection with that house: what the hell was it to cause such a reaction?

'C'mon, buddy, let's go,' came a voice from the vehicle behind. Leroy looked into the rear view mirror and saw two cars in the right turn lane. He glanced up and saw the light had turned green. He lifted his right hand up to acknowledge the driver behind, then made the right. As he completed the turn, he heard a man's voice shouting: glancing round, he saw that the third car behind had not been able to make the turn before the light went red again. Instinctively, he felt down for his service weapon – just in case there was trouble ahead.

There was no trouble, and Leroy arrived home around ten-thirty. He parked, and paused before going indoors. Looking around, he slowly walked in the direction of the beach. As he came to the first cross street, he paused again and looked around. It was a quiet night: the normal rows of cars parked along the streets, but only the occasional vehicle moving past. There was normally more road and foot traffic: maybe it was because it was mid-week. As he turned to walk back to his building, a warm gust of wind hit him. He lifted his chin so his whole face caught the gust, and adjusted his collar. It was going to be a warm, humid night tonight: he was thankful his building superintendent had renewed the air conditioning earlier in the year.

Once in his apartment, he got himself a tall glass of iced water and lay on his bed. What would he do next? Tomorrow he needed to check out that house again. Of course, in his capacity as a private citizen that would be more difficult. He could still use his police identification, but only as a last resort. He could find himself facing disciplinary action if he did that, and got found out. He would have to think of another way.

He lay back and tried to figure out his next move.

Then fell asleep.

CHAPTER FORTY-FOUR

THE ALARM ON Leroy's phone went off at ten minutes after midnight. A shrill noise, sounding something like a coyote's bark, only much higher pitched, it caused him to lift an inch or so off the bed. He was wide awake in seconds, which was the effect he had intended.

In his small kitchen he made a brew of very strong black coffee and filled a vacuum flask. He checked himself in the mirror: he was already wearing black pants, so he pulled a black leather bomber jacket from his closet to finish the ensemble. Then put his phone to silent. A bathroom stop later, he was walking downstairs to his car. He opened the trunk and checked he was still carrying the Yukon night vision goggles, which he normally kept in the car, in case they were needed unexpectedly. He took the goggles out and threw them onto the front passenger seat, next to the coffee, then set off.

Just as he was approaching his intended destination, he

pulled over. There was hardly any traffic here on Mulholland Drive at this time of night: one car passed in either direction while he was stopped. He checked his bearings: the turning he wanted was the next right. Just after the turning the road took a sharp bend to the right; he pulled away and, at no more than twenty-five, took the bend. Fifty yards or so further on, there was another turning to the right. He took this turn, and drove along this road for the next hundred yards.

This street was longer than where the mansion was situated: it was not a dead end. On one side there was a row of single storey houses, mainly in darkness. Now and again, a house would have a window illuminated; on some, the bushes in the front yards would be lit up. On the opposite side there was an embankment of about fifty feet, on which there were trees and bushes.

Leroy stopped the car, and switched off the engine. He looked over at the houses immediately opposite. They were all bathed in darkness. He waited a couple of minutes just in case a light went on, or he saw movement. He wanted to avoid bumping into anybody. There would not be a problem for him if he did meet anybody; after all, he was carrying his LAPD identification and would be able to bluff his way out of any questions, but it would be an inconvenience.

He opened the flask and took a drink of coffee, savouring the strong caffeine, then looked around again. After satisfying himself that nobody was aware he was there, he got out of the car, and quietly closed the door.

The tracker binoculars were attached to hands-free head gear, and Leroy pulled them down over the top of his head, fastening the straps. He adjusted the binoculars themselves, so they were directly in front of him, and looked through them. The view through the lenses was similar to a black and white view, with a heavy green tint. As he looked across the street at the houses, he could clearly see the detail of the three buildings. There was still no light or movement.

Except….

He could see a large dog walking around in front of one of the houses, slowly making its way across the yard, putting its nose down to the ground every so often. This particular house was surrounded by high walls, and Leroy could only make out the dog as he had climbed slightly up the embankment and the house itself was above street level. Thank God the animal hadn't heard him pull up, he thought: a dog that size would have a loud bark and that could have put paid to what he had in mind.

He swung round and climbed further up the hillside. Even though the embankment was filled with trees and undergrowth, he easily made his way up the slope. A great advantage of his night vision apparatus: such a climb would be very difficult in complete darkness.

At the summit he paused and looked around. In the distance, all around, he could see the green tinted gridlines of the streets below. On the freeways, he could see a steady stream of head and tail lights, even at this hour.

He walked a few yards along the peak of the embankment, and looked directly down. Down the hill slightly, and around half a mile away across scrubland, was the rear of the mansion.

He carefully set off down the hill, making a sweep of the ground in front of him as he walked. At the foot of the hill the grass gave way to sand and shrubs, which made it easier to see what was ahead. As he walked along, he noticed some movement out of the corner of his eye, to his left. He froze. Looking down he saw the tail of a snake disappear under a clump of bushes. The body was slender and the tail pointed. It was probably a gopher snake.

The pacific gopher snake is indigenous to the region. Non-venomous, it tends to produce a loud hiss when agitated; sometimes it will inflate its body, flatten its head, and vigorously shake its tail to and fro, which may produce a rattling sound if done in dry vegetation. For this reason, it is sometimes confused with a rattlesnake, also found in these parts, except for the shape of the head and absence of a rattle at the end of the tail.

The confusion is two-way: Leroy was reminded of a night a couple of years back, when two fellow detectives were on stake-out duty. One of them needed to pee and went behind some bushes and came across what he assumed was a gopher snake. The rattler bit him on the calf before fleeing. The officer needed prompt medical attention: having been administered antivenom by the paramedics attending, he made a full recovery, although it was not a pleasant experience, and one which Leroy intended to avoid.

Slowly moving, keeping a lookout for hazards, natural and human, Leroy reached a fence. Or rather, a row of bent wooden poles connected by razor wire. Beyond the fence there were trees, and further still, the house. He felt he recognised the edge of the grounds from the other day when he and Domingo visited.

There was one factor which Leroy had to take into account: security. It was one of those known unknowns of Donald Rumsfeld again. He knew there would have to be some kind of security in effect, maybe some kind of surveillance. He noticed a discreet camera at the gates the other day, and more obvious cameras at each corner of the mansion, but what about out here? The wire fence looked too neglected, too run-down to be part of any security. He leaned down to listen to the wire. If it was electrified, which was unlikely, there would be a faint hum, easily heard in the silence of the dead of night. There was no hum, and no sign of any electrical equipment anywhere. Pressure pads would be out of the question, as they would be set off every few hours by the local wildlife. For the same reasons, detection equipment in the undergrowth would be unlikely.

Leroy walked along the fence to a spot where he could get a better view of the house. He adjusted the focal length of the binoculars and looked. He could make out the detail of the rear of the place. Lights were on on both first and second floors.

He looked around and found a small boulder, about a foot square, flattish on the top. He pulled his leather gloves down and grabbed the stone, pulling it away carefully. He took a deep breath, half expecting a snake to be underneath, breathing out when he could see there was not. He pulled the rock to just by the fence, and stood on it. This made it easier for him to step over the fence without snagging his clothing. Once over the fence, he carefully made his way towards the house.

Approaching the mansion from the rear, he came first to the pool house. This was in darkness, even with the NV apparatus. The pool itself was in darkness. Crouching behind a small wall, he looked at the house. One light was on: through illuminated double doors facing the pool, he could see two figures - male, he assumed – walking around. 'God, don't you guys ever sleep?' he muttered, as he looked up at the floor above. Lights were on in three windows, although in the case of the last window, this was fainter, as if it was from a bedside lamp. The size of these windows suggested bedrooms. He looked up at these rooms and scratched his very stubbly chin. What the hell was going on?

Still crouching, he made his way away from the pool but still parallel with the house, heading for the side of the place where he noticed the other day several cars parked. Four cars were there tonight. He walked into the bushes and along past the cars, checking the licence numbers. He noted down the numbers; this may be useful information in the morning. As he did this, he noticed a side door open. He hit the deck, and looked up, watching. A man - Leroy didn't recognise him, even in NV mode - left the house, and walked towards one of the cars, his feet crunching on the gravel. He paused at the car to light a cigarette. Leroy stayed crouching, not moving an inch.

After a moment, the man got into one of the cars, started

the engine and drove off. Leroy remained crouching. He saw the tail lights of the car disappear into the distance The brake lights came on for a second, then the car turned to the right, heading to Mulholland Drive, he guessed.

He moved his position from crouching to sitting, carefully positioning himself on a raised part of ground. Through the Yukon, he looked up at the house. This side, the place was in darkness, except for the light coming from behind the door through which the man had just left.

Leroy waited for five minutes: in this time, there was no activity. He returned to a crouch position and started to make his way towards the front of the house. As he reached a spot parallel with the corner, he paused again. He could hear voices.

He took a step back and positioned himself in some undergrowth. Two figures were standing at the main door chatting. He leaned slightly from behind the bush and adjusted the binoculars. He could clearly see the faces of the two men. One looked as if he was leaving; the other had his back to the open door.

He recognised one of the faces. Looking through the binoculars, a broad grin appeared on his face.

The man leaving walked across the gravel to another of the cars. As he did so, the other figure turned and went indoors. Leroy waited until the second man drove off, then slowly stood up.

He turned left to go back towards the pool, and started to move. Then froze again.

Through the night vision binoculars, he saw a figure, twenty feet away and also in the undergrowth, coming towards him.

CHAPTER FORTY-FIVE

LEROY HIT THE deck. Or, rather the soil behind a large bush. As his gloved hands touched the ground, it occurred to him how ironic it was that just before she died yesterday, Marisol was probably in the same position as he was now.

He remained in the kneeling position, not daring to move a muscle. Through the NV binoculars, he could see that the figure was not equipped as well as he was, although he - if it was a he - was holding a flashlight.

The figure was stepping slowly through the trees, moving the beam from the flashlight to and fro. It was not clear to Leroy if the figure was looking for something in particular, or just checking the grounds. Surely if he had unknowingly activated some alarm, there would have been more than one guy with a flashlight out searching.

With the black jacket, pants and boots, Leroy felt he was reasonably well camouflaged, and the beam was quite narrow. The Yukon and its headgear were black and covered most of his face, so Leroy lowered his head slightly and waited for the figure to pass by. He did, his feet no more than six inches away from where Leroy was kneeling. He clearly hadn't seen Leroy.

Leroy had positioned himself kneeling but facing the direction the figure had come from. He made no sound as he walked past, so without moving - something Leroy wanted to avoid doing for the time being - there was no way of knowing how far away he was. Leroy remained in that position for a full minute, which is a very long time if you are in an uncomfortable position and trying at all costs not to make a sound.

Leroy mouthed the seconds, and on sixty-one slowly inclined his head so he could get a view of where the figure was headed. The angle was not right, so he slowly shifted his body to the right. He froze as he heard a faint clicking sound. Not a twig or a branch, but a bone in his ankle clicking. He cursed silently and waited another half minute. No sign of the figure. He turned forty-five degrees and peered round the side of the bush. In his enhanced view of the darkened undergrowth, of this figure there was no sign. He stood up, stretched, and looked around again. Through the Yukon, the light at the side of the house bathed the parked cars in an eerie green light: now there were two vehicles left. To whom did they belong, Leroy thought, and what were the owners doing in there? A simple explanation was that this was some fancy whore house, but that Counsel to the Secretary was so evasive, that Leroy had a gut feeling there was more to it. And clearly Dwight Mason was up to his scrawny neck in it. Whatever *it* was.

He took a few steps in the direction the figure had gone, craning his neck to see as far as he could. There was no sign of him; not even the beams from the flashlight waving to and fro.

There was no sign of anything going on outside the house. The next logical step would be to get inside but Leroy was wary of doing this: he was on leave, not on official police duties, a private citizen, as Perez had stressed. If he was caught inside, he could be charged with all manner of misdemeanours; felonies too most likely, as the owners and occupants would probably have access to highly skilled lawyers who would argue that Leroy had a personal vendetta against Dwight Mason, and that he had entered the building to harm the man. He adjusted the Yukon headgear: the same lawyers would probably also argue that possession of the binoculars was an inchoate crime, as he was wearing them for the sole purpose of getting to Mason.

He was not sure what to do next. His plan was always to come here at night and to see what he could see. Not looking for anything specific; just to sniff around and see what came up. That was the way he often tackled cases at work, successfully too. Those known unknowns again.

He decided he would make a complete circuit of the house, then call it a night. He had already had confirmation that Mason was involved in whatever was going on here, which he was still convinced was connected to the three deaths the other night. All on the same night. But it was a matter of getting evidence. He had a record of the licence plates of the cars: officially he could do nothing about that until he returned to work, but Quinn was due back the next day, so he would call him and ask him to check the plates. Leroy had noticed that the car on the far end - one of the vehicles which had already left - had D.C. plates: that may or may not be significant, but it would be the first one he would ask Quinn to check.

He looked around again: no sign of any activity in the house, and no sign of the other figure. He started to resume his circumnavigation of the mansion.

As he reached the front corner, the foliage stopped. Or rather it continued away from the house. At the front of the building, there was a gravel roadway leading from the entrance gate, a large formal lawn, and more gravel leading back to the gate. Goddamit, he thought: gravel was the worst surface to cross silently. The roadway was around twelve feet across. He looked around again, took two steps back and leapt. He managed to cross the roadway only touching the surface once. Louder than if he had walked, but only one fraction of a second of sound. Once he landed, he lay face down on the lawn. After a few seconds, he looked up at the house. No reaction from there. Then looked around the grounds. No reaction there either: just darkness.

He slowly stood up, and walked, continuously looking around, across the lawn. As he approached the second gravel roadway, he broke into a run and leapt again. Again, he was able to cross with only one step on the gravel. Once he landed on the verge, he rolled over and lay still again, still looking around.

This side of the house was a mirror image of the other wing: the gravel extended around to the back; one car, a dark coloured Mercedes was parked here, at a one hundred and eighty degree angle from the house. Leroy knelt down and checked the tag. It was another DC plate.

He returned to the undergrowth and resumed his circuit. He took no more than five paces when he froze again. He had heard what he had dreaded most: the barking of a dog. He swung around, and in the green tinted view from the binoculars, saw the shape of a dog, on a lead, but dragging a man's form across the lawn. It had picked up his scent!

Just as he turned back to run, he saw the figure lean over and release the animal from its collar. Immediately, he turned and ran, as fast as he could. Once more, he was thankful for the Yukon, but he knew that this would not give him any advantage over the dog. He knew from numerous conversations with officers in the dog unit that dogs have evolved to see well in both bright and dim light, whereas humans do best in bright light. Apparently, nobody is sure how much better a dog sees in dim light, but one handler told him that dogs can see in light five times dimmer than humans. They have many adaptations for low-light vision, he had been told. A larger pupil lets in more light. The centre of the retina has more of the light-sensitive cells, which work better in dim light than colour-detecting cones. The light-sensitive compounds in the dog's retina respond to lower light levels, and the lens is located closer to the retina, making the image on the retina brighter.

But the dog's biggest advantage is called the tapetum, which is a mirror-like structure in the back of the eye which reflects light, giving the retina a second chance to register light that has entered the eye.

And then there was the question of speed. Leroy knew from medicals that he could sprint at about 12 miles per hour. However, that was in a straight line, without any obstructions: this was on uneven ground, and through trees and bushes. He calculated he was doing no more than seven or eight. He knew than the dogs in the canine unit could clock over thirty, and this animal would have the added benefit of soft ground to propel itself along. He had no chance: his only hope was that he had enough advantage and would reach a wall or fence before the dog reached him.

As he tried to figure out how long it would be before the dog caught up with him, he heard a deep growl behind, and felt two blows, one on each shoulder, as Sam Leroy and guard dog fell to the ground.

CHAPTER FORTY-SIX

THERE IS A difference between a guard dog and an attack dog. You want a guard dog to scare people away, not to scare you. Guard dogs are not generally trained to attack. Rather, a guard dog's task is to alert its owner to a stranger's presence, by barking or growling. Contrary to popular belief a guard dog does not make a good attack dog, and vice versa. Typically, small breeds are used as guard dogs.

Attack dogs are different. Police dogs are trained attack dogs. In recent times of war, dogs were trained as sentry guards, protecting troops from attack. They were also used as silent scouts, warning troops of the presence of enemies, reducing the likelihood of an ambush. Properly trained, an attack dog is loyal to its master, and totally obedient. It will not attack unless its owner is facing a threat or has commanded an attack. An attack dog is trained to bite on command, as well as to stop biting on command. Of course, some attack dogs are not properly trained. The most common breed of attack dog is the German Shepherd.

Leroy's training as a police officer had included how to deal with an attack by a dog. The first thing to remember is not to panic. The urban legend that dogs can sense fear has some truth. If you become agitated and scream, the dog may become more confident, or feel threatened. Neither is a good place to be. If a dog approaches, you should remain still, not waving arms and legs, which the dog could perceive as a threat. Leroy was also trained to avoid eye contact, as this could cause a dog to lunge. Never run away: this could awaken the dog's instinct to chase, and a dog could even outrun a man on a bicycle. If a dog persists, face it, and command it to back away, still without making eye contact. If the dog does lunge, fight back. A dog attack can be fatal, so you have to defend yourself. Hit or kick the dog in the nose, throat, or back of the head. Even in the genitals. Don't bother to hit it over the head: they have thick skulls, and this will make it angrier.

The training also advised if you can't escape from the dog's grasp, use your entire body weight on the animal. Dogs can't wrestle, and you will break their bones easily. If you can get on top of the dog, apply pressure to the throat or ribs.

All this went through Leroy's mind as he fell to the ground. He guessed from the size and weight the animal was a German Shepherd, a young adult. As he hit the deck, the animal went for his left arm and started gnawing at his jacket. Leroy had two objectives here: one was to get away from the dog for its own sake, the second was not to allow the dog to delay him so one of the guards or anybody else from the house was able to detain him. There was only one way. He managed to push himself up a few inches above the ground so he could reach inside his jacket with his right hand. He pulled out his Glock and fired. Instantly the dog made a high pitched yelp, and collapsed on the ground. Leroy leapt up, took one look at the dead animal, put the Glock back into its holster and began running again. As he ran his first few steps, he adjusted the Yukon's headgear as it had been dislodged by the fall.

He was now past the house, and running past the pool: only a few hundred yards to go. He felt pain from his left arm where the dog had bitten him, but there was no time to stop and check. As he ran he could hear voices shouting behind him in the distance. Clearly the alarm had been sounded; either by the dog's handler, or by the sound of his gun going off. For obvious reasons, LAPD officers are not provided with silencers for their service weapons.

He carried on running, through the green tinted undergrowth. Only fifty yards to go, he guessed. Then, about twenty feet ahead, a figure stepped into his line of sight. Leroy guessed it was the same person he had seen earlier on, the other side of the house, as he was carrying a small flashlight. Through the NV glasses, he could see this figure was dressed in not a dissimilar way to him: wearing black, or at least very dark clothing, and his face covered by a balaclava, a thin slit for eyes and nose.

The figure put up one hand as if requesting Leroy to stop. No way, he thought. He was running down a slight slope and must have been hitting ten miles per hour: even if he wanted to stop, he probably was going too fast to. He kept up the momentum, and ran straight at the other figure, barging him out of the way as he passed by.

Instead of at least staggering a few steps back as Leroy had expected, the figure almost held his ground. Leroy thought he heard the figure cry out something like, 'Hey'; then he felt him grab his arm - the arm the dog had bitten. Leroy winced: partly in pain and anger, he swung round and gave the figure a right hook to the chin. The figure recoiled, and while he was clearly preparing for a counter blow,

Leroy lashed out with his right foot and hit him on the left thigh. The figure cried out and collapsed to the ground. Leroy turned and carried on running. A few seconds later he reached the wire fence and climbed over. As the fence was razor wire, he climbed over carefully, but as quickly as he could. He snagged his pants on the wire, just below the groin, crying out in pain. Once over the fence, he found himself in the scrublands, but he carried on running, albeit with a slight limp. He was safe from any more dogs now, but there might be human guards who felt like following him. He carried on running: once he was back in the car, he could check out his wounds, although they did not feel serious.

He clambered up a small slope, then half ran, half slid, back down to the road where he had left the car. He caught hold of a bush to stop as he got to the pavement.

Then a feeling of panic overtook him: the car had gone.

CHAPTER FORTY-SEVEN

LEROY ADJUSTED HIS headgear; during his descent down the slope, it had moved slightly. He looked over at the houses across the street. The houses across from which he had parked were single storey; this one directly opposite had a second floor. As did the next. On the other side, the house was of a modern, almost square design, not as the others in the street. Leroy realised what had happened: in his run across the scrubland he had followed a different route to his way to the house. He looked down the street, adjusting the focal length of his binoculars. In the distance, parked on the left hand side of the road, was the shape of a car. There was the Taurus. Breathing a sigh of relief he stepped back into the undergrowth and, at a slow pace, walked towards his car, looking around all the time for any sign of light or movement from the houses opposite. He definitely didn't want to disturb the dog in the house opposite the car. With much relief he got to his car.

He lifted his hands up to the Yukon to release the headgear, but out of the corner of one eye he picked up headlights in the distance. Immediately, he dove to the ground, behind the Taurus. Assisted by the NV binoculars, he could make out the lights get brighter and larger as the car approached. A worse case scenario would be for this to be a patrol car: being found by two fellow officers in a situation like this, and having the embarrassment of explaining to the watch commander and Lieutenant Perez what he was up to was the last thing he wanted. If it was a patrol car, it would probably slow down as it got nearer. Otherwise, it would drive straight past.

'Shit,' he whispered as the car began to slow down. He rose slightly to prepare for his encounter with the officers. The patrol car had slowed to a crawl, and by the angle of the headlight beams, he could see it was pulling to the left. It was going to stop behind the Taurus.

He took a deep breath, but then the red lights on the car roof began to flash, and it pulled away. It must have reached Mulholland when he heard the siren start. He sat back down on the grass and breathed out with relief. Pulled off his NV apparatus, and ran his hand through his wet hair. He was quite warm, and sweating profusely.

Leroy climbed into the car, tossed the Yukon onto the passenger seat. Started the engine, and drove away. A couple of hundred yards up there was a side street, so he turned the car around then, not wishing to set off anybody's alarm by using their driveway. Within minutes, he was back on Mulholland Drive, heading home.

During the last part of the journey, traffic had started to pick up: the morning's rush hour was beginning, and as he walked from the car to his building entrance, he could see the beginning of the sunrise over the city. He checked his watch: it was 6:28. He hadn't realised how long he had been out. Once in his apartment, he poured the cold coffee from his thermos. He had only drunk a little of it: the adrenalin must have kept him going.

Leroy slowly made his way into the bedroom. Sitting on the bed, he rubbed his chin; he could hear his hand running over twenty-four hours' stubble. Lay back, resting his head on his pillow. He slowly closed his eyes. The effect of the adrenalin had worn off.

CHAPTER FORTY-EIGHT

WHEN LEROY AWOKE, it was almost two in the afternoon. He rubbed his eyes, squinted as he tried to focus on the bedroom wall opposite as the afternoon sun was streaming into his bedroom. When he had got home the previous night - or early that morning, to be precise - he had not bothered to draw the blinds. He put his hand to his chin, and heard a scratching sound as he did so. He got off the bed and looked in the mirror: his chin was dark with two days' growth. Lifted one arm and sniffed his pit, then pulled a face. He needed a shower, and quickly.

After twenty minutes in the shower, he stood naked in front of his wash basin and shaved. He had always preferred a wet shave: an electric shaver was fine for everyday use, particularly when he was in a hurry, which he normally was;

but whenever he had the time, he would use an old-fashioned razor. Once done, he rubbed his chin again and smiled: as smooth as a baby's ass. He applied some aftershave and deodorant, and returned to his bedroom. Still naked, he sat back on the bed and picked up his phone. He had three missing calls: two from Joanna and one from Ray Quinn. They had both called just after nine. He had put the phone to silent before he went out the previous night, and was too tired when he got back to remember to change this. In any case, he was probably in too deep a sleep to hear even if it had rung.

He also had one text message, and that was from Joanna, received 09:12, just after she had called. *Hey Sam*, it read, *hope ur ok. Call me. J x*. She had rung again at 12:16, this time leaving a voicemail. He listened: she was just getting concerned that she hadn't heard from him. Please would he call or sms as soon as he got this message. He tabbed down to her name in his contacts list, and was about to dial, then realised she would be teaching, so sent her a quick message: *Hey, yes am ok, was working last nite @ short notice call u 2nite. S x*. Within seconds, he got a reply: *ok cu x*. While she was in a classroom, she was not allowed personal calls except in an emergency, but could get away with text messages.

The voicemail from Quinn was of a similar theme. 'Hey Sam, it's Ray. I'm back in today, but I see you're not. You want to give me a call - let me know what's going on?' Leroy returned Quinn's call, only to get voicemail as well. He left a message to the effect that there was a lot to tell him and could he call back.

He got dressed and went into the kitchen to make coffee. It was then he realised how hungry he was: in the last twenty-four hours he had only eaten a mediocre burrito. He looked around his kitchen: he couldn't be bothered to cook or prepare anything, and it would take too long, anyway.

Café 50s on Santa Monica Boulevard was probably

Leroy's favourite local eating place, somewhere he had regularly frequented for many years. Located on the historic Route 66, it was popular with locals and tourists, selling merchandise like vintage postcards and Route 66 pins. When Leroy first moved to LA, he collected all the merchandise, but once it was no longer a novelty, he gave it to his nephew back in New York for a Christmas present.

There were plenty of empty tables when he arrived, so, after purchasing a newspaper outside, he made his way to a booth, and studied the menu. As it was his first meal of the day, he opted for a breakfast, served all day; a *3+3+3*: eggs, pancakes and link sausage. He added potatoes and coffee.

As he munched through the breakfast, he scanned the newspaper to see if there were any reports on the John Does. There were none; after all, they were now closed cases, but there was always the chance that it had happened again. Not finding anything, Leroy turned to the Politics section. Not a section he normally went to, but he noticed there was a report of a speech Secretary of Defence Davison had made, this time about the need to curb healthcare costs. Leroy failed to understand how that came within Davison's portfolio, and merely grunted and turned the page.

On the next page he found an article about how Texas, the nation's most active death penalty state, was running out of pentobarbital, its execution drug. The problem had arisen, the article said, because some drug suppliers, especially those based in Europe, had barred the use of their drugs for executions either, as a spokesman for one of the companies said, 'we manufacture drugs to prolong life, not to end it', or were now refusing to sell or manufacture drugs for use in executions on account of pressure from death-penalty opponents. Leroy skimmed through the entire article, drank more coffee, then turned to the cartoons.

Being a regular, he normally got an extra refill of coffee and as the server poured more coffee into his *Café 50s* mug, he sat back and began to ponder on what his next move should be.

First would be to make sure he and Joanna got hold of each other.

Second, speak to Quinn. Update him on the story so far and see if there had been any developments while he had been off. In particular, he would get Quinn to check those licence plate numbers. He was particularly interested in those with DC plates.

He also wanted to visit the site where Domingo was murdered, not out of a morbid desire to pay his respects where she died, but he was convinced her murder was connected somehow with the John Does. If he was investigating the case himself, the first port of call would be the crime scene, even though now it would have been cleaned up. That was just the way he worked.

He settled his bill, walked round to the parking lot, then headed off to Erwin Street. Erwin Street was a residential street, filled with a mixture of houses and condominiums. Beginning a few hundred yards from the *Arroyo Calabasas*, the Calabasas Creek, a seven mile tributary of the Los Angeles River, the street pointed eastwards. After passing under State Route 27, the residential buildings slowly gave way to light industry, a couple of gas stations and car dealers, and a church. Enadia Street, the place where the shooting occurred, was some ten blocks further on from the 27 overpass.

Leroy briefly waited for a gap in traffic, then turned the Taurus left to go into Enadia. On one corner of this dead-end street was a small factory building, long since derelict. A small store stood on the other corner, its windows plastered with posters advertising discounts off its various items.

The street itself was only a hundred yards or so long. The factory building stretched down the entire length; at the end of the street was the back wall of the building facing the next street. There was a small window about ten feet above

263

the pavement, barred and filthy. On the other side of the street, there was a wall, six feet high, a roll of barbed wire on the top. Next was a shop premises, closed and boarded up, then the store on the corner.

Leroy turned the car round so it was facing Erwin Street, needing to reverse and forward five times, owing to narrowness of the street, and on one kerb were the smashed remains of a brown beer bottle. He parked the car outside the derelict shop, and looked around. There, right under that small skylight, was where Domingo and her partner were gunned down. But how? Why?

He walked up to the corner store; a tinny bell rang as he opened the door. The shop was empty of customers; a small Hispanic looking woman stood behind the counter. '*Hola,*' she said.

'Hello,' replied Leroy, looking around. She appeared nervous. Even though he was a private citizen at this time, he showed her his identification. Seeing this, she appeared more relaxed. Smiling he stepped over to the counter. 'I'd like to ask you a couple of questions.'

'*Sí.*'

'Are you in here every day?'

'*Qué?*'

Leroy paused a moment, then asked, '*Trabajas aquí todos los días?*'

She nodded eagerly. '*Sí, señor.*'

Leroy spoke slowly, searching for the right words. '*Dos agentes de policía fueron asesinados por ahí por otro día.*'

She shrugged and shook her head. '*No, no lo sé.*'

Leroy tutted, then, '*Fuera di aquí, un tiroteo.*'

'*No, lo siento, señor.*'

This was a waste of time. '*Muy bien, gracias,*' Leroy said, and left the shop. Went back to the Taurus, leaned on the hood and scratched his head. Maybe he should come back with an officer who could speak Spanish better than he could.

Like Domingo.

He was sure, though, that the officers from the Major Crimes Division would arrange for a translator; they probably had already.

He stepped away from his car and walked down to the end of the street. Stood where Domingo's patrol car would have been. He stood and tried to visualise the scene. Domingo would probably have been driving, so she would have been sitting on the left. They both died from one shot to the head, so the shooter must have been standing further to the left. He had not had sight of the official report, so had no idea of the range involved, or whether any gunshot residue had been found. If there had, then the shooter would have been up close; if not, then further away, but the factory wall was fifteen, twenty feet away. If he was that far away, then he must have been a skilled marksman, as two shots of that accuracy would have been difficult. And if he was closer, why did Domingo and Connor let him get that close?

He took two steps back, and looked around again, scratching his smooth chin. Then his thoughts were interrupted by a voice.

'What the hell are you doing here?'

CHAPTER FORTY-NINE

LEROY SPUN ROUND.

'Well, you're a sight for sore eyes,' he said, taking off his sunglasses. He went up and shook Ray Quinn's hand. 'I might ask you the same question. Where's your car, by the way?'

His partner inclined his head towards the store. 'Just around the corner. I wanted to surprise you.'

'You certainly did that. When did you get back to work?'

'First day back today. I got in start of shift, expecting to find you. Then I heard you been taken vacation time suddenly, away for a week, just like that. The station house is buzzing with speculation as to what's going on. So I rang you straightaway.'

'Yeah, I saw you'd rung. Had my cell on silent.'

'So what is going on, Sam? *Are* you on vacation? If you are, what are you doing here? This is where Domingo and Connor were killed, isn't it?'

'To answer those questions in order,' Leroy said, walking back down to the end of the street, 'yes, I am on vacation.' He paused. 'You remember, at your wedding, I had to go to a crime scene?'

'Er – yes, just about.'

'Well, I'll give you the short version now. If you're free for a drink later,' - Quinn nodded - 'I'll give you the full picture. But for now: that night, there were three John Does brought in. All with the same COD.'

'Which was?'

'A massive ingestion of drugs. Recreational drugs.'

'All the same?'

'You got it. Domingo had a similar case, so we kind of partnered up. You were away, and Connor had something on - I forget what it was. But after a day or so, we got word from Perez that the verdicts were death by misadventure, and the cases were closed.'

Quinn looked puzzled. 'But even if that was the case, somebody had supplied the stuff.'

Leroy shrugged. 'All about priorities, apparently. Would cost too much, and to quote the lieutenant, or Captain Patterson, I suspect, there are more pressing matters to investigate.'

'Sam, that's bullshit.'

'I know that. You know that. Domingo knew that.'

'Is that why the lieutenant put you on vacation?'

'I don't know. You know how difficult he is to read. I kept banging on about it, so it might have been a case of fuck off for a week, I'm sick of listening to you, or go on vacation, Sam, what you do in your own time is your affair, wink, wink.' He paused a second. 'How did you know I'd be here, anyway?'

Quinn laughed. 'The lieutenant told me you'd gone on vacation, I'd heard talk of your views on the John Does. I kind of guessed what you'd be up to. And yes, it seems likely that it wasn't a coincidence that Domingo gets killed – lucky you weren't the first. Perez put me on some admin for the next few days, so as you didn't answer my call, I thought I'd come and find you. I had a look outside *Whiteleaf* but there was no sign.'

'*Whiteleaf*?' queried Leroy.

'The house on Mulholland you visited with Domingo.'

'Oh. Never knew it had a name.'

'Hm. So anyway, I know how you work, so I tried here, in the absence of a call back from you.' Quinn looked around the dead-end street. 'So you think the two of you were on to something, and that's what got her killed?'

Leroy looked around too, and then up at the sky as an airplane flew overhead. 'I'd take book on it.'

'Sam, if you're right, you could be next,' said Quinn.

'The thought had occurred to me. Look,' Leroy said, turning to face his partner, who was standing just where Domingo's car would have been. 'Her car was there, right where you are. Both she and Connor took one bullet here,' - he put his forefinger on his forehead – 'so I figure the shooter was either right up close, or fired from around here.'

'But must have been some shot,' added Quinn, 'to fire from over there with that accuracy.'

'And in such a short space of time,' Leroy said. 'It would have taken two seconds for one of them to draw their weapon.'

'So our marksman would have had to have gotten off two rounds in less than that time. Sam, our best guys couldn't do that.'

'I don't know of anybody who could. So that means the shooter was up close. But there was no way Domingo and Connor would have let an armed man - let's assume it was a man, one man, for now - get that close. They were both sitting in the front of their car.'

'Unless they knew the shooter,' said Quinn.

'Mm?'

'They would let him get that close if they knew him. Had no reason to be concerned, even if he was armed.'

Leroy took a step back and scratched the back of his head. 'Yeah, guess so.' Then something hit him. He looked up Quinn. 'My God, Ray; you realise what that means?'

Quinn returned Leroy's stare, then finished his partner's sentence. 'Sam, they were shot by another cop.'

CHAPTER FIFTY

QUINN SLID A beer over to Leroy's side of the table. A few hours earlier, after they had come to their conclusion about Domingo's killers, they agreed their next steps.

'Look,' Leroy said. 'We need to keep this between ourselves. I certainly didn't shoot them, and neither did you, so I guess for now we can only trust each other. What time do you have to be back at the station house?'

Quinn checked his watch. 'As soon as, I guess. Before I'm missed. You want to meet up in Martha's after the shift finishes?'

'Best not there; you never know who'll see us. Do you know The Daily Pint? It's on Pico.'

'Yeah, I know it. See you there about six?'

'Fine. There's one more thing.' He gave Quinn a slip of

paper. 'Could you get these licence numbers checked out? They're off the cars I found at *Whiteleaf* last night.'

'Last night?' Quinn frowned and looked at the numbers on the paper.

'Long story. Fill you in later. I'm particularly interested in those two there.' He tapped the paper with his finger.

'DC plates?'

'You got that right.'

When they met up later, the first thing Quinn did was slide the list of numbers over to his partner. Leroy read the notes Quinn had made.

'I knew it,' he said. 'I damn well knew it.'

'Knew what? Obviously I know who George Davison is, although I've no idea why his car is parked outside a house in LA, but who's Dwight G Mason?'

'Let me tell you the whole story,' said Leroy. He sat back, and related the whole sequence of events, right from the Quinn's wedding night.

Quinn sat back, and listened, occasionally softly whistling at what Leroy was saying. When Leroy had finished, Quinn asked, 'So you think Davison and Mason are involved?'

'To be honest, I can't say for Davison. I've no evidence of him being involved at all. I've never even seen him. Just because he owns the place, it's not evidence that he's personally involved. As for Mason…'

'Who is the guy, anyway? And why do you think he's involved? And involved in what, anyway?'

'Dwight Mason is Secretary Davison's private counsel, and is the most obsequious, smarmy, condescending bastard I've ever met.'

'You're not a fan, then?' asked Quinn, deadpan.

'No, absolutely. Apart from him lying to us when Domingo and I went to the house, I saw him there the other night. He was kind of hosting things.'

'I get it. But hosting what?'

'Don't know for sure, but we're talking hookers and drugs; so go figure.'

'What are you going to do tomorrow, then? I'd better stay at my desk; don't want to arouse any suspicions.'

'Not sure. I might go over to the house in daylight, see if I can see anybody going in or out. Then there's those other names on this list. I think I'll pay them a call, see what I can get from them.'

'Be careful, Sam. Remember you're on vacation.'

'I will. As the lieutenant told me, I'm just a private citizen right now. But I might be able to bullshit something out of them. If they're men with families, I might be able to… you know.'

'Okay, Sam: if you need anything, let me know. And keep me in the loop, won't you?' He emptied his glass. 'Another?' he asked.

'Sure, go ahead.' Leroy studied the list again while Quinn went to the bar. He frowned: apart from Davison and Mason, the names meant nothing to him.

Shortly, Quinn returned. He passed Leroy his beer and sat down. 'So,' he said, sipping from his own glass, 'anything you want to tell me?'

Leroy frowned. 'Say what?'

'There's talk around the station house that you've gotten yourself a lady friend.' Quinn grinned slightly as he spoke.

'Oh, is there?' Leroy took another mouthful of beer.

'Come on, then. Out with it,' Quinn persisted.

Leroy shook his head as if in exasperation and took another sip. 'Nothing to tell, really. For once, the gossip's right. I've only known her a short while, couple of weeks, maybe less.'

'What's her name? How'd you guys meet?'

'Her name's Joanna. Joanna Moore. She's a school

teacher.'

'Oh yeah?'

'That's right. For young kids. Fourth graders, she said. She works somewhere in Culver City. Did tell me the name of the school, but…'

'So, tell me how you met. Where's she from?'

'San Fran originally, but she has an apartment in Venice. Not far from me, as it happens.'

Quinn took some more beer. 'Go on.'

'I'd just gotten home one night. It was quite late – about eleven, I think. Had just parked outside my place when I heard some screaming coming from a few blocks away, from the direction of the ocean.'

'Still night, then?'

'It was. Anyhow, I ran in the direction of the commotion, and found her in the process of being mugged. Two guys. I cuffed them and called for a patrol car. She told me she didn't live far, so I walked her home.'

'Very gallant, Detective Leroy.'

'Just as well I did. She passed out just as we got to her building. I saw her indoors, then left. Next morning, she called me to say thanks and invited me round to dinner. Her way of showing her appreciation, I guess.'

'And how much appreciation did she show?'

'Nothing like that. I was only there for a couple of hours.'

'No breakfast, then?' Quinn smirked.

Leroy turned to his beer. 'Shit, that was what Domingo used to say.'

'Jeez. Sorry, Sam. I had no idea.'

Leroy shook his head, took some more beer, and continued. 'She's a vegetarian, so what we had wasn't what I'm used to. She served hot baked vegetarian chimichangas.'

'Burritos, I like, but not sure about vegetarian. What was in it?'

Leroy shrugged. 'She said it contained mushrooms, chillies, refried beans.'

Quinn pulled a face.

'No,' said Leroy. 'It was okay.' He laughed. 'Surprisingly enough. Cheesecake afterwards.'

'That's the only time you've seen her?'

'Couple of times since.'

'You guys…?' Quinn raised his eyebrows.

'The day Domingo and Connor were killed. We had already arranged to meet up; this time go out for a meal, maybe a movie at the AMC or something. I said I would pick her up. When I did, we started chatting some more at her apartment. I don't know, Ray – it was one of those nights when I didn't want to be alone.'

Quinn nodded. 'You seeing her again, I guess?'

'Sure. Maybe later tonight. Will certainly speak to her. But definitely next weekend. We're planning on going away somewhere for Saturday night. Catalina, maybe.'

His partner nodded again. 'Should be good. Better than mine.'

'Oh? How so?'

'Holly wants us to spend the weekend at the Meriwether family residence. Her old man's birthday.'

Leroy laughed and raised his glass. 'I'll take Catalina.'

CHAPTER FIFTY-ONE

ON HIS WAY home, Leroy made a detour to Joanna's apartment.

'My God, Sam,' she said. 'You look like shit. What's going on?'

'Nice to see you, too.' Leroy kissed her on the cheek and slid past her into her apartment. He passed a mirror and stopped to check his reflection. She was right. He thought that by having a really close shave a few hours earlier, the effects of many hours' sleep deprivation would not show. He was wrong. He had the beginnings of shadow on his chin, but he looked pale, and he looked dark around the eyes. 'Hm,' he said. 'See what you mean.'

'Sorry, baby; that wasn't a very nice greeting.' She embraced him and they kissed again, this time on the lips.

'Anything I can do?' she asked, as their mouths parted.

He looked around her apartment. The floor, the table, and the sofa were covered with dozens of sheets of paper, neatly arranged in piles, each pile a different colour. He was certain if he sneezed, or if there was a sudden gust of wind, the place would be in complete disarray.

'It looks like your hands are full already,' he replied.

'Test papers,' Joanna explained. 'Each year has a different colour. As I think I told you already, a teacher's day doesn't finish when the kids go home.'

'Yes, I think you mentioned that,' said Leroy, not without irony.

'I could use a break,' said Joanna. 'You want a coffee?'

'Wouldn't say no. Want me to get it?'

'You sit your ass down, Detective. I'll get it.'

He found a space between a pile of buff paper and salmon paper and sat down.

'You eaten yet?' Joanna called out from the kitchen.

'Yes, I have, thanks.'

Joanna joined him shortly, passing him his coffee. She sat down cross-legged on the floor with her cup, then opened a bag of potato chips.

'You have to do this sort of thing every night?' he asked, indicating to the numerous coloured piles.

She shook her head. 'This is a one off. These are all the test papers for each year, and going back five years. So thirty sets of test papers. They were in a mess at school, you know – not filed in any order, that sort of thing, so I said I'd get them sorted out. Prefer to do it here than stay late at work.'

Leroy sipped some coffee and closed his eyes. He had to make an effort to open them again.

'You look bushed,' she said. 'So what's going on? I assume something's up at work. You got my messages, then.'

'Yeah, yeah I did.' He then related to her about his

vacation time, the visit to *Whiteleaf*, and his meeting with Quinn.

'My God, Sam; so you were up all night?'

'More or less, yes.'

'So you think that the Secretary is involved?'

'Somehow, yes.'

'You said that your boss told you that those cases had been considered closed at the highest level, or something?'

'Er – yeah, he said something like that. What are you getting at?'

'Well, if you're right and he is involved, then maybe he could have influenced that decision. You said there was enough evidence to proceed with the cases.'

Leroy rubbed his eyes and suppressed a yawn. 'I guess that's possible; I hadn't really considered that. What I don't get about Davison, though, is: he comes from Arizona - Flagstaff - and began his political career there. Then moved to DC when higher office beckoned.'

Joanna nodded, sipping her coffee.

'So I've been trying to figure out the LA connection. Why would a guy who's spent all his life in Arizona or Washington either own or lease a house over here? It's not like it's by the beach or anything.'

Joanna frowned in thought. 'I think there's a family connection.'

'No, it's not that. His parents are both probably dead by now, and he was an only child.'

'I'm not sure about that,' said Joanna. 'Couple of years back, the kids in the 8th grade I think it was had to research and prepare a paper on major government figures. You know, the guys who run our country, that sort of thing.' She looked around the apartment. 'I don't think I have a copy here. But I'm sure that they said that he had relatives here.'

'What sort of relatives?'

She shook her head. 'Can't remember. Sorry. In any case, why do you think he was an only child?'

He laughed. 'The other morning, I went to the library and Googled him.'

Joanna nodded her head, smiling. 'Sam, when I was at college, one of our professors said that information technology and the internet are wonderful tools, but beware of the temptation to confuse proper research with Google. Just because something's on the internet, it doesn't mean it's true.'

'Yes, I know that. So there might be a connection after all. I'll check it out in the morning.' He yawned and rubbed his eyes again.

'Is your car out front?' she asked.

'Yes, why?'

'Then leave it there. There's no way you can drive in the state you're in.'

'I'll be okay. It's only -'

'A short drive, but if that was me sitting there half asleep, would you let me drive home?'

He smiled and shrugged his shoulders. 'No.'

'Then go in there are get some sleep. I won't disturb you.'

He sighed. 'Okay, I'll go quietly.' He laboriously got up off the sofa and stepped over the stacks of paper and headed for the bedroom. As he passed Joanna, he brushed the top of her head with one hand. Once in her bedroom, he sat on bed, took off his shoes, and lay down.

Through half-closed eyes, he saw Joanna peep into the room, then close the door, leaving him to sleep.

Which he did.

He awoke later. It was dark. He was still sleepy but the four or five beers he had had with Quinn a few hours earlier had worked their way to his bladder. He sat up, allowing his eyes to adjust to the darkness. It took him a few seconds to figure out where he was. He looked over his shoulder, and saw Joanna's form under the sheet, sleeping soundly. He stood up and shakily made his way to her bathroom. When he returned, he saw that she had changed position and now had her back to him. Standing over her, he checked the time. It was 2:55. He briefly contemplated quietly leaving and going home, but thought again. Then undressed and joined her under the sheet. He lay down close to her, the position of his body the same as hers. He put his arm round her. She moved around a little, her body pressing against his. He settled down to go back to sleep. He snuggled closer to Joanna. This felt good.

This is what kids call spooning, he thought, before falling asleep again.

'Eggs?'

Sam Leroy opened one eye, and tried to focus on the woman standing over him. It was daylight, and the sunlight was strong.

'Say what?'

'Do you want eggs? And if you do, are they scrambled, fried, poached…?'

He rubbed his face and sat up. 'Er – scrambled would be good.'

'Or French Toast?'

'Yes, yes. French Toast.'

'Coming up. Coffee's there.'

'Oh, thanks. What time is it?'

'Seven,' Joanna replied, on her way out of the bedroom. 'Get your ass in gear, Detective; I need to leave in thirty minutes.'

'As you obviously won't be ready to leave at seven thirty,' Joanna said, as Leroy munched on a strip of bacon, 'I'll leave you to take a shower and go when you're ready.'

'Thanks. I'll clean up here before I go.'

'You don't need to, Sam.'

'I will.'

'You going straight home when you're done here?'

'Thought I would. Get some clean clothes on.'

'Then what?' Joanna asked, as she looked in the mirror to apply some lipstick.

'Just have a couple of people to see. Then catch up with Ray.'

'Your partner?'

'U-huh.'

'Will I get to meet him one day?'

'I guess so. His wife - Holly – will certainly want to meet you.'

'Look forward to that.' She leaned over to kiss him. 'Have to go now, baby. Have a good day. Speak to you later.'

'Sure,' he said, watching her walk to the door.

'Oh, by the way,' she said, stopping and turning round. 'I was right about Davison. He does have a sister. I found that paper the 8th graders did while you were asleep. I left it there on the sofa. Have a look.'

'Okay, I will. Thanks.'

After she closed the door, he stepped over to the sofa and picked up a small file. It comprised half a dozen sheets of letter-size paper, neatly bound together. He sat back down at the table and opened it. Joanna had left a post-it note on the page containing Secretary Davison's details. In the personal details section, it mentioned a sister. Nothing out of the ordinary, he thought - like she said last night, just because something is on the internet is no guarantee it is correct – until he saw the sister's name: Emma.

Emma. Emma.

He scratched his temple, racking his brains. He didn't know anyone called Emma, but he was sure he had heard the name recently.

But where the hell had he heard it?

CHAPTER FIFTY-TWO

LEROY DECIDED HE would shower at his own apartment. There was no Joanna there to shower with him, and in any case, he preferred his own: the water was faster and the temperature easier to control. He made himself more coffee, dressed in the previous day's clothes, and walked back to his own place, taking with him the file Joanna had left out for him.

Once home, he showered and shaved, dressed, fixed himself some more eggs and more coffee, and sat down with the file. While he was in the shower, he remembered where he had heard the name Emma recently: when he and Domingo visited Lance Riley's workplace in Century City, they were met with the office manager. Her name was Emma. Emma Kennedy. Could she be Davison's sister? He recalled that there were no bands on her left hand, so she appeared unmarried. So, why Kennedy, not Davison? Also, unless she looked remarkable well for her age, she seemed too young to be the Secretary's sister. But there had always been something about her that didn't quite ring true.

He swung round and switched on his laptop. While he waited for it to boot up, he rang Quinn. Much to his surprise, his partner answered immediately.

'Hey there, big boy,' came Quinn's cheerful voice. 'How you doin'? Where you calling from today?'

Leroy laughed. 'Still at home. Was just about to leave to see those other guys on that list. Was just wondering if you knew much about Davison.'

'About him personally, you mean?'

'U-huh. In particular about his family.'

A moment's pause. 'As far as I know, he's a pretty normal family life. Married a dozen years or so, a couple of sons.'

'No,' said Leroy. 'I was thinking siblings.'

'Siblings? Don't know, off hand. I'm sure there's something on the internet; you want me to -?'

'No, it's okay; I'm online here now. I'll search.'

'Sure. What you getting at, Sam?'

'It's something that came up last night. I was trying to figure out what connection Davison has with out here.'

'Yeah, go on.'

'It turns out that he had family out here. A sister. She's called Emma.'

'And?'

'One of the John Does worked in an office in Century City. Domingo and I went to visit the place early on in the investigation, and the person in charge there, the office manager, was a woman called Emma Kennedy.'

'And?' repeated Quinn.

'It's just a theory, I know, but when we visited the offices, she seemed a tad obstructive.'

'Obstructive? How so? Don't tell me, Sam: somehow she managed to piss you off, and so she's your number one suspect. Been here before, haven't we?'

'Maybe so. Yes, she did piss me off somehow; I think it was her superior attitude. But there was one tangible thing. We were asking about sites the vic might have been visiting.'

'You mean like that dating place? Dates 4 you or something?'

'Yeah. He'd wiped the search history on his device. I asked her if there was any way we could retrieve what he had deleted. I'm no computer geek, Ray, as you know, but I'm sure I had read that a computer retains everything, even though it's been deleted.'

'That's right; it does.'

'Well, we asked her that, and she said it was possible. Offered to check the device for us.'

'Go on.'

'She's the manager of an office in an IT firm, for Christ's sake. Surely she'd know everything would be retained? It's on the hard drive, or something, wouldn't it?'

'It would. So, where are you going with this, Sam?'

'Not quite certain, yet. Look, a few days back I passed the guy's laptop over to the CCU to get it checked out. Has anything come back from them?'

'CCU. Hold on.' There was a short pause. 'Sam, there is something. I guess so, anyway. It's a laptop, sealed up. Hold on.'

While he waited, Leroy typed into his search bar: *George Davison family*. There were 1.7 million results. He started tabbing down.

'Sam, you still there?' Quinn asked.

'Yeah, still here.'

'Well, the CCU retrieved the last three months' searches.'

'Great. Anything of any interest?'

'Well, out of the last fifty or so, there were at least one, two, three, four….ten visits to arrangeadate.com.'

'That's the place,' Leroy exclaimed.

'Okay; well, he was a regular visitor.'

'I guessed as much. So - he was a visitor to the site, met up with someone -'

'And ended up dead,' said Quinn.

'Yeah. Full of drugs.'

'So,' Quinn went on, 'he used that site, deleted it from the search history to cover his tracks, as it were.'

'And Emma Kennedy didn't want us to retrieve that information from the hard drive. '

'You said she offered to check it out for you?'

'She did. And you can bet your ass she'd come back and say, "Sorry, Detective, we can't find anything."'

'So - next steps? Anything you want me to do?'

'Not sure if there's anything you can at this time, but I'll call you if there is. Keep you in the loop.'

'Sure. You going to see Kennedy, then?'

'Thought I'd start with her, yes. See what I can stir up.'

'Okay, but take care, Sam.'

'I will. Call you later.'

'Yeah, speak to… hold on, Sam; there's something that might be of interest.'

'What's that?'

'I came across a report last night. It was a guy who was picked up the other night at the Blue Line stop at Florence and Graham. He was caught carrying out a scam with vehicles in the parking lot. When he was questioned, he gave the officers some story about a van pulling up, a guy falling out and puking up in the lot.'

'Right…'

'I'm wondering, it seemed from the kid's story that the guy was thrown from the van. What if he was pumped full of drugs like the others, but survived somehow. A smaller dose, maybe. He would have thrown up, wouldn't he?'

'It's possible, I guess.'

'You want to speak to the kid? He's been released, but we have his address.'

'Did he get the van's licence number?'

'No. Just heard the other guy puke up.'

'Has the other guy's body been found?'

'No, not as far as we can tell.'

'So he might still be alive. It's worth a shot. I don't think it's worth speaking to the kid, but a sample of that vomit might be useful, if it's still there. It's not rained for a while, so there might still be traces there. Maybe we could get a match to the stuff we found in the others. If you can, take a look at any CCTV for that area; see if you can see where he went. You might also get a shot of the vehicle he arrived in; maybe get a plate number. Anyway, you've got your day job, Ray; once I've spoke to Ms Kennedy, I'll call the hospitals nearest to that part of town and see if they treated the guy.'

'Sounds a plan. Will be in touch.'

'By the way: Major Crimes are going to be investigating Domingo's shooting. Any word on how it's going?'

'Not really. Only that a couple of detectives are around. Have they contacted you yet?'

'No, nothing.'

'That's odd. I would have thought you'd be one of the first they would want to speak to.'

'Yeah, so would I. Anyway, I'll speak to you later. What cases you dealing with by the way?'

'It's a stabbing at Grand Central Market. In fact, Sam, I think -'

'I did. Good luck with that.'

As Leroy hung up, he clicked on an entry entitled *Secretary of Defence George Davison spends Christmas in California.* The article itself was from a DC newspaper. At the start of the text was a photograph of the Secretary and his own family.

And his sister, Emma Kennedy.

At the end of the article, there was a link to *Family History*. He clicked on that.

'That explains it,' he muttered as he read that she was in fact his half sister. His own father died when he was fifteen years old. His mother had remarried, and had a daughter with her second husband. Leroy frowned: but that differed from the official online biography he had read previously. Was Davison trying to airbrush part of his life out of the public domain? It was just as Joanna had said: just because something's on the internet, it doesn't mean it's true.

CHAPTER FIFTY-THREE

BY NOW, LEROY knew the way to the Century City office. He parked the Taurus in the same spot he and Domingo had used previously. He walked past the sign for Culver Technologies and called the elevator.

At the sixth floor, he got out and walked down the hall to Emma Kennedy's office. The frosted glass door was closed, but he could see two silhouettes sitting either side of her desk. Surprised nobody had approached him, he knocked on the door and opened it.

A wide-eyed Emma Kennedy was sitting behind her desk; opposite was the other employee they saw at their last visit.

'Detective Leroy,' she said, forcing a smile. 'This is a surprise. Give us a moment, Rolando, would you?'

Rolando stood up. 'Sure thing, Emma.' He turned and left, nodding to Leroy as he passed him.

'How can I help you, Detective?' she asked. 'I thought we were done.'

'Just a couple more questions. Concerning Lance Riley's laptop. You might recall we were interested in the websites he visited before he died.'

'Yes, I do.'

'And that he had deleted his search history. Maybe to cover his tracks; he was in a relationship, you know.'

She adjusted her jacket and shifted some papers on her desk. 'I know that. What does this have to do with us here?'

'You very kindly offered to check out his laptop for us. You know, to see if the addresses he had deleted could be retrieved.'

'That's right, I did.'

'Well, my colleagues at the Computer Crimes Unit checked his hard drive and found his last three months' history.'

'And where did he visit?'

'That's neither here nor there. What I'm interested in, Ms Kennedy, is how you appeared to imply that the history might not be retrievable, when in fact, the hard disk retains everything.'

She shrugged. 'Oh, I didn't know,' she replied nonchalantly.

'Come on, Ms Kennedy. This is an IT company, isn't it? And you're the office manager, aren't you? Are you telling me-?'

'I'm not telling you anything, Detective,' she replied angrily, rising from her chair. 'Now leave my office.'

Leroy said nothing; did not move.

'I said leave this office,' she repeated, becoming angrier. 'Why are you here anyway? You've no right to be here! The case is closed, and you're on vacation!'

CHAPTER FIFTY-FOUR

LEROY SAID NOTHING.

Not in order to be macho, or intimidating, or to make her speak next, but for the simple reason that he could not think of what to say. This outburst from Emma Kennedy took him by surprise, although it may have answered a few questions.

'I said what do you think you're doing here?' she repeated.

Leroy said nothing.

'I think you'd better leave this minute,' she said. 'Or shall I ring your Captain?' Her hand wavered over the telephone on her desk.

Leroy straightened up. 'Keep your shirt on. I'm leaving. I only had a couple of questions.'

'Not for me,' she said. 'Now, leave.'

He turned to leave. As he rested his hand on her office door handle, he paused, turning back. 'Don't worry. You've already answered them.' He waited a second for some facial reaction from her, then left. As he walked back down to the elevator, his phone beeped. As he waited for the elevator to reach the floor, he checked who had sent him a text. It was Quinn. The elevator arrived; as it took him down to the first floor, he checked the message. *wasn't sure what youd be doin rite now call me asap.*

As he walked back to the car, he rang his partner, groaned when he got voicemail, then left a message for Quinn to call him.

He sat quietly in his car before turning on the engine, leaning forward in his seat, craning up to get a view of the building windows. He counted up to the sixth floor, and squinted. He would have liked to say he could see Emma Kennedy looking out of her office window at him, but the windows were tinted and merely reflected the morning sunlight.

He sat back in his seat, thinking. How the hell could she have known about the case being closed and that he was on vacation? There was only one answer: someone in the Department had told her. Or certainly told somebody outside the LAPD; how else would she have known? That would certainly tie in with his theory that Domingo and Connor were murdered by another cop.

He needed to think, and thought best after a large cup of strong coffee, so started up the car, and pulled away. Ten minutes later, he pulled up outside *Food*, a red fronted building on West Pico. He found himself a single table near the rear of the café, and paid his $2.75 for a large coffee. In normal circumstances, he might have also ordered a Danish pastry or a muffin; however, this establishment was an eclectic café serving seasonal and healthy food, so today it was just coffee.

He sat back in his red chair and thought through what had happened so far today. He had gone to that office with the knowledge that Emma Kennedy was George Davison's younger sister, or half-sister to be precise. He was seventy-five percent certain that whatever was linking the deaths of Lance Riley, Ted Parker, and Guy Robbins, it was taking place in the house off Mulholland Drive. That house was owned by Davison. She was Davison's half-sister; very early on in, she tried to obstruct the investigation. And someone, somewhere, had given the orders that the cases were unrelated and accidental death. That would suggest somebody high in the food chain, and logic would say that the most senior person involved in all of this was the Secretary himself. But they needed evidence; something concrete and tangible, not just theories.

He was not quite sure what he expected to get out of his second interview with Emma Kennedy; frequently, if a case had stalled, he would go on a fishing trip with one of the suspects, just to provoke a reaction, and to see what they did next. So from one point of view, his visit there this morning was a success: it had confirmed all his suspicions. The question now was: what next?

He checked his phone again for word from Quinn. There was none. For a moment, he considered calling his partner again, but stopped himself. He knew Quinn well enough to know he would return the call as soon as he could, and did not want to disturb him while he was working, presumably at Grand Central Market, carrying on from where Leroy himself had left off.

Next step would be to visit the three others whose cars were parked outside the mansion. Then he would check out the hospitals nearest the Florence and Graham Blue Line station. He checked the list. First there was a Jamal Edwards, down in Culver City. That's useful, he thought; only a short drive away. He finished his coffee and returned to his car.

'Well, I'm damned,' he said aloud as he set Jamal Edwards' address into his GPS. The address was on Barman Avenue, Culver City, just across the street from a Clover Park, not the Clover Park he had visited a few days earlier. Maybe that's good karma, he wondered as he set off; or maybe bad karma, as his enquiries at the other Clover Park proved fruitless.

Jamal Edwards' house was a small, single storey dwelling at the end of a narrow but long front yard. There was a neatly cut lawn out front, with a flagstone path leading through the middle. At the side of the lawn, separating it from the long driveway, was a modest flowerbed, with pink flowers and small shrubs dotted around. Leroy was unable to park the Taurus directly outside as the front was blocked by three trash bins, green, black, blue. Instead, he parked on the house's driveway.

The fact that there were three Herbie Curbies outside in common with other houses in the street suggested that somebody was around, although there was no vehicle on the driveway leading up to the garage, and all the windows were shut.

He stepped up to the front door and pressed the bell. He could hear it ring faintly inside, but that was the only sound he could hear. He waited a moment, then rang it again. Still no answer. He stepped along the front patio to a window and looked in. The house certainly looked occupied. Maybe he was at work. He had no idea of Edwards' marital status, but all of the victims from the other night were in a stable relationship. Family maybe, but this house looked too small for a family, just large enough for a couple.

He walked round the side of the house. There was a small, brick-built chimney attached to the side: too small to be a traditional chimney; maybe an air-conditioning flue, or maybe just cosmetic. A large bougainvillea bush with pink flowers clung to the side of the house.

The garage was at the end of the driveway; its brown

293

metal door was closed. Leroy tried it; it was locked. A black wrought iron gate separated the garage and drive from the back yard. Through the gate Leroy could see a neatly mown lawn matching the one out front, with neat flower beds either side. From the rear, the house looked empty.

A neat, tidy house, a neat and tidy garden, Leroy thought. Obviously Jamal Edwards was not a drunken drug addict. Fits the profile of the others; respectable family man with a dark secret.

Leroy tried the gate - it was locked – then returned to the front of the house. In all probability Edwards lived here with his wife or partner, and they were both out. It looked like a one-bedroom place, so there were probably no children; therefore they were both at work. Left the trash out for collection this morning, then left for work. He opened his glove compartment and took out a business card. Wrote a note on the reverse asking Edwards to call him on his cell and put the car in the mailbox.

A gust of warm air caught him as he opened his car door; he paused and lifted his head to take in the draft. It was a warm, humid day, and the warm wind did nothing to temper that.

Back in the car, he checked the next name on the list. 'Oh shit,' he said aloud as he read the address: it was Oakland. No way was he going to drive there; a phone call would have to suffice. Something he would do later. Or maybe not: if one assumed he was in LA on business, then he might still be; a call to the home address might reveal where he was working and staying. He got into the car and dialled Information. Got the number, and dialled. He immediately got the ringing tone, but nothing else. He let it ring for a full minute, when he heard somebody knocking on the car roof. He hung up. An elderly man was standing by his door. 'Can I help you, son?' the man asked.

Leroy took out his identification; the man stiffened when he saw it.

'I'm looking for Jamal Edwards,' Leroy said.

'Looking for Jamal? Why, he's not in any trouble?'

Leroy shook his head. 'It's just routine. I guess I have the right house then? Would he be at work?'

'Sure, sure. He left this morning, around six thirty.'

'Do you know where he works?'

'Sorry, son; I know he works in an office Downtown somewhere. Don't rightly know where.'

'When's he normally home?'

The old man shrugged. 'Normally around seven, I guess.'

'What about his wife?'

'Wife? No, Jamal ain't married.'

'Okay. Girlfriend, then.'

The old man laughed. 'You got it all wrong, son. Jamal lives with another guy.'

'Oh. Right.'

'Yeah, a really nice white guy. Frankie.'

'I see. And when will Frankie be back?'

''bout six thirty. Just before Jamal gets in. Shall I give them a message?'

'No, it's okay, thanks. I put a note through the door already.'

'That's good.' The old man finished talking and stood by the car.

Leroy looked up at him. 'Thanks for all your help. I'll let you get on.'

The old man got the hint. 'No worries, son.' He knocked on the car roof and shuffled off.

Leroy watched him disappear round the corner, then leaned forward to start the engine. So, Jamal Edwards was gay. Did that make any difference to things? Probably not: if the mansion was a high class whore house, then they might cater for all tastes. Some places also provide male hookers. Or Edwards might actually be bisexual.

He decided to get something to eat before he went to see

the third name and called the hospitals. He turned out of Barman, into Overland. There were plenty of eating places he knew on Venice Boulevard, so headed up there.

Traffic on Overland was heavy, and he had only gone a hundred yards or so when his phone rang. It was Quinn.

Leroy snatched the phone off the seat. 'Talk to me Ray.'

'Sam, are you driving?'

'Yeah, why?'

'You need to pull over.'

'Huh?'

'Pull over now.'

Leroy indicated and jerked the wheel to the right to get the Taurus on the side of the road. A car horn blared at him; Leroy gave the driver his middle finger. The other driver pulled up alongside to remonstrate, but pulled away one Leroy showed him his badge. He picked the phone up again.

'Right, I'm pulled over. What's up?'

'You remember that incident at the Blue Line station?'

'Sure. Any luck there?'

'Yes. I got hold of the parking lot CCTV and made the vehicle.'

'Well done.'

'It was a Ford E-350 wagon.'

'Did you get the licence plate?'

'Sure did.'

'And?'

'It was registered to a company called GD Enterprises.'

'Oh. Do we know anything about the company?'

'Only who owns it.'

'And who's that?'

'Think about it, Sam. GD. Secretary of Defence George Davison.'

CHAPTER FIFTY-FIVE

'WELL, HERE WE go again,' Leroy said to himself as he donned the Yukon binoculars for the second time that week. It was just after midnight. He had parked the Taurus in the same spot as he had parked the other night. Once again, he looked around before setting off; there was no sign of the dog in the grounds of the house opposite. Satisfied that there was nobody around, he set off up the hill.

Once at the summit, he carefully made his way across the scrublands in the direction of the grounds of the house. As he got nearer to the broken fence, he paused again, looking around. Even with the advantage of his NV apparatus, he still felt vulnerable: as well as the Yukon, he had his service weapon and some other items, but these would be ineffective against more than one guard, or one with a dog. He was lucky last time; it was likely that after that night the guard would be increased. In the distance, to the north, he could see the head and tail lights of traffic moving along a freeway. Even at this time of night, the highways were far from empty.

He stood, hands on hips, staring through the trees into the grounds of the mansion. He nodded, clear on what he had set out to achieve that night. His conversation with Quinn earlier in the day confirmed everything he had suspected about Secretary Davison. He had long suspected that Davison was involved in this somehow; now that he had confirmation that Davison, or at least Davison's company, owned the Ford wagon, that was it as far as he was concerned. Quinn had floated the idea that one of the Secretary's employees was actually involved rather than Quinn himself and was using the 'company car', but there was also the question of who saw to it that his investigations were halted. It would have needed to be somebody with considerable influence, and for Leroy, that spelt Davison himself, and nobody else. He was not quite sure where Dwight Mason fitted in to all of this, but Davison himself was the prize. Before he left home, he did an internet search on *GD Enterprises*, and found it was a tiny concern, presumably set up for tax reasons. So, *GD Enterprises* meant George Davison himself.

'Is it worth speaking with the lieutenant?' Quinn had asked. 'He might reopen the investigation and get something done officially.'

'No,' Leroy had said. 'It would make things easier I guess, but there's still the question of whoever in the Department is involved as well.'

'Domingo's killer, you mean? You can't mean the lieutenant?'

'I don't know what I mean. That's the most logical assumption about Domingo, and - I forgot to tell you - Emma Kennedy, Davison's half-sister, let it slip that she knew I was on vacation and the cases had been closed.'

'Jesus Christ; how would she have known?'

'Good question. Who in the Department knew? Me,

you, Perez himself. Maybe others, I don't know. So: no, keep Perez out of the loop at this time.'

'Sure. What are you going to do then? What do you need me to do?'

'I'm going back to the house tonight. Do what I did the other night, but this time I'm going to break in.'

'Sam...'

'I know, I know. It's a calculated risk, but unless we make a move like that we're going to go round and round in circles.'

'Okay, but be careful. Call me the minute -'

'I will. Don't worry,' Leroy had said, then hung up. He decided against calling the third name on the list and the hospitals: the guy was probably dead by now, anyway. Maybe Hobson was cutting him up right now.

Leroy adjusted his headgear and carefully stepped over the wire fence. He moved slowly through the trees and undergrowth, moving his head 180 degrees left to right for any signs of movement or sound. After five minutes he reached the pool house. He crouched down beside a low wall adjacent to it. He inclined his head: he could hear voices. He concentrated: the voices were coming from inside the pool house. Slowly he raised his head above the wall. The French windows at the front of the pool house were ajar; thin, white under drapes were blowing out in the warm breeze. Leroy waited for more sounds. He could hear two voices, a man's and a woman's. They were laughing and talking: Leroy was unable to hear what they were saying. Suddenly the woman's voice changed from talking to moaning. Leroy felt relieved: they should be occupied long enough for him to get past the pool house.

Keeping his body low, Leroy sprinted round the pool and across some gardens to the double doors at the rear of the house. In the still night air, the woman's cries were getting louder. He hoped this would not attract any attention, then reflected that it could be a common occurrence, and might make good cover for him.

He reached the house and pressed himself in one of the dark corners of the double doorway. He noticed that one of the doors was half an inch open. So he wouldn't need to actually break in: that might make a difference if the shit hit the fan.

He slowly opened the door further. Inside, the lights were off, so he kept on the NV gear. The double doors opened into a kind of utility room: there were two white washing machines against one wall, some closets and shelves on the other. There were what looked like towels folded on the shelves.

He stepped across the room and came to a single door. He gripped the handle and slowly pushed down. The door opened. He waited for a creak but one never came.

The door led to a passage way. It was lit. Leroy removed the Yukon, blinking as his eyes adjusted to the light. With it hanging round his neck, he walked along the corridor. There was another door at the end; he knew he was headed to the centre of the house, so he guessed this door led to the main hall, some stairs maybe. As he crept along, he slid the Glock out of its holster.

He gripped the handle of this door, and cautiously opened it. He had opened it no more than two inches when he heard two voices, one of which he recognised. It was that of Dwight Mason. From the sound of it, Mason was walking upstairs. Leroy strained to hear what Mason was saying, but by the time he felt able to open the door further, Mason and the other person had reached the top of the stairs. Then the other person spoke: again, Leroy was unable to make out what they were saying, but could tell the other person was a man.

Leroy waited a few moments, then opened the door further. Now he was in the main hall. It was lit by five or six small lamps on the walls, but he recognised it from his 'official' visit here. Nobody was around, so he stepped into the hall. Now standing at the foot of the wide staircase, he looked around. This floor was deserted.

One hand on the stair rail, and one on his revolver, he slowly climbed the stairs. Half way up, there was a small landing, then the stairs did a ninety, then a dozen steps to the second floor. It was as he expected: as in any large house, a wide corridor with doors either side. Probably five doors either side, with an ornate window at the end.

'Here goes,' he whispered again, made for the first door. He paused at the door, his head pressed against the dark oak. If this place was, as he had guessed, a high class whore house, he knew what he could expect to hear, but from this room there was nothing.

He slowly opened the door. The room was in total darkness. Disregarding how ridiculous he must have looked, rather than switching on a light and disturbing anybody sleeping, he looked though his binoculars. The room was set out like a bedroom, and the bed was empty. He put down the Yukon and switched on the light. The bedroom reminded him of a quaint old bed and breakfast he had visited some years back. A high, four poster bed, a round table with a lacy cloth, and two old fashioned armchairs. He switched off the lights, and closed the door behind him, then moved to the next room.

He did the same at the next door: again he could hear nothing from inside. Suddenly, he heard another door open, further down. Instinctively, he grabbed the brass handle, and opened the door. The room was also in darkness. He quickly and silently closed the door and remained up against the door, listening, and praying that whoever had left that room was not headed to this one.

He could hear footsteps pass the door and go downstairs. He took a deep breath, and felt down in front of him for the Yukon so he could check this room for any occupants.

He was just about to put the lenses to his eyes when a light came on. Leroy swung round.

Sitting on the bed, wearing a white vest, and black pants with matching socks, and pointing a gun directly at Leroy was Captain Patterson.

'You!' Leroy exclaimed. Suddenly, all the missing pieces of the jigsaw fell into place.

Patterson said nothing.

Just fired.

CHAPTER FIFTY-SIX

LEROY FELT A stab of intense pain in his left leg as he collapsed to the floor, dropping his weapon. The pain, severe as it was, was coming from the side of the leg; he could not be certain where Paterson was aiming, but it seemed to be a flesh wound. He looked down and could see a small dark patch appearing on his inside leg, just below the thigh.

Depending on the location, gunshot wounds may not always bleed profusely: most of the damage is internal, and inherently more serious than typical wounds. Bullet wounds can be especially damaging as they penetrate deeply, take an unpredictable path through the body and are accompanied by a shock wave. When, as here, a handgun is used, injury will result from direct effects along the track of the bullet. Leroy's injury appeared to be in a fleshy part of his leg, so not as serious as it could have been. It still hurt like hell.

Leroy had been trained in circumstances like this to apply pressure directly to the wound with the heel of his hand; if he kept this pressure up for at least ten minutes, several blood vessels would have closed by spasm and there would be early blood clot formation. He should have also removed clothing around the wound to check for entry and exit points, but there was not way he was going to do that. Just by feeling the other side of his trouser leg, he could tell the bullet was still in his leg.

Once Leroy had collapsed to the floor, Patterson stepped over and kicked the Glock out of his reach. 'You won't need that ridiculous thing any more,' he said, ripping off Leroy's night vision apparatus and slinging it onto the bed. He picked up Leroy's weapon and tipped the shells into the palm of his hand, then tossed them on the bed too, dropping the Glock back onto the floor. He sat back down on the bed, still covering Leroy with his weapon.

'Just a flesh wound?' he asked.

Leroy nodded, still applying pressure to his leg. 'Is that where you were aiming?'

'Tell you the truth, I wasn't aiming anywhere in particular. It will all be academic soon. You won't be leaving here.'

'If I'm missed, others from the Department will come.'

'Bullshit,' spat Patterson. 'You're on vacation, my friend. Nobody knows you're here.'

Leroy was about to say Quinn did, when the door opened. Leroy turned and looked up to see Dwight Mason standing in the doorway.

'I heard a shot,' he said. 'Why, Detective Leroy; you're back. Very persistent, aren't you?'

'Fuck you,' Leroy replied.

Mason grimaced slightly, then asked Patterson, 'What

are you going to do with him?'

'Kill him of course; but I just want to talk to him for a while. I shan't be long; you carry on.'

'I'll have to tell GD about him.'

'You go do that then. Then get one of the guys to bring a car round front. Once I've done with him here, we need to take a drive.'

Mason frowned. 'A drive?'

'To get rid of the body.'

'Why don't we do the same as we did the other night?'

'Mason, you're an idiot. What better way is there to tell the LAPD that Leroy was right all along?'

Mason nodded. 'Very well. I'll call GD then arrange a car.'

'You go do that.'

Mason looked down at Leroy one more time, then closed the door.

'Putz,' Patterson muttered. Then he looked down at Leroy. 'So, Sam; when did you first guess it was me?'

'When orders came down the line to close the cases. I smelt a rat then; the evidence was so overwhelming. I take it GD is George Davison: you in bed with him, then?'

'In bed with him?' Patterson repeated, laughing. 'Yes, I guess you could say that. I've known George Davison for many years. We met at school.'

'In Flagstaff?'

'My, my; you have been doing your homework, haven't you? Yes, we met at school, became friends there. We kept in touch while he was in Oxford, England, and got together again when he returned to the States.

'George always was a strange, complex, character, but when he came back here from England, I noticed he was shall we say different from the rest of us.'

'Different? What do you mean?'

'What do I mean? He never wanted to get himself laid, like the rest of us did. He just liked to watch.'

'Oh. Kinky,' said Leroy through gritted teeth. The pain was worsening, although the bleeding appeared to be lessening.

'Yeah; he did it a bit at school. Ask one of us to leave the door open slightly while we were entertaining, you know. Wasn't fussy who he watched: one of our classmates, Mason out there, is a homosexual and old George would watch him at it too.

'Well, when he got back from England, he got more sophisticated. Got one of bedrooms in his place fitted with a two way mirror, and invite guys to make use of it. He'd sit behind the mirror with his box of Kleenex: do I need to draw you a picture, Sam?'

'But he's married with a family.'

Patterson sniffed. 'All show. He always wanted to have a career in politics, but a weird little pervert wasn't going to get very far. The Davison family and the LaHood family were always very close, and Barbara always had ambitions to be First Lady, so accepted that she would have to put up with his tastes.'

'What about his kids?'

'Are they his, you mean? Not sure, to be honest. I'll wager they're not. His wife was always known locally as the Trampoline, so who knows? I think both of them just wanted the appearance of conformity and respectability so he could pursue his political ambitions, so accepted each others' - what's that phrase? Lifestyle choices.'

'So, where does this place come in, and those four guys who died the other night?'

Patterson cleared his throat. 'As he progressed up the career ladder, he found he had the money to indulge his tastes. He bought this place some years back, when Barbara had the idea of him becoming Governor. Wouldn't listen when he tried to explain that Sacramento is the capital, but that's by the by. Mason had already gotten him into using the internet to find couples who didn't mind him watching

- nobody realised who he was.

'So, eventually, he had that website set up. Paid a lot of money to get control of a team of hookers, and got them to work out of the rooms here, while he sat and watched.'

Leroy looked around. 'Mirrors?'

'No; he'd moved on by then. Had lots of miniature cameras installed everywhere: under the beds, in the ceilings, in the bathrooms. Had a room fitted out with one of those screens with half a dozen images, and he'd press the one he wanted to see in close up. Got himself hours of it.'

'I still don't get it: what about those guys the other night?'

Patterson coughed. 'There were lots of drugs involved. Mason had known him for years, and Davison hired him as his Counsel. Mason had connections and was able to get all that stuff in large quantities. George never used any; it was just for the guys who saw the hookers.

'The other night: yeah. Well, six months or so back, George seemed to find that watching wasn't enough. He wanted to join in. Not bed a hooker, a threesome; nothing like that. He wanted to try dressing up and posing as a hooker. Figured if a guy arranged to come here, he'd be so fuelled up with booze and drugs, they'd not notice the hooker was a United States Secretary of Defence all dressed up, with five o'clock shadow and all.'

'What? Are you telling me nobody noticed it was him? That's crap.'

'Think about it, Sam. It depends on what type of sex the client wants. As long as... get it?'

'Guess so. Still seems hard to believe.'

'It all ran smoothly for a few months. The original girl would find out what the john was after, then say something like, "I'll introduce you to Georgina".'

'Georgina? You must be kidding!'

Patterson waved his hand in dismissal. 'Something like

307

that. I never got involved.'

'Yeah. You just made sure the LAPD never got involved either.'

'Yes, that was my contribution. Well, the other night, George was all dressed up, and the guy recognised him. Don't know how, but did. I think he realised it was a man, and pulled the wig off and recognised him. Then the shit really hit the fan. This guy made such a hullabaloo, it only took five minutes for all the other guys visiting to know what George liked doing.

'So, George and Mason had to think on the spot. There was no way these johns could leave here knowing what they did: it would be all over the front pages the next day, and Davison could kiss goodbye to - well, everything. They couldn't use one of these,' - he held up the handgun - 'as that would arouse suspicion, so they had the bright idea of mixing up some of the drugs we had here and injecting the guys. So George held them at gunpoint while one of the girls used the needle. Mason told her to inject them between the toes, as the mark might not get discovered. That way, he figured, when the bodies were found, they might be considered death by misadventure. Which it was, until you and Domingo got involved.'

'Who killed Domingo and Connor, then?' Leroy asked. 'You?'

'Had no choice.'

'Give me a break,' said Leroy. 'You had a choice.'

'I had no choice,' Patterson repeated. 'We managed to get anyone who mattered to accept the death by misadventure verdict - even the coroner - but when you and Domingo started snooping around, we had to act.

'I found out where they were at that time - they were following up a rape enquiry - and happened to be there at the time. She wound down her window to talk to me...'

'And you executed them both, you bastard. I guess I was next?'

Patterson nodded. 'You were, but I had to tread more carefully. For a start, you're more experienced than Domingo was, and after her and Connor, I knew you'd be more alert. Maybe I should have taken you out first. My mistake.'

'Big mistake, Patterson.'

'All academic really, now.'

'So, you used a vehicle owned by Davison to get rid of the bodies. Smart move,' Leroy said sarcastically.

'Patterson shrugged. 'They're both out of their depth.'

Leroy stretched out. The pain was easing, and the wound was starting to clot. 'One more question. Actually, two more.'

Patterson looked at his watch. 'Go on, then.'

'Where does Emma Kennedy fit in?'

'Emma Kennedy?'

'Yes, Davison's half-sister, apparently.'

'Oh, yes; that's right. The IT woman. She actually gave details of the website to a couple of her employees. She knew about George's tastes, but went along with it. That's right: she tried to stop you checking a hard drive or something.'

'When I went to see her the second time, she knew about the cases being closed, and my being on vacation. I guess that came from you?'

The captain shrugged again. 'I guess so. I told George; he must have told her. Yeah, when the guy died, I guess she was stuck between a rock and a hard place, but stuck by her brother.' He paused a second. 'What was the other question? The last question.'

'Are you the only one from the Department involved? What about Perez?'

'No, it's just me. Perez is clean: he just follows orders blindly. Not like you. That's why he's the lieutenant, and you're not.'

'So, what now?' Leroy asked.

Patterson replied, 'First, we need to get rid of you. Leave your body in the desert somewhere, I reckon. Then I guess that's up to George. He's the one calling the shots.' He looked down at his gun and sniggered at his pun. He stood up and stepped over to the window, still covering Leroy. Glancing out of the window, he said, 'The car should be out there by now.'

In the second it took Patterson to look away, Leroy had grabbed his own pistol and now had it pointed at the captain.

Patterson sneered. 'What's that going to do? I emptied the magazine, remember?' He pointed over to the shells lying on the bed.

'You did,' Leroy answered. 'But you forgot the one in the chamber.'

Patterson did not even have time to react before Leroy fired. A small black hole appeared in Patterson's forehead before he crashed to the ground. Leroy pulled himself up using a chair and limped over to the window. He switched off the small recording device Quinn had given him earlier, and looked out. In the distance he could see the red flashing lights of three patrol cars as they approached the house.

'Just in time,' he whispered, before he passed out over Patterson's body.

CHAPTER FIFTY-SEVEN

SECRETARY OF DEFENCE George Davison closed the study door behind him. He leaned with his back against the door for a moment, then took a deep breath. He could hear the sound of chatter and laughter coming from the dining room. The dinner party his wife had arranged was in full swing. The sort of event he hated: even since the late seventies, when they were newly married, he and his wife had different circles of friends; they would each go their separate ways, with their own interests, only meeting up when a public appearance was involved. This particular evening was supposed to be a fund raising event for something his wife was involved with. She had told him what, but he had forgotten; he didn't really care, either. The day after tomorrow there was another dinner, this time at the White House. It was to honour the former Ambassador to Belarus, or somewhere. Barbara would go along to that with him, of course; she lapped up all that bullshit. He, on the other hand, got bored rigid by 'her' events. This one was going on so late: it was way past one, for Christ's sake.

Normally, he would excuse himself after the brandy and cigars were brought out to his study, and take a look at some footage from Los Angeles. Sometimes pre-recorded, sometimes a live feed. He pushed himself off the door and stepped wearily over to the brown leather armchair in front of the fireplace, slumping heavily into it.

Tonight was different. A slightly inebriated local dentist had told him a joke which he thought hilarious and Davison just didn't understand when his phone rang. In the early hours of the morning, Dwight Mason had called him. Something had happened at *Whiteleaf* last night. Ever since they first met, Mason was cool, calm and collected; always knew what to do in a crisis. When Mason called him the second time last night, he was anything but cool, calm and collected. Where was his loyalty now?

The call tonight was different: not Mason, who seemed impossible to contact during the day, but Harry DuPont, another old friend, but also the CEO of *The Washington Herald*. DuPont was so sorry, but there was nothing he could do. He had wind of the story that would be in the paper in the morning.

Davison sighed. Got up and stepped over to a bureau and poured himself another brandy. Then another. Then another.

He walked over to the cabinet the other side of the study. Fished a little key out of his waistcoat pocket and unlocked the glass door. He took an old shotgun off its hook and studied it. It had been in his family for years: when he was growing up, his father kept it at home 'just in case', as he used to say; when he himself moved to DC, the gun came too and sometimes left the cabinet when Davison hunted deer.

He took out another small key and unlocked a drawer in his brown oak desk. Took out a small white box, and out of this box two shells. Loaded the gun.

Shoulders slumped, he returned to the leather chair. Rested his head back on the leather, and stared up at the portrait of his father which hung above the fireplace. Then leaned forward and put the shotgun barrel in his mouth.

He took one look at the black and white picture which stood on a table next to the chair. It was of him, Barbara, and his two sons on vacation many years ago in the Caymans.

Happier times.

Maybe.

Then he squeezed the trigger.

CHAPTER FIFTY-EIGHT

'SAM, DON'T ARGUE. You're going to need a wheelchair. At least for the time being. Not for ever. You heard what the doctor said.'

Joanna Moore had spent the last fifteen minutes arguing with Leroy over how he would get out of the ER room at Los Angeles County Hospital and into her car. He eventually gave in.

'Is there anyone who can look after you?' the well-meaning doctor had asked him. Leroy explained quite patiently and calmly that it was only a flesh wound on his leg and he was still mobile. He would be living at his apartment, Joanna at hers, but she was only ten minutes away in an emergency. Anyway, he would be back at work soon. The doctor wisely chose not to argue.

'You sure you'll be okay?' Joanna asked, as they drove back.

'I'll be fine. Don't worry. Ray's off today, so he's coming round later.'

'Hey, Sam - remember what the doctor said: no alcohol while you're on those pain killers.'

'Oh, yeah. I forgot. Great.'

They arrived back at Leroy's building and she helped him up to his apartment.

'You sure you need to go straightaway?' Leroy asked, patting the seat next to him.

'Yes, I am. Remember what the doctor said. Take it easy and rest your leg.'

'Wasn't going to use my leg,' Leroy grinned.

'Sure. Just save your energy for Catalina,' Joanna said, leaning over to kiss him. 'I'll call you later.'

Just as she was leaving she bumped into Quinn at the door. 'I have to go back to work,' she said. 'Make sure he rests, and no booze. He's on painkillers.'

Quinn gave her a mock salute. 'Yes, ma'am.' Once she had gone, he slumped down in a chair opposite Leroy. 'Is that true?' he asked. 'No booze?'

Leroy pulled a face. 'Seems so. While I'm on these painkillers.'

'It doesn't apply to me, does it?' Quinn asked, getting up and heading for Leroy's fridge.

'Yes, it does,' Leroy called out. 'If I can't, you can't.'

'That's not fair.' Quinn said. 'Coffee, though?'

'Yeah, go on.'

'When do you expect to get back?' Quinn asked once had made coffee.

'Couple of weeks, I guess.'

'Need any physiotherapy?'

'A little, maybe. The doc said to do plenty of walking for a start, then see how things go.'

'Lucky it was only a flesh wound.'

'Yeah. Though I've still got no idea what Patterson was aiming for.'

'Lucky.'

'How's married life?' Leroy asked. 'Still good?'

'Of course. Holly says the two of you must come over for dinner. While you've got time on your hands.'

'Thanks.'

'She moving in yet?'

'No. Let's change the subject: how's things at the Department?'

'Much the same, really. Obviously there's no captain.'

'Obviously. Perez having to make decisions all by himself?'

'Yeah. Just like he did the other night.'

Leroy nodded. 'True,' he said quietly.

Quinn asked, 'Is Joanna going with you to Domingo and Connor's funerals?'

Leroy nodded. 'Said she would. Domingo was Catholic, so may be a large affair. Both would be, I guess. What about Patterson's?'

'Haven't heard anything.'

'Will be a low-key thing, I would think. Just family. Just like the other guys: Guy Robbins, Lance Riley, and Ted Parker. What about the fourth one? The one at the Blue Line station?'

'Haven't heard anything. Maybe he survived. Maybe they haven't found the body yet. By the way,' Quinn added, 'Emma Kennedy isn't being charged.'

'No?'

'The DA said insufficient evidence.'

Leroy shrugged. 'Well, I guess having your brother blow his brains out is enough.' He paused. 'Any word on that little prick Dwight Mason?'

'Nothing yet, as far as I know. He seems to have gone aground.'

Leroy leaned back and rested his head on the back of

the sofa. 'Well, it's only a matter of time before he's picked up.' He yawned.

'You know, it all started on one night,' said Quinn. 'Just one night.'

'Say what?'

'Well, think about it: Davison and Patterson had this little enterprise going; for some time, by all accounts. Then one night, it all went tits up. If that one guy hadn't spotted that his hooker -'

'Was the United States Secretary of Defence in drag? Yes, that had occurred to me.' Leroy paused again. 'I guess the case really is closed now.'

Quinn nodded. 'It is, now Davison's gone. He was the last man.'

Leroy yawned again. 'Apart from Mason.'

'Apart from Mason,' agreed Quinn. He stood up. 'I think it's time to go, Sam. You need to rest. I'll give you a call in a day or so, and we can all get together.'

Leroy looked up at his partner. 'Sure, I'd like that. Give Holly my love. Let yourself out, will you?'

Quinn did so, and left Leroy on the sofa. He leaned back again and closed his eyes.

Leroy was awakened by the sound of his phone ringing. It was Joanna. Or so the phone said.

'Hey, baby,' he said, answering.

Only it wasn't Joanna.

'Hello, Detective,' said a familiar, sneering voice.

'Mason?' Leroy said, manoeuvring himself up. 'What the hell are you -?'

'Don't worry, Detective, she's okay. In fact she's twenty feet away in the park with a friend. She doesn't even know I have her phone. The silly bitch just left her bag open on the seat next to her.'

'What do you want? If you -'

'You think you've been so clever, don't you, Detective? Have you considered what you have done? You single handedly destroyed the life of one of the best politicians this country ever had. One day he would have been President of the United States of America.'

'I don't think so, Mason. And it won't be long before you're picked up. Now, I asked you where's Joanna.'

Mason laughed. 'Now it's time I gave your girlfriend her cell phone back. I think I'll say she dropped it on the ground.'

'Where are you, Mason?'

'I have to give her the phone back. Can't have you using it to trace me, can I? But it just goes to show one thing, doesn't it?'

'What?'

'How close I can get to your girlfriend.'

THE END

SAM LEROY WILL RETURN

WRONG TIME TO DIE

'I don't think I've ever seen so much blood.'

Los Angeles, California

When LAPD Detective Sam Leroy is called to a murder scene, even he is taken aback by the ferocity and savagery of the crime.

Furthermore, there seems to be no motive, which means no obvious suspects.

Believing the two victims themselves hold the key to their own murder, Leroy begins his investigations there, and before long the trail leads him to the island of Catalina, where a terrible secret has remained undiscovered for almost thirty years...

www.amazon.co.uk/dp/B00VPKN4TI

www.amazon.com/dp/B00VPKN4TI

NO PLACE TO DIE

Los Angeles, California
A severed head is found beneath the Hollywood Sign.

Fresh from wrapping his previous case, LAPD Detective Sam Leroy is called to the scene. Now he is tasked with identifying the victim, and finding the rest of him. Not necessarily in that order.

Following up on the few leads they have, Leroy and his partner, Detective Ray Quinn, find themselves unravelling a complex puzzle, one which began two thousand miles from home, and which involves sex, extortion, and ultimately murder.

While Leroy follows the trail, he is feeling himself coming to the end of a relationship, and may possibly be making decisions he might later regret.

www.amazon.co.uk/dp/B01N38CZNJ

www.amazon.com/dp/B01N38CZNJ

ALSO BY PHILIP COX

AFTER THE RAIN

Young, wealthy, handsome - Adam Williams is sitting in a bar in a small town in Florida.

Nobody has seen him since.

With the local police unable to trace Adam, his brother Craig and a workmate, Ben Rook, fly out to find him.

However, nothing could have prepared them for the bizarre cat-and-mouse game into which they are drawn as they seek to pick up Adam's trail and discover what happened to him that night.

http://www.amazon.com/dp/B005FZ0RAI

http://www.amazon.co.uk/dp/B005FZ0RAI

DARK EYES OF LONDON

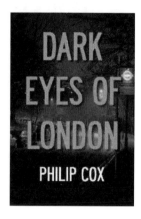

When Tom Raymond receives a call from his ex-wife asking to meet him, he is both surprised and intrigued – maybe she wants a reconciliation?

However, his world is turned upside down when she falls under a tube train on her way to meet him.

Refusing to accept that Lisa jumped, Tom sets out to investigate what happened to her that evening.

Soon, he finds he must get to the truth before some very dangerous people get to him…

www.amazon.com/dp/B007JMWBM2

www.amazon.co.uk/dp/B007JMWBM2

SHE'S NOT COMING HOME

EVERY MORNING
At 8.30 Ruth Gibbons kisses her husband and son
goodbye, and goes to work.

EVERY EVENING
At 5pm she finishes work, texts her husband leaving now,
and begins her walk home.

EVERY NIGHT
At 5.40 she arrives home, kisses her husband and son, and
has dinner with her family

EXCEPT TONIGHT

www.amazon.co.uk/dp/B009US94U0

www.amazon.com/dp/B009US94U0

DON'T GO OUT
IN THE DARK

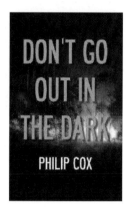

A WET AUTUMN NIGHT
Newspaper reporter Jack Richardson lends his coat and car
to a friend

AN ACCIDENT
Within thirty minutes, Jack's car lies in flames

The crash seems suspicious, and Jack wonders if it was an
accident, or murder.

But if it was murder,
Who was the intended victim?

www.amazon.co.uk/dp/B00LG005GM

www.amazon.com/dp/B00LG005GM

SHOULD HAVE LOOKED AWAY

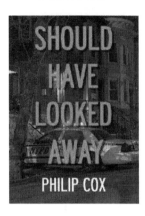

It began on a Sunday. An ordinary Sunday, and a family trip to the mall.

Will Carter takes his five-year old daughter to the bathroom, and there he is witness to a fatal assault on an innocent stranger.

Over the next few days, Will tries to put the experience behind him, but when he sees one of the killers outside his home, he becomes more and more involved, soon passing the point of no return.

Becoming drawn deeper and deeper into something he does not understand, Will feels increasingly out of his depth and is soon asking where this is going and was the victim as innocent as he first thought...

www.amazon.co.uk/dp/B01C4VVWUY

www.amazon.com/dp/B01C4VVWUY

THE ANGEL

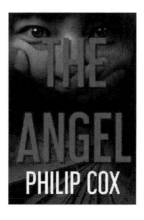

Investigative reporter Jack Richardson is assigned to a story involving sleaze and a prominent Member of Parliament.

During the investigation, Jack receives a call relating to an old case, one involving the murder of a twenty-year-old girl, suggesting that the case might not be as closed as everybody thinks.

Torn between his assigned story, and one where there might have been a terrible miscarriage of justice, Jack must make a choice.

His decision leads him into a dark place he never knew existed, and which puts him in great personal danger...

www.amazon.co.uk/dp/B07BR2YQGG

www.amazon.com/dp/B07BR2YQGG

Printed in Great Britain
by Amazon